W9-AFR-882

THEORY OF
PSYCHOANALYTIC
TECHNIQUE

*the text of this book is printed
on 100% recycled paper*

THEORY OF PSYCHOANALYTIC TECHNIQUE

Karl Menninger, M.D.

THE MENNINGER FOUNDATION

Harper Torchbooks ❦ THE ACADEMY LIBRARY
HARPER & ROW, PUBLISHERS
NEW YORK, EVANSTON, AND LONDON

THEORY OF PSYCHOANALYTIC TECHNIQUE

© Copyright 1958 by Basic Books, Inc.

Printed in the United States of America.

This book was originally published in 1958 by Basic
Books, Inc., and is here reprinted by arrangement.

First HARPER TORCHBOOK edition published 1964 by
Harper & Row, Publishers, Incorporated
10 East 53rd Street
New York, N. Y. 10022

Library of Congress Catalog Card Number: 58-9932.

PREFACE

"It is amazing how small a proportion of the very extensive psychoanalytic literature is devoted to psychoanalytic technique and how much less to the theory of technique."—OTTO FENICHEL

NEARLY TWENTY YEARS HAVE ELAPSED SINCE THE LATE OTTO FENICHEL recorded these words of astonishment. The situation he described then still obtains, although training in psychoanalysis, including technique, has expanded manyfold. The formal teaching of psychoanalytic theory and practice was inaugurated in 1920 in Berlin. The New York Institute was founded in 1929, the Chicago Institute in 1932, and the Institute in which I now teach in 1938. Today there are fourteen such institutes in America, in addition to those of England, Austria, Holland, Belgium, France, Germany, Italy, Sweden, Switzerland, India, Israel, Japan, Argentina, Brazil, and Chile.

All over the world, in these small, hard-working units, psychoanalytic theory and practice are systematically presented by carefully selected teachers to carefully selected students. This educational edifice has been the envy and the model of educators in other fields, particularly in medicine. Repeatedly idealists have urged the assimilation of psychoanalytic training into the graduate programs of medical schools, but with few exceptions this has been resisted—first because of the peculiar nature of the content and of the teaching method, and second, because of the intensity of the teaching program, which is so much greater than in other graduate medical curricula.

Almost from the beginning it was recognized that the process to be understood had to be experienced. However beneficial it might be in the training of the budding surgeon for him to be obliged to undergo a major operation in order really to know how the patient feels, it is not as yet required anywhere, so far as I know. In psychoanalytic training this experience is of the essence. It precedes all theoretical training and all practice. But it does not replace them.

The general theory and practical methods of psychoanalysis are now common knowledge in scientific circles. They can be learned about in a hundred volumes, best of all in the collected works of the founder. All psychiatrists become familiar with them in the course of their basic psychiatric training. But one who has undergone the experience of a personal analysis studies and comprehends psychoanalytic theory in a different way. It further illumines the past—his own experience—as well as the future—the experiences of his practice. Psychoanalytic practice begins as a supervised training, but it is based on the theory that has been studied and the process that has been experienced.

This book is about theory—the theory of the therapy. It is not a manual of practice, but an examination of some of the psychodynamic principles operative in the practice. It is the product of subjective experience and of objective experience—the latter with both patients and students. These experiences were shaped and enlightened by the guiding words of the many who have written for us to read. It has long been one of my functions in the Topeka Institute for Psychoanalysis to teach a course on the subject of technique; what follows in the pages to come is a written version of my seminar presentations. I have revised and enlarged my notes each year, and in doing so I have had the invaluable assistance of many students and faculty colleagues. I shall expressly acknowledge the assistance of some of these later.

But first I feel that I should say something more general to set the tone for the teaching spirit in which this material was prepared. It was my good fortune to grow up with psychoanalysis in America. The year the Berlin Institute was being formed, I was a young psychiatrist just getting acquainted with such leaders as Adolf Meyer, Smith Ely Jelliffe, A. A. Brill, Adolph Stern, C. P. Oberndorf, William Alanson White, and many others. My great teacher, Elmer Ernest Southard, had just died. Although he approved of the emphasis that psychoanalysis gave to psychology, which was ignored by most scientists of the time, he felt that psychoanalysis was pessimistic, that it dealt too little with constructive, practical, directive techniques. Had he lived longer I am sure he would have changed his mind, for he was the most open-minded man I ever knew, and saw in 1920 a vision of the potentialities of psychiatry that we are only now beginning to realize.

I can recall hearing one of our most promising young colleagues, just back from Vienna, describe to a small group of us at one of the annual meetings of the American Psychiatric Association his personal experiences in being psychoanalyzed by Freud. There were very few psychiatrists in those days, and few of these few would admit to an interest in psychoanalysis. We were all "neurologists," or "neuropsychiatrists" perhaps, or state hospital superintendents, or assistant physicians! Neurosyphilis rather than neuroses or "schizophrenia" was our most exciting area of interest. New diagnostic techniques had just been introduced, and those of us who could use these and who knew something about how to administer the wonder drug of the day (not penicillin, not chlorpromazine, not Salk vaccine—but arsphenamine!) were busy indeed. Untreated syphilis was then very common, and hence both acquired and congenital neurosyphilis were also abundant, although frequently masked. The reader will recall that Freud commented upon the large number of his neurotic patients who came from syphilitic parents, with the implication that congenital syphilis was a contributing etiological factor.

Psychotherapy of various sorts, although undoubtedly administered with good effect to many patients by the neurologists, was not regarded as really scientific. The neuroses were neatly packaged into "psychasthenia," "neurasthenia" and "hysteria." The reader will re-call here how much Freud was influenced at first by this classification. And as for treatment, the Weir-Mitchell complete-rest-and-force-feeding regimen was far better known than the more rational pro-grams of Janet, Dubois, Ribot, and others. Various placebo proce-dures—electrical, thermal, and mechanical—were prescribed and administered in the good faith that their suggestive value accom-plished good in some mysterious way. The state hospitals were in a most pessimistic mood of therapeutic nihilism; no one was expected to recover from mental illness of any kind, and when recovery did occur, it was considered a miracle or a misdiagnosis.

And then, under the influence of Brill, Jones, Jelliffe, and others, psychoanalysis came to America and combined with the psychology of William James, the philosophy of Josiah Royce, the psychiatry of Ernest Southard, and the psychiatry of Adolf Meyer. William Alan-son White had much to do with the constructive fusion of these points of view through his diplomacy and leadership. He was friendly with everyone—the conservative hospital superintendents, the dignified neurologists, the effervescent and often provocative psychoanalysts, and the youngsters like himself who didn't know *what* they were. It was he who engineered the affiliation of the American Psychoanalytic and the American Psychiatric Associations and, with Brill, fathered the psychoanalytic section in the latter organization.

Nevertheless, it was a long time before psychoanalysis was really accepted. Indeed, at first its attraction for some of the younger phy-sicians (as well as intelligent laymen) only heightened the opposition. Ridicule, scorn, and denunciation met any attempt to apply the new theories. No doctor with academic or social aspirations could afford to be associated with psychoanalysis or "the psychoanalysts." This, of course, made it all the more attractive to some alert and independent —and, we must add, rebellious—souls, and an element of martyrdom furthered the spirit of adventure in investigating the new theories and practices.

I well remember my own distrust of the new science, and my ultimate change of attitude. A patient came to me who proved to be, in many respects, similar to Freud's case of "Dora." She was a perceptive young woman, much troubled by various nervous symptoms. One of these was sleepwalking. I conscientiously made careful physical, neurological, and psychological examinations and came to the conclusion that she was suffering from either epileptic equivalents, as we called them in those days, or major hysteria. I conveyed this information to her and mentioned that, in case it proved to be an instance of the latter affliction, there were certain schools of thought which held that verbal ventilation as a therapeutic procedure might yield some results. I suggested the possibility that she and I might experiment with it.

She bravely elected to undertake this, and I wrote posthaste to my mentor, Smith Ely Jelliffe, asking for instructions. He said to "put her on the couch." I wrote him that I had no couch, but that I might be able to borrow a chaise longue. He wrote back for me to use anything convenient, but just get her to talk and listen to what she said.

This I did. And of course (although to my astonishment) she began to tell me in her weekly (!) two-hour (!) sessions all the details of her sleepwalking, how she prowled about her house with a recurring tendency to go stealthily into her parents' bedroom, where she sometimes awoke in considerable embarrassment. It seemed to her in the dream thoughts that accompanied the sleepwalking that she was on a perennial search for something mysterious, hidden, secret. It was something that should have been hers, something her father intended her to have but never gave her, something that, if it could but be found, would change her entire character and personality. It seemed to her, furthermore, that it was in some way connected with her parents' bedroom and was perhaps even hidden in the bed. It was wrapped in an elongated package, she believed, but she wasn't quite sure about its size because she had never seen it clearly. She had a feeling that she had a right to have it and was prevented from doing so by her mother. But always, when she awoke from the sleepwalking, all these things which then seemed so clear became vague and senseless.

All of this sounded amazingly similar to the "nonsense" that I had read in some psychoanalytic journals contemptuously scanned from time to time. But however skeptical I might be of psychoanalytic articles, I could not doubt my patient. She was sincere, she was intelligent, and she was articulate. She ultimately told me more than the books had. And she got well! So did a few others to whom I cautiously applied the same method.

Here and there physicians over the country were, like myself, becoming "convinced" about the new method and wondering how and where (and whether) to obtain systematic training in its modus operandi. Everywhere—in psychiatric circles—it was being debated whether or not a personal analysis was a necessary prerequisite of the use of the method. The New York Psychoanalytic Society was almost torn asunder over the question, "with one crisis after another for five years," as Oberndorf described it in his history. My "success" with a few patients had almost convinced me that this special training was unnecessary, but it was being recommended. A few young psychiatrists undertook the trip to Europe, but formal training was begun in this country in 1929, in New York. In 1930 Franz Alexander came to Chicago as the first full-time psychoanalytic teacher (and university professor of psychoanalysis) in America. He offered didactic analysis to a group of us who two years later assisted him and Lionel Blitzsten and Ralph Hamill in organizing the second American psychoanalytic institute in 1932.

The prerequisite of a personal analysis, which so disturbed our psychoanalytic beginnings, has turned out to be the keystone of psychoanalytic training. More and more clearly we recognize that Freud's decisive step toward his greatest achievement was his courageous self-examination, his unparalleled self-psychoanalysis. More than anyone who ever lived, he followed those great historic adjurations, "Know thyself" and "Physician, heal thyself." Because of what Freud discovered, no psychiatrist today need be quite so much at the mercy of his own unconscious as in the days before Freud undertook this historic task and unveiled his revolutionary findings about the human personality for us all to see, and to test and to work from.

This book was written for students of the psychoanalytic method. Most of these will be candidates in psychoanalytic institutes. But there are many others who want to know what mysteries go on in the consulting rooms of the psychoanalyst! Time was when we would have considered it very bad indeed for prospective psychoanalytic patients to be told explicitly "what goes on"; we considered that it would work against the very effects of the treatment, by arming such readers with intellectual resistances. Today, however, such procedure of psychoanalytic sessions are so well known to most literate people from innumerable case reports that anything as dry and technical as these pages can scarcely make matters worse. Knowing from a book on botany that a green persimmon is astringent is quite different from knowing it by biting into one. Indeed, the essence of the psychoanalytic process is that reading about it and experiencing it are two quite different ways of "knowing."

Furthermore, I think the attitude of psychoanalysts has changed in regard to who should be given the experience of being psychoanalyzed. I am sure my own opinion has changed. I once regarded it not only as a great educational experience but as also a therapeutic program par excellence. True, Freud warned us against the emphasis on the therapeutic effect. Now I know he was right; therapeutic effect it does have, but, in my opinion, were this its chief or only value, psychoanalysis would be doomed. Surely the continued development of our knowledge will help us to find quicker and less expensive ways of relieving symptoms and re-routing misdirected travellers. Psychoanalysis essays to change the structure of a patient's mind, to change his view of things, to change his motivations, to strengthen his sincerity; it strives, not just to diminish his sufferings, but to enable him to learn from them.

The educational value of psychoanalysis grows, in my mind. It is an intensive post-academic education, albeit an expensive one. We used to discuss whether or not it would be desirable for all those who could afford it to be psychoanalyzed. The better question is how to make it financially possible for all those who teach psychiatry and the social sciences to have the experience. I think it is more important for them to get a new concept of themselves, of human beings, and of the world so as better to guide their students than for a similar number of sufferers to be relieved of their symptoms. I trust this will not be taken to indicate hardness of heart; I have spent a lifetime attempting to relieve suffering. But as I see it now, the greatest good for the greatest number depends upon the application of the principles and knowledge gained from the science of psychoanalysis rather than upon its therapeutic applications in particular instances. To the educational value of psychoanalysis we must add its value as a research tool. No other therapeutic method has taught us so much about the human mind.

I shall, therefore, continue to teach and to search. This implies my continuance as a student. I am indebted to the teachings and counsel of my fellow workers Otto Fleischmann, Director of the Topeka Institute for Psychoanalysis, Rudolf Ekstein, Herbert Schlesinger, and H. G. van der Waals of our faculty who have sat in on the seminar discussions and have also gone over various drafts of the manuscript with helpful suggestions. Earlier drafts were carefully examined by Maxwell Gitelson of Chicago, Norman Reider of San Francisco, and Ralph W. Gerard of Ann Arbor. And when I think of the help I have had in various ways from other present and past associates—Robert Knight, Frederick Hacker, Jan Frank, William Pious, Merton Gill, Elizabeth Geleerd Loewenstein, my brother Will, and many others—I am loath to close these brief words of acknowledgment without naming many more. But the reality principle must prevail!

I give particular thanks to Philip S. Holzman of our faculty, who for the past two years has led the discussions of assignments which follow my sessions of the technique seminar. Doctor Holzman went over the manuscript carefully and made numerous suggestions and corrections.

Harry Roth, himself an author as well as an artist (and the husband of a psychoanalyst!), attended innumerable sessions of our seminar in order to grasp my intentions in the use of the blackboard and many colored chalks. The beautiful color transformations which he made of my highly schematic diagrams had to be abandoned for black and white drawings. These please me, and will—I trust—be helpful for some readers; by others they can be ignored.

The references and quotations will be found accurate, I believe, because they were conscientiously checked by librarians Vesta Walker of the Menninger Clinic Library and Elizabeth Rubendall and Bernice Stone of the Winter VA Hospital Medical Library. Mary Douglas Lee of our Publications Division helped me indefatigably with the proofs and index.

My final words of gratitude must be to Kathleen Bryan, who has typed each page of this book no less than ten times, but each time with care and alertness for repetitiousness and other blunders. Those that remain will, I hope, be forgiven us and called to our attention for elimination in a later printing. With such fond hopes of a gentle, corrective reception, I join that great company of wistful authors who diffidently commit their fledglings to the skyways.

KARL MENNINGER, M.D.

Topeka
March 17, 1958

CONTENTS

THEORY OF
PSYCHOANALYTIC
TECHNIQUE

I

INTRODUCTION
and
HISTORICAL REVIEW

IT IS A QUESTION WHETHER ONE SHOULD SAY THAT FREUD *invented* THE technique of psychoanalysis, or *discovered* it.

Clearly he began with familiar tools and procedures—a consulting office, a chair, a couch, an attitude of concern regarding the sufferer's problem, an avowed effort to help solve it. The maneuvers of hypnosis, imperfectly understood as they were, he borrowed and modified and ultimately abandoned. Gradually he put together a new method of gaining access to the unconscious, of hearing from it, as it were, and then of translating its language into terms that both he and the patient could understand.

From the beginning he followed the scientific ideal of describing his procedures to colleagues as accurately as he could, hoping that they would make use of them and confirm or refute his findings. His original advice to those who would learn the technique was that they should follow the road that he had traveled, analyzing their own dreams. It was not until 1912, when he recalled having given this advice, that he explicitly recommended that those who aspired to become psychoanalysts should themselves be psychoanalyzed.* It was much later [55] that he modified this by the caution that acquiring the technique required considerable *training*. Even then it was obviously the effect rather than the theory of the technique of which he was thinking.

Freud's earliest expressed theory of technique accompanied his therapeutic explorations reported in 1895.[59] His theories at that time were that in hysteria an idea becomes painful because it conflicts with the patient's values, ideals, and moral standards—*i.e.,* his "ego." The ego then exerts a counterforce ("defense") that pushes the idea out of awareness. The idea becomes pathogenic *because* it is repelled. (Later Freud concluded that the repelled idea became pathogenic only if it could be associatively connected with early sexual traumata.) Treatment is properly directed toward overcoming the repelling force, the "resistance." The idea then emerges and the symptom disappears.

Freud's technique for overcoming resistances was to insist that an idea would come to mind, accompanied by pressure with his hand upon the patient's forehead. When a link to the forgotten idea emerged, as a fantasy, idea, memory, it was then discussed with the patient, and "worked through."

Freud lectured on the technique of psychoanalysis before the College of Physicians in Vienna in December 1904. He described what he and Dr. Breuer had observed, and gave Breuer credit for introducing a "novel therapy for the neuroses." Freud admitted with some pride that the theory, if not the practice, had gained ground with the profession. The technique, he said, had not been in a state of development such that he could give systematic directions. He reminded them that physicians may not discard psychotherapy, since patients have no intention of permitting that and actually do suffer

---

* "I count it one of the valuable services of the Zurich School of Analysis that they have emphasized this necessity and laid it down as a requisition that anyone who wishes to practice analysis of others should first submit to be analyzed himself by a competent person . . . not only is the purpose of learning to know what is hidden in one's own mind far more quickly attained and with less expense of affect, but impressions and convictions are received in one's own person which may be sought in vain by studying books and attending lectures." [58]

from conditions amenable to it. He spoke well of hypnosis, encouragement, "exercise," and other types of psychotherapy but gave preference to his own "cathartic" method which, like sculpture, "does not seek to add or to introduce anything new but to take away something, to bring out something." He assured them that it was not an easy technique, "to be practiced offhand, as it were." He reminded them that Hamlet's uncle appointed two psychotherapists who were so clumsy in their efforts that Hamlet exclaimed, " 'Sblood, do you think I am easier to be played on than a pipe? Call me what instrument you will, though you can fret me you cannot play upon me." [55]

The most important thing about this early paper was Freud's explicit statement that psychoanalytic treatment makes great demands upon the patient as well as upon the physician—from the former, sincerity, time, and money and from the latter, laborious application and study. Some psychoanalysts have forgotten his next statement, which, I think, should be emphasized: *"I consider it quite justifiable to resort to more convenient methods of healing as long as there is any prospect of attaining anything by their means."*

To fully amplify my emphasis upon the importance of this statement would require a digression from our main thesis many pages in length. It would involve a discussion of the essential meaning of treatment—historically, universally, and in our present culture. It would inevitably lead us into questions of medical economics: How much does an illness cost? Whom does it cost? How much is treatment worth? What are the motives of the therapist? What is the goal of therapy? How effective do we consider psychoanalysis to be therapeutically? Is what the psychoanalytic patient gains health or is it wisdom? Is it a freedom from pain or an increase in self-knowledge? Is it a treatment or an educational process?

Now, we believe that there are indeed some conditions for which psychoanalysis is the most effective treatment. Conditions which in Freud's day were regarded as incurable can be ameliorated, if not entirely dispelled, by psychoanalytic treatment. But there are other conditions for which we are not sure psychoanalysis is the best treatment, and still others for which we are quite sure that it is not the best treatment. But psychoanalysis is a radical procedure in that it involves great changes in one's living habits; it is a long treatment; it is an expensive treatment. The financial burdens which it imposes sometimes cause more pain to the members of the family, if not to the patient himself, than did his original symptoms. The magic of the word psychoanalysis attracts patients and gives them a secret hope that if they can only be *psychoanalyzed* they can be cured of all their ills. The patient is eager to be analyzed, the analyst is eager to assist. The combination leads to a scotomatization of the practical fact that the patient may not be benefited clinically and will certainly have to spend a great deal of time and money finding this out.

There is an additional complication, less true today than twenty years ago, but still valid. Some psychoanalysts, having acquired some skill in the use of psychoanalytic technique, tend to want to specialize —and to restrict themselves to doing that and nothing else. The patients who can be helped by other less expensive and less time-consuming methods of therapy are apt to be sent away, and sometimes they are sent away without very much direction. More and more, however, psychoanalysts are giving at least a part of their day to psychotherapy and psychiatric therapy of other kinds, so perhaps this tendency is diminishing.

This problem of length and expense of treatment has been a thorn in the flesh of psychoanalysis since the earliest days. Time after time exponents of brief or briefer methods of psychoanalysis have arisen and, after a temporary spate of interest and notoriety, disappeared. Those of my generation will remember the three-month analyses promised and dispensed, for a time, by Otto Rank. On the other hand, psychoanalysis has been sharply criticized, for example, by Macalpine and Hunter,[101] who point out that as we learn more about the theory we should be able to make the practice shorter and more effective. Instead, analyses which formerly averaged a year or two in length now average twice that long. The treatment of tuberculosis, pneumonia, other medical and many surgical conditions has been shortened as we have learned more about them. The same is true of *most* hospitalized psychiatric illnesses. But psychoanalytic treatment has lengthened, and this we can only justify if we can regard it as educational (in the broad sense) and preventive rather than merely therapeutic.*

---

* Piers, Bornstein, E. Sterba, and others have addressed themselves to this problem as summarized by Rudolf Ekstein.[26]

Indeed, in his second paper on technique, a section on psycho-therapy in a textbook by Loewenfeld (1904), Freud himself took the position that psychoanalysis should be considered a reeducation. He mentioned that it might require from six months to three years. It was in this paper that he first described the basic rule specifically.*

It was to be some years before Freud and other psychoanalysts became more specific about who might advantageously be psycho-analyzed and who might advantageously psychoanalyze them. Freud [53] himself published no more papers on technique until six years later, when he ventured a view of the "future prospects" of his therapy and mentioned countertransference and modifications of the technique required for certain conditions.

Freud's 1912 paper on dream interpretation—a reprise of the famous study published in 1900—emphasized again the fact that not every dream can be or should be interpreted, but that probably each dream contains an image or a reflection of the total neurosis. There were to be two other dream interpretation papers, one in 1923 and the other in 1925. He wrote on "The Dynamics of the Transference" (calling it a resistance, "the *strongest* resistance"). Further recommendations on technique came from Freud in 1913 and dealt essentially with the practical problems of the initiation of treatment. Papers with the same title followed in 1914 and 1915, discussing remembering, repetition, working through, resistance and transference "love." Then came a long silence, as far as technique was concerned, except for a paper on "Turnings in the Ways of Psychoanalytic Therapy" in 1919, which stressed a state of abstinence as a fundamental requirement of analysis,† and the two dream papers mentioned. Freud wrote no more papers on technique for more than twenty years—when he published the famous "Analysis Terminable and Interminable," another shorter paper on "Constructions," and the chapter on technique in *An Outline of Psychoanalysis* in 1937.

Thus technique, as such, was an early—and then a late—preoccu-

---

* "In order to secure these ideas and associations he asks the patient to let himself go in what he says, 'as you would do in a conversation which leads you from cabbages to kings.' Before he asks them for a detailed account of their case-history he admonishes them to relate everything that passes through their minds, even if they think it unimportant or irrelevant or nonsensical; he lays special stress on their not omitting any thought or idea from their story because to relate it might be embarrassing or painful to them." [45]

† I shall discuss this at length in Chapter III.

pation of its discoverer. This is the more interesting in view of the fact that it may be this—the creation of an instrument of investigation —which may ultimately rank as his most important single contribution. Freud never devoted a book to technique, although dozens of his followers have done so.* The first of these was Smith Ely Jelliffe, whose *The Technique of Psychoanalysis* was published in 1920. Jelliffe was a vigorous, forceful, eloquent leader whose basic training and early practice had been in neurology and whose prodigious acquaintance with both the literature and the leaders of the profession in all countries gave him a place of pre-eminence. He was early alerted to the importance of psychoanalysis and was personally acquainted with Freud, Jung, and the early psychoanalysts. His written productions had a quality of condensation and elision such that they never quite did justice to his profound grasp of the subject matter, and his textbook, although occupying a unique position, never quite caught on. Ernest Jones described the technique of psychoanalysis in a book published the same year in this country, followed two years later by a book with the same title as Jelliffe's but written by David Forsyth; it was so clear and didactic that it immediately became popular. Ferenczi was the first of the early group of psychoanalysts to publish a collection of papers on technique. This appeared in English in 1926 as *Further Contributions to the Theory and Technique of Psychoanalysis.* It was followed by the first edition of Glover's book in 1928, which again had the same title as Jelliffe's and Forsyth's. An excellent review of "The History of Development of Psychoanalytic Technique" was published by Dr. Sylvia Payne.[120]

For nearly ten years there were no books on technique. Then the eminently practical manual by Lawrence Kubie, *Practical Aspects of Psychoanalysis,* was brought out as a guide to candidates and intelligent laymen as well as colleagues to justify certain of the apparent rigidities and novel conventions of psychoanalytic procedures. Some of these still excite comment and dispute—for example, the fluctuating fee scale and the charging of medical colleagues for therapeutic

---

* Those available in English are by Alexander,[1] Balint,[4] Berg,[10] Braatöy,[15] Deutsch,[17] Fenichel,[32] Ferenczi,[34] Forsyth,[40] Anna Freud,[42] Fromm-Reichmann,[63] Glover,[70] Jelliffe,[80] Jones,[82] Kubie,[88] Lorand,[99] Nunberg,[115] Reich,[129] Reik,[132, 133] and Sharpe.[143]

assistance, which some consider to be in violation of the Hippocratic oath.

Kubie's guide is based upon principles Freud clearly laid down. In his 1913 paper, "Further Recommendations in the Technique of Psychoanalysis: on Beginning the Treatment, etc.," Freud presented advice that has not yet been superseded. For example:

> In regard to time, I adhere rigidly to the principle of leasing a definite hour. A certain hour of my available working day is appointed to each patient; it is his and he is liable for it, even if he does not make use of it. This arrangement, which is regarded as a matter of course for teachers of music or languages among our upper classes, perhaps seems too rigorous for a medical man, or even unworthy of the profession. All the many accidents which may prevent the patient from attending every day at the same hour will be referred to, and some allowance will be expected for the numerous intercurrent ailments which may arise in the course of a lengthy analytic treatment. My only answer is: no other way is practicable. Under a less stringent regime the "occasional" non-attendances accumulate so greatly that the physician's material existence is threatened; whereas strict adherence to the arrangement has the effect that accidental hindrances do not arise at all and intercurrent illnesses but seldom.
>
> [And further], By voluntarily introducing the subject of fees and stating the price for which he gives his time, he (the analyst) shows the patient that he himself has cast aside false shame in these matters. Ordinary prudence then demands that the sums to be paid should not be allowed to accumulate until they are very large, but that payments should be made at fairly short, regular intervals (every month or so). . . . [The analyst] may refrain from giving treatment gratuitously, making no exceptions to this in favor of his colleagues or their relatives. This last requisition seems to conflict with the claims of professional fellow feeling; one must consider, however, that gratuitous treatment means much more to a psychoanalyst than to other medical men—namely, the dedication of a considerable portion (an eighth or a seventh part, perhaps) of the time available for his livelihood over a period of several months. Another treatment conducted gratuitously at the same time would rob him of a quarter or a third of his earning capacity, which would be comparable to the effects of some serious accident.[48]

In this paper Freud discussed many very important practical matters, such as the trial period of analysis, the effect of long preliminary discussions, difficulties encountered when friendship already exists between patient or his family and the analyst, the evaluation of the patient's attitude towards treatment, the frequency of appointments, the length of treatment, the use of the couch, the first communications, the wording of the fundamental rule, and the use of medical treatments during an analysis.

Since then many books on technique have appeared, emphasizing the principles and describing the practices of technique.* Most of them discuss the theory implicitly, and of course it is also dealt with in the various textbooks. But certain aspects of the theory back of the technique, although implicit in all of these books, have not, in my opinion, been dealt with sufficiently. The second generation of psychoanalysts is now made up of men in the fifties and sixties, many of whom have developed certain special points of view or emphases in the utilization of the basic psychoanalytic principles. These make for slightly differing concepts of the technique of psychoanalysis, sometimes overemphasized as unique departures (which they rarely are). Some of these systems have become so divergent as to pass beyond the definition of psychoanalysis originally formulated by Freud and adhered to by the great majority of psychoanalysts.

Quite aside from the various radical departures from psychoanalytic technique such as those of Jung, Adler, Ferenczi, and Rank, I have in mind those analysts whose theory of psychological dysfunction implicitly forces them into one-sided therapeutic measures. For example, Wilhelm Reich's character analysis, with its exclusive attention to the analysis of the patient's character armor, and the techniques of those analysts who emphasize only the interpersonal dynamics of their patients, neglect much that is essential in a psychoanalysis. It is the persistent exclusiveness of each of these emphases that makes them divergent.

In my opinion, the most important thing in the acquisition of psychoanalytic technique is the development of a *certain attitude or frame of mind* on the part of the psychoanalyst toward his task in the

* The excellent clinical review of "Recent Books on Psychoanalytic Technique" by Dr. Helen H. Tartakoff [151] is recommended to all readers.

psychoanalytic situation. It was perhaps essential to the discovery of the psychoanalytic method that Freud was so little driven by the *furor sanandi* that he was able to restrain himself from the compulsion to do (or even to say) something to the patient struggling through the various steps of self-discovery. This restraint is very hard for the average young doctor, particularly for the psychiatrist, to exercise—with the exception of those constitutionally passive individuals who seem to operate on the theory that healing rays emanate from them so that patients should get well by virtue of merely being exposed to those benign influences.

Groddeck had a wisdom in this respect which paralleled Freud's. Durrell quotes and paraphrases him as in the following eloquent words:

> Death is always voluntary; no one dies except he has desired death. . . . The It is ambivalent, making mysterious but deep-meaning play with will and counter-will, with wish and counter-wish, driving the sick man into a dual relation with his doctor so that he loves him as his best friend and helper, yet sees in him a menace to that artistic effort, his illness.
>
> The illness, then, bears the same relation to the patient as does his handwriting, his ability to write poetry, his ability to make money; creation, whether in a poem or a cancer, was still creation, for Groddeck, and the life of the patient betrayed for him the language of a mysterious force at work under the surface—behind the ideological scaffolding which the ego had run up around itself. Disease, then, had its own language no less than health, and when the question of the cure came up, Groddeck insisted on approaching his patient, not to meddle with his "disease" but to try and interpret what his It might be trying to express through the disease. The cure, as we have seen above, is for Groddeck always a result of having influenced the It, of having taught it a less painful mode of self-expression. The doctor's role is that of a catalyst, and more often than not his successful intervention is an accident. Thus the art of healing for Groddeck was a sort of spiritual athletic for both doctor and patient, the one through self-knowledge learning to cure his It of its maladjustments, the other learning from the discipline of interpretation how to use what Graham Howe has so magnificently called "The will-power of desirelessness": in other words, how to free himself from *the desire to cure*.[20]

To know when to wait, to know when to clarify, to know when to answer or to remind or to emphasize or to question—these are torturing problems for the beginning analyst. Most of them melt if this attitude which Groddeck has verbalized can be acquired. And certainly one cannot expect to find definite answers to such questions in the books. Indeed, Glover [70] and again Bellak and Smith [7] have amply demonstrated that, although certain general principles and conceptions are held in common, for the most part, by psychoanalysts, they do not agree very closely when pinned down to specific matters of formulation, definition, prediction, and procedure. All the more reason, therefore, that a theoretical schema be set forth, as I am trying to do, which serves to map the way for the student. Older travelers will neither follow it nor need it.

There is another attitude which I believe it important for students to acquire. We regard the patient as telling us about himself when he talks, but we may take the view that the patient, during silences or other periods of strong resistance, is concealing information from us and from himself. I have found it helpful to teach that the patient is *always* communicating something, always revealing himself * even during periods of silence and even when he is less than candid. It is part of the art and technique of psychoanalysis to be able to realize what the patient is saying during these periods. Such an attitude toward the patient on the part of the analyst effectively prevents him from assuming the role of a detective or a cross-examiner. The burden is on the analyst to discover what conflicts, impulses, defenses, resistances, attitudes, themes, etc., the patient is expressing via these various verbal and nonverbal forms of communication. This attitude helps the analyst to remain the ally of the patient's ego as it struggles with the id.

---

* The following remarkable comment on the patient-physician relationship occurs in *The Scarlet Letter* by Nathaniel Hawthorne,[77] written approximately in 1850.

"He deemed it essential, it would seem, to know the man, before attempting to do him good. Wherever there is a heart and an intellect, the diseases of the physical frame are tinged with the peculiarities of these. In Arthur Dimmesdale, thought and imagination were so active, and sensibility so intense, that the bodily infirmity would be likely to have its ground work there. So Roger Chillingworth—the man of skill, the kind and friendly physician—strove to go deep into his patient's bosom, delving among his principles, prying into his recollections, and probing everything with a cautious touch, like a treasure-seeker in a dark cavern. Few secrets can

The question is, how can one help candidates to acquire an "attitude"? Can it be taught? If so, how? Certainly the example of their own analysts is not sufficient. It seems to me helpful for the candidate to get an over-all understanding of what he is trying to do from some other source and vantage point, as one might belatedly acquire a map of an area which had been traversed in a cross-country trip. Learning to "do" analysis is not like learning to ride a bicycle which moves over familiar terra firma; it is more like learning to fly an airplane (or to soar in a sail plane). Air is very different from solid ground, and one must get a sense of the new and relatively strange medium in which he is operating. He must learn to think in terms of the unconscious motivation and "unconscious language" of the patient and his own unconscious—as well as conscious—reactions to this language and the communications made to him. Freud himself compared analysis to learning to play a game of chess, with certain concepts of power and movement to be learned and fairly stereotyped opening moves to be memorized but increasing originality required in the midgame.

I think one very helpful device in teaching is to provide a working model of the way in which psychoanalytic therapy operates. To do this requires one to resort to certain schematizations in the interests of developing a consistent skeleton of theory and practice. I shall make no effort to develop the many subtle implications and variations and complications of the psychoanalytic process, referring the student and the reader to some of the literature on these, and leaving

---

escape an investigator who has opportunity and licence to undertake such a quest, and skill to follow it up. A man burdened with a secret should especially avoid the intimacy of his physician. If the latter possess native sagacity, and a nameless something more,—let us call it intuition; if he show no intrusive egotism, nor disagreeably prominent characteristics of his own; if he have the power, which must be born with him, to bring his mind into such affinity with his patients, that this last shall unawares have spoken what he imagines himself only to have thought; if such revelations be received without tumult, and acknowledged not so often by an uttered sympathy as by silence, an inarticulate breath, and here and there a word, to indicate that all is understood; if to these qualifications of a confidant be joined the advantages afforded by his recognized character as a physician,— then, at some inevitable moment, will the soul of the sufferer be dissolved, and flow forth in a dark, but transparent stream, bringing all its mystery into the daylight."

them for subsequent study in the course of the candidate's maturation.

What I propose to do is to examine the essential dynamics of the interpersonal situation involved in a two-party contract or—to use the word preferred by Dr. Maxwell Gitelson—compact. I shall apply these dynamic principles to the psychoanalytic treatment situation, pointing out the pressures and values which can be mobilized to favor communication by the patient to the listening therapist and the extent to which these are followed by gratifications and frustrations which alter the balance in such a way as to determine a progressive course. If the reader will note the topics of the chapters listed he will observe that the reactions of both patient and therapist to each other in the interactive process or compact are carried systematically and successively to a point where separation of the contractees is logical.

This over-all view will permit us to examine such familiar phenomena as transference, regression, resistance, interpretation, and so on in a perspective which gives them a clearer meaning. It will be objected that this sharpness or clarity involves certain distortions or misrepresentations, dependent upon oversimplification. But this is the perennial dilemma of the teacher: the teaching of facts and figures versus the teaching of truth. To convey a model, a teacher must reify and diagram and declare clearly what cannot be seen at all. The student must "learn" things in order to realize subsequently that they are *not* quite the way he learned them. But by that time he will have gotten into the spirit of the matter, and from this he may arrive at some approximation of the truth, an approximation he will continue to revise all his life long.

II

THE CONTRACT

The Psychoanalytic Treatment Situation
as a Two-Party Transaction

THE WORD PSYCHOANALYSIS HAS COME TO HAVE TREMENDOUS VALENCE
and importance. When an interview with a psychiatrist or a session of
psychological testing is described by a layman as "being psychoanalyzed," we overlook the blunder indulgently. But it should make us
alert to the magic implications of the word. Although given a specific
definition by Freud, it has been used in all kinds of ways and carries
with it an aura of mystery and transformation.

Any word of such profound implications, such varied applications, and such undisputed popularity can be exploited, and it is to
the credit of some dissidents like Adler and Jung that they made
explicit declarations that what they were doing and thinking was not
psychoanalysis. In more recent times it has been the tendency of some
who branch off in autistic tangentials and sales-package distortions to
continue to use the designation psychoanalysis for their concepts and

practice. The word is, to be sure, not copyrighted, although the British Medical Society long ago made a definite pronouncement that clarified the meaning of the word in England as the Freudian interpretation of personology and the Freudian technique of treatment. This book is in that tenor.

Historically, psychoanalysis described first of all a mode of access to the unconscious. In this sense it was comparable to dissection or perhaps we should say, more accurately, anatomical exploration in the living. From such exploration was derived a body of knowledge based on the data that had been obtained by this method. In this sense psychoanalysis might correspond to anatomy or histology. But extending this knowledge further, we have constructed a system of hypotheses to describe psychological function more broadly, a science of personology, as it were, which perhaps corresponds more nearly by analogy to physiology. And finally, there is what most people think of first, namely, the use of this approach to the unconscious and this knowledge of psychological function and this concept of personology to describe a philosophy and technique of treating certain kinds of patients in a certain way. It is this therapeutic technique that we are now examining.

The adjective psychoanalytic is often used loosely to describe various psychological approaches which emphasize motivation, and more precisely the viewpoint in psychology and in psychiatry that unconscious psychological forces, mechanisms, and processes are recognized as the basic material of psychological functioning. Perhaps the common factor in all of these meanings or uses is the recognition of the existence and importance as well as the availability of unconscious motives and memories. Since we consider psychoanalytic treatment something essentially scientific, although not excluding art and skill in its application, we must do everything possible to exclude the element of magic.

Psychoanalysis as a treatment method comes logically within the broader genus of psychotherapy. Psychotherapy is formal treatment of patients distinguished by its dependence upon psychological rather than physical or chemical agents. Several hundred definitions have been offered for the term psychotherapy which seem to blink the obvious differentiation just made. The psychological methods referred to are conventionally understood to be those using principally verbal communication. All treatment aims at ameliorative change of the patient by something done or said by the therapist, and *this* is true of psychotherapy. All treatment is transactional and contractual and this is no less true of psychotherapy.

Psychoanalysis, like other forms of psychotherapy, is a long continued two-party contract or compact. In all such two-party contracts, as we have seen, the interaction is a complicated one. Imagine how this might look to a man on Mars with a very powerful telescope: Out of a mass of milling, struggling individuals, two of them—here and there—are engaged in a regularly discontinuous series of vis-à-vis meetings. They come together, both remaining relatively motionless; they apparently engage each other in a communication; they exchange something. A balance of some invisible kind is established, and the two separate.

TWO-PARTY CONTRACTS

Let us examine a few typical two-party interchanges or compacts of this sort. Suppose a vendor, whom we shall call V, is offering for sale some apples and that he is approached by a potential customer, C. We must assume, of course, that V actually possesses some apples, and that he is at the same time relatively short of or in need of money; the purchaser, on the other hand, presumably wants apples (*e.g.*, he is hungry). We must also assume that he possesses something to be offered in exchange for the apples in case a transaction can be established.

A transaction usually begins in a tentative way when the purchaser notices and approaches the apple vendor. It is continued, still without commitment, when the apples are offered, when they are inspected, and when they are priced; there is still no contract.

If it is mutually agreed that a fair exchange can be effected, the transaction is definitely consummated as follows: The vendor gives an apple to the purchaser; the purchaser, in exchange, gives the vendor something *—*e.g.*, money. The purchaser is now in a position to relieve his hunger; the vendor is now in a position to increase his stock. In other words, the vendor now has fewer apples but more money; the purchaser now has less money but more nutriment. An even exchange has taken place; a balance has been struck; needs have been reciprocally satisfied, the transaction is closed, the vendor and purchaser part company.† The vendor has also rendered some service, and gained some satisfactions of achievement. (See Figure 1.)

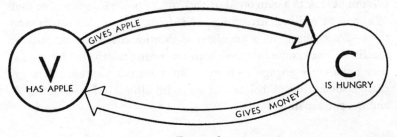

FIGURE 1

Here and later on I shall refer to and include diagrams which have been useful to me and to some of my students in visualizing in abstract form the principles to be described or emphasized. For some people diagrams like this are clarifying; for others they are confusing. The reader (or the teacher or the student) may therefore "take it or leave it." The diagrams are not essential to the text.

Let us change the situation slightly now and assume that the vendor has no excess of goods but possesses certain skills and the ability and willingness to perform certain services. Whether such services are as menial as scrubbing floors or as highly technical as

* Money is used here, as indeed in our economic life, only as a symbol. Some individuals, such as Albert Schweitzer, Johnny Appleseed, and many others, are so constituted and so situated that various direct satisfactions suffice and symbolic stored value (money) is unnecessary. But with them, too, there are "contracts" and exchanges.

† Even in such a simple bargain as this, various abstruse and recondite problems in psychology are involved such as the theory of decision-making in risky choice and in riskless choice, and the theory of games. For a discussion of these, see Ward Edwards.[21] For our purposes we shall pass over this question of choice for the present.

surgery of the heart valves, the structure of the contract is the same. Let us assume, for the purposes of illustration, that the services to be rendered are those of barbering. A general announcement has presumably been made that Barber *B* is able and willing to perform such services for a price. Customer *C* finds he needs a haircut. He approaches the barber, submits to the physical requirements of sitting in a barber chair and holding still; the barber wields his scissors. The performance finished, the barber accepts money and the transaction is completed (Figure 2).

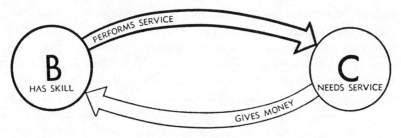

FIGURE 2

Here again we can assume that an even balance has been achieved. Each has gained by the transaction. The barber has gained another client, another opportunity for exercising his skill, the special situations of prestige which may relate to a particular customer, the pleasure of his company and interest of his conversation, and other intangibles. In addition he has received money. The customer, on the other hand, has been improved in looks and hence presumably in self-esteem. He too has had the pleasure of companionship and a few minutes' rest. Both are "satisfied." If they were otherwise, either this particular contract would have been broken off or continuance of the relationship threatened.

One can readily see that much the same process occurs when the personal service is rendered by a physician, but it is more complicated for various reasons. For one thing, the "customer" (patient) is—in this case—never so sure of just what he wants or of what he gets. For this reason, in part, the physician must have announced that he is *qualified* (medically trained), *authorized* (certified by the state), *pre-*

pared (in the way of equipment and time), and *willing* to render services to anyone considering himself "sick." Learning this, a sick man then approaches the physician and states his problem or complaint. In a sense this is a preliminary and tentative step in the contract. The physician gives the patient his attention and, having heard what the patient complains of, makes a decision as to whether or not he—the doctor—can justifiably accept the responsibility of attempting to help this person as a patient. If the physician's decision is in the negative, no further contract exists; if he accepts the petitioner as a patient, he has, as we say, "taken" the case. He promises to seek the best way to help the patient. He will proceed, then, to get a history of the illness and of the patient; he will make various examinations. To questions and examinations the patient submits passively, contributing his cooperation to the utmost of his ability. Except in pediatrics and psychiatry the refusal of this cooperation automatically terminates the contract.

As a result of the information obtained both by inquiry and by examination, the physician comes to certain conclusions. In the vernacular, he has "found out what is the matter." He then calls upon his experience and his knowledge of the procedure indicated by the pathology that he has discovered and formulates a plan of action. This is usually put in the form of a proposition. This proposition may be called an opinion, recommendation, prescription, medical order, or something else, but whatever it is called, it amounts substantially to recommendations as to a procedure of intervention, the intent of which is to relieve the patient of suffering or disability. The doctor says, "I have found so-and-so about you; on the basis of these findings it is my conclusion that such and such a condition is present; for the treatment of such a condition, such and such a procedure has been found effective."

The procedure may require further services from this physician or may require the services of another physician or may be something which the patient himself can carry out. In the first instance the contract continues; in the latter two cases it usually terminates after the advice is given.

Thus the patient-physician contract is never specifically for the removal of symptoms, a wished for eventuality which actually may not occur. The patient buys a "package"—the examinations, the information translated to him by the physician from the latter's findings in that examination and the advice drawn from the physician's knowledge as to what can be done about the condition discovered. If the treatment plan is accepted and treatment actually administered, he will pay for these services also. The similarity of the differences in the contract to those described above (and those to be described below) is apparent in Figure 3.

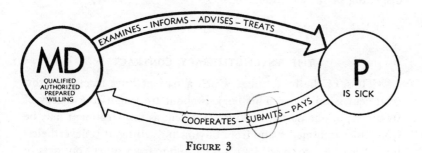

FIGURE 3

The trend of all that we have been saying (and drawing) is to emphasize the following points: First of all, in any engagement between two individuals in which a transaction occurs there is an exchange, a giving and a gain of something by both parties with a consequent meeting of needs in a reciprocal, mutual way. When this balance is not achieved, either because one does not need what the other has to offer or because one does not give what the other needs or because there is the feeling on the part of one or the other that the exchange is not a fair one, the contract tends to break up prematurely. This is not to say it does break up, because the first effect of the awareness of dissatisfaction will be for one or both parties to attempt an improvement of the fault. In one sense, therefore, its incompleteness and in that sense its unsatisfactoriness may be the very basis for its continuance. This obvious and apparently trite fact is important in the consideration of the nature of psychotherapy.

If one goes to a doctor to have a boil lanced or to a barber for a haircut, though the boil recur and though the hair grow long again, there is no sense of dissatisfaction with the contract. But in the case of the man with tuberculosis or some other chronic medical illness, the treatment is a long, drawn-out affair in which presumably the doctor is paid not so much for doing something as for trying to arrange and maintain a situation. He is paid, nonetheless, and thus he gains something, while the patient gains nothing he had hoped to get beyond the attention and observation of the physician. A point is reached at which the patient must realize that it is for these intangibles that he is paying and not for the relief of suffering or the dispelling of his affliction.

THE PSYCHOTHERAPY CONTRACT

Thus, of the four things which a patient buys from a doctor, treatment is only *one*. This book is about treatment—the theory of treatment of one particular kind. Different as this treatment may be from other treatments, and from buying and selling, it is nevertheless formalized by a contract. Its contract differs from other contracts in several respects:

1. In a sales transaction, be it of goods, of skills, or of advice, the relationships between the two parties are rather incidental to the goal. One buys an apple, one gets a haircut, one obtains an X-ray whether one feels friendly or unfriendly toward the vendor; one takes the advice with a smile or in somberness. But in psychotherapy the relationships between the two parties come very close to being the goal themselves. They are by no means incidental, they are not even in the strict sense of the word a vehicle for the transaction. The relationships are the most tangible elements of the transaction.

2. Ordinarily, transactions between people have defined time limits. A contract starts at some time and becomes consummated at another, specified time. When the apple has been bought, when the X-ray has been taken and paid for, when the lawyer's advice has been obtained, the contract is consummated—it ends then and there. When the need is felt anew, another transaction may be planned and a new contract made. Despite similarity between and repetition of such transactions, every new transaction is indeed a separate one, which will again have a practically or formally defined time limit. Not so

with psychotherapy. As long as the goal of psychotherapy is betterment—or amelioration or growth or maturation—it is by definition an
open-ended venture. It is essentially interminable, since there is no
predetermined specification of what is meant by mature, healthy, or
comfortable. In a way, the termination of the contract in psychotherapy is decided upon retrospectively, when the patient decides that
from now on he can manage alone, but even then this decision will
be no more than a venture. In this respect, psychotherapy is very
much like learning: even when one may set a seemingly defined goal
such as "obtaining the doctor's degree" or "finishing college," the
essence of learning is that it is open-ended; it can never be consummated.

3. Whereas most contractual relations are confined to two parties, who are named and described and identified in the contract, the
transaction between a psychotherapist and his patient need not be
confined to these two; it may often involve other people to whom
the patient is related. Perhaps the major part of all psychotherapy is
at least focused on the patient's relationships with others, and the
transaction between the two parties of the contract consists largely
in an account of the patient's extracontractual relations. Often, the
therapist must also relate himself directly or indirectly to some of

FIGURE 4

the people in the patient's sphere of living: to his spouse, his parents,
etc. Though the focus is on the two parties, the transactions are not
limited to a two-party space. In modern psychiatric therapy the "case
work" done by the social worker with various human elements (persons) in the environment serves this function of making the two-party

contract a triangular or polygonal one, or a parallel one. (See Figure 4.)

All treatment can be classified into *subtractive* treatment, the removal from the patient of something unwanted such as a tumor from a woman's breast, or a cinder from a man's eye; *additive* treatment, in which the doctor instead of taking something away from the patient gives something to him which the patient assimilates in a way to nullify the symptom—*e.g.,* a capsule of medicine or a pair of spectacles; and *manipulative* treatment, in which the doctor neither gives anything to the patient nor takes anything from him but does something to him which effects the meliorative change; the doctor may, for example, reduce a dislocation or massage stiff muscles (Figure 4).

The particular kind of treatment in which we are here interested, psychotherapy, may be *additive* in the sense of giving a patient hope, *subtractive* in the sense of removing a fear, or *manipulative* as in the case of redirecting a patient in regard to a goal. Thus psychotherapy partakes of the same modalities as medical and surgical treatment. It differs from medical and surgical treatment in that the addition, subtraction, or manipulation might be considered to be figurative. Nothing material is given or taken away from the patient, and nothing is done to him physically. There is no laying on of hands, no utilization of instruments, no administration of medicines. What passes between the doctor and the patient are such things as words, gestures, smiles, nonverbal sounds, and the like. Patients sometimes distinguish between "talking doctors" and "real doctors," doctors whose contracts with the patient are physical and material. Even by some physicians, psychotherapy is considered scarcely "treatment"; it seems to them more accurately a kind of "counsel" or "re-education."

PSYCHOTHERAPEUTIC DYNAMICS

This book is not about psychotherapy in general, but about psychoanalysis. Nevertheless it is necessary at this point to describe briefly one aspect of the dynamics of psychotherapy, to serve as a background for the subsequent discussion of the psychodynamics of the special form of psychotherapy represented by psychoanalysis.

Psychotherapy is of many kinds, not sharply differentiated from one another. The basic principle in all of them, however, is something like this: A patient comes to a person trained as a "psychotherapist" because of some kind of distress which the patient has been advised (or come spontaneously to recognize) is referable to the area that we call psychological. His symptoms may be psychological or they may not be; they may be physical symptoms or social ineptnesses. But the patient realizes or is told that these symptoms are connected with his thinking and feeling—in short, with his psychology. He is prepared, therefore, to accept treatment in psychological terms, to have certain false ideas taken from him, new ideas given to him, certain other ideas modified. (I have used the word "ideas" with the understanding, of course, that emotions and behavior are always associated with them.)

Usually the patient does not clearly understand just how this ameliorative process is to occur or to be effected. But having told the doctor the nature of his distress, he is prepared for a response from the doctor in the direction of identifying or explaining psychological connections with this distress. The patient complains, for example, of attacks of headache; the physician may not need to say that perhaps these headaches are associated with disturbing experiences; the patient often takes this for granted or, if he does not, will assume it as a hypothesis. When the doctor asks him what events seem to have precipitated the headaches, the patient does not (usually) describe falling down the stairs or being hit on the head with a brick; he mentions the visit of his mother-in-law, or the approach of certain examinations. This gives the doctor a clue, and he asks more pointed questions, which in turn give the patient directives for further recollection or organization of his experiences in a way that leads to an explanation of the symptom.

Parenthetically, let me comment that it is useless to attempt to dispel the philosophical fallacy that one in this way discovers the "cause" for a symptom. No one thing, such as a symptom, is caused by any one other thing, such as an event. In the alphabet regularly *C* follows *B* but is not caused by *B*, nor *B* by *A*. Many things contribute to a totality of stress, which may become "symptomatic" with or without certain additional and "specific" precipitants. But the average patient simply cannot grasp this point. When headaches are found to be related to an inexpressible hostility felt for the mother-in-law, this means to the patient that the mother-in-law "causes" the headaches, or at least that his hatred for the mother-in-law "causes" the headaches. Of course, both statements are false, but there is no use in attempting to dispel this falseness by direct or didactic tactics. As Tolstoy [153] so eloquently expressed it in his intuitive perception of all that Hume arrived at so elaborately, "The combination of causes of phenomena is beyond the grasp of the human intellect. But the impulse to seek causes is innate in the soul of man."

It is an empirical observation that a patient will frequently come to "understand" the origin and meaning of a symptom and, simultaneously, feel better to an astonishing degree. Is the process of discovery the "cause" or the "result"? Something must have changed in his defensive structure to permit the formerly forgotten or neglected unconscious bit to become conscious. And then the discovery may assist him in rearranging his life in such a way as to avoid the specific precipitant. Or he may go on to further discoveries.

This, to be sure, is a greatly oversimplified "case." Most psychotherapy is a *continuing* process, rather than a single-step event. The medical or surgical patient, having accepted a treatment program in principle, submits to it in practice in the form of an operation or a medication which, after a few days or weeks, has presumably accomplished its effect; the patient, having yielded up his illness as it were, recovers, pays his bill, and separates himself from the physician—and the transaction is closed. In psychotherapy, however, the treatment is not a passive submission but a give-and-take exercise which is apt to be long-drawn-out—if not, indeed, interminable—and might be experienced at times as a kind of extended examination. The "irritating points" of the disadvantageous pattern have to be sought for mutually by the patient and the physician in order for a change to occur.

I would not leave the impression that psychotherapy consists only in such a search. As everyone knows, much of the activity of psychotherapy has to do with the repeated correction of certain patterns of reaction (behavior) which lead to the production of the "symptom." We sometimes refer to this in rather grandiose unclarified terms; we speak of strengthening, expanding, or reinforcing the ego, making it more elastic and better able to handle the inevitable tensions of variable life experiences. This involves such things as repeated clarifications of purpose, pointing to unrecognized self-destructiveness, recalling neglected considerations, freeing of energies for constructive activities and more expeditious planning for the future.

But the process of doing this can, I insist, be brought back to a kind of continuous, progressive, mutual exchange and stimulation. The patient presents the doctor with a fact—let us say, a complaint; the therapist is given thereby a certain partial orientation and is enabled to ask a more pointed question of the patient. This directs the patient's attention and thinking toward a further self-exploration, the communication of which to the therapist in turn enables the latter to make a comment. This comment throws a new light on something for the patient and enables him to add further material which then still further enlightens the physician who may then still further assist the patient objectively to appraise himself, and so on.

This differs from an ordinary conversational dialogue in that both the physician and the patient have a definite and identical purpose, that purpose being to change the patient's ideas or emotional reactions or behavior or all of these in such a way as to diminish his suffering. In this, it is the physician's responsibility to watch the compass and guide the direction of the process. He is, at all times, "in charge" of the general situation; how he manages this relationship, including the verbal interchange, differs in psychoanalysis most conspicuously in his much greater relative inactivity, but the responsibility is still his.* (See Figure 5.)

* I quote here a comment by my colleague, Dr. Herbert J. Schlesinger:
    "One of the difficulties in teaching analytic technique stems from the series of dilemmas in which the would-be psychoanalyst is placed. These represent paradoxes, or as I prefer to think about them, 'dialectics,' the synthesis of which must be accomplished individually by each psychoanalyst. For example, you state here that the physician is 'in charge' and yet, of course, his purpose is to demonstrate to the patient that he (the latter) is really in charge not just of the treatment but of his life. Elsewhere it was implied that the physician must sincerely want to get the patient 'well.' Yet, to accomplish this, he must achieve an attitude of 'desirelessness.' There are, I believe, a number of such paradoxes, the continuous

FIGURE 5

Even though the psychotherapy is continuous, each separate session is a partially completed contract. The patient pays his money and presents his problems and answers the questions posed; in return he is listened to, questioned further, and instructed, advised, or at least talked to. He may or may not feel any better, but in this respect he is no different from many medical or surgical patients who go to their physicians for treatment. It should be remembered that he is not paying money for relief; relief is what he wants, but what he pays for are the professional services of the physician.

This is a good place to emphasize, too, that the money paid by a patient to a psychoanalyst is *not* in payment for the analyst's "time." Many psychiatrists fall into an error of thinking in this regard. Time is not for sale; it belongs to the universe, not to the physician. The physician may measure the price of his services by the clock, but this is merely a convenience. He is no more selling "his" time than is a silk merchant selling "his" yards. He is selling his professional services for so and so long a period.

---

effort at resolution of which leaves its mark on the self-concept of the psychoanalyst. Incidentally, I believe it is the last mentioned 'dialectic' that perhaps makes many 'old-time psychoanalysts' suspect the orthodoxy of those analysts who also do psychotherapy, as if to do mere psychotherapy would imply too much 'wanting the patient to get well' on the part of the psychoanalyst.

The whole question of the meaning of activity and passivity (or inactivity), with respect to the analyst's functioning deserves a careful discussion. I think one must distinguish sharply the analyst's relative inactivity, meaning that he does not often say or do very much that could be identified as such by an outsider, from the enormous effects that his judicious abstention from interfering can have. By way of an extravagant analogy, a person who watches another commit suicide without interfering would not be adjudged to have been 'inactive.' "

It will not have escaped the reflection of the thoughtful reader that in these various illustrations of transactions between two individuals, the apple vendor to the psychoanalyst, something has been omitted. Even in the case of the man buying an apple, something else takes place than the mere exchange of money and goods. In the course of every transaction, in addition to the exchange of that which is lacked by the one and possessed by the other, there are certain intangibles which are also exchanged. These are not measured or balanced, but they improve or injure the flavor of the transaction. One apple vendor will far exceed another in his sales, even in the same location. Why? One barber will be far more popular than another without necessarily being any more skillful. There is, as everyone knows, a certain factor of satisfaction or dissatisfaction in a transaction which is only partly dependent on the quality of the goods or services dispensed and paid for. In business affairs this is encompassed by the concept of "good will." This factor of good will is really not less important to doctors than to merchants, but in scientific discussions it is apt to be discounted because it is not tangible and because it is often illogical. We know that it is a much more complicated matter than might be derived merely from adjectives describing the likability or alacrity of the vendor. Conscious factors of liking and disliking certainly enter the picture, but one of the greatest discoveries of Freud was precisely to this point; namely, that *unconscious factors of a powerful sort are always operating in a transaction and operating in both directions.*

My point in these examples is that psychoanalysis, like all other psychotherapy, like the employment of a dermatologist or of a barber or like the purchase of an apple from a street vendor, involves a certain balance of giving and of taking. And like all these other transactions, it also involves unconscious exchanges. In these everyday transactions, the intangibles cannot always be studied; in psychoanalysis they *must* be studied. Indeed, the observation and understanding of these intangibles constitute the essential uniqueness of psychoanalytic treatment, the way in which it differs from all other transactions. As we shall see, it is in respect to these intangibles, and particularly the extended unconscious meanings of them, that the psychoanalytic patient discovers himself increasingly frustrated by the treatment, in contrast to the tendency in all other forms of treatment to be increasingly satisfied in the normal progress of the treatment. Of this we shall have much more to say in the next chapter.

THE PSYCHOANALYTIC CONTRACT

In the concept of psychoanalytic treatment as a two-party contractual relationship in which each party expects something of the other, to be delivered over a period of time, the indefiniteness of this time period is one of the great complications in the contract. It makes it necessary for the party of the first part to pay his money (which is admittedly not *all* of his contribution to the contract) in divided portions against the expectation of an *ultimate* fulfillment of obligation by the party of the second part. This is not a simple case of open-end contract, because the party of the first part pays in full, hour by hour, as he goes along, but the party of the second part seems not to! The party of the second part (the psychoanalyst) delivers immediately and from the beginning one very essential factor in the fulfillment of the contract, in that he sets up the unique situation of psychoanalytic treatment. The audience room, the couch, the insured privacy, etc., are the mechanical elements in this. Then and thereafter the therapist stands by, *ready* to serve, doing so largely by listening, occasionally by speaking. Someone has facetiously likened the therapist's role to that of a fireman. His verbal participation is relatively sporadic and irregular, and its full value depends upon a continued, developing process in which he participates all the time.

All this is well known to every psychoanalyst, but it is not known (or clearly understood) by the patient at the time he starts. Thus the "party of the *first* part" enters into the contract more than a little blind, which makes it all the more important that the established "rules of the game" be conscientiously adhered to by the therapist, even and especially in the *pre*contractual period.

These "rules of the game" were worked out empirically by Freud, and they have been little improved upon or changed since his formulations of 1913, in "The Further Recommendations in the

Technique of Psychoanalysis," [48] a paper which every candidate should almost memorize. The tentativeness of the contract, the avoidance of lengthy discussions of the prognosis, the irrelevance of conscious attitudes favorable or unfavorable toward analysis and the analyst, definiteness regarding time and money arrangements, the clear option of the patient to stop whenever he wishes, the use of the couch and the elimination of the analyst from the patient's vision, the assignment of complicating medical problems to a colleague, and finally, the clear enunciation of the basic rule—these are features which the candidate will have learned by precept and example. But in spite of such instruction, the beginning analyst will often fumble the preliminary arrangements through a failure to understand the peculiar nature of the contract involved in psychoanalytic treatment. For this reason it is my own teaching practice to use role-playing by various pairs of candidates in our seminars, various practical problems being assigned them for solution, the candidates acting as prospective therapist and prospective patient.*

Perhaps the most important rule is that the therapist must be careful as to what he promises to deliver. From one point of view the essence of psychoanalytic treatment is intellectual honesty, and no one in honesty can predict with definiteness what the future will bring. Yet if the analyst did not *expect* to see improvement, he would not start—and so taking the case *is* an implied prediction. The analyst cannot promise cure; he cannot even promise relief. He can only promise to try to help the patient by a method which has helped others and on the condition that the patient try to help himself.

In this sense, every psychoanalysis is a "trial analysis." But while this should be made clear to the patient before he starts, to emphasize it sounds too threatening, and certainly no special point needs to be made about it. In making the preliminary arrangement, discussing the probable length of treatment, and so on, the analyst should use care that he does not give the impression that although he calls the first months of the treatment a trial period, he has actually made up his mind already.

---

* The reader is urged to read Kubie's excellent book [88] on the practical aspects of treatment and Greenacre's wise counsel in her article on transference.[73]

MONEY

A very important problem in the setting up of the original contract is the question of money. Freud reminded us of how hypocritical and evasive we all are about payment for getting and giving help. This is less of a problem today than it was twenty years ago, because patients have learned about what to expect in the way of psychoanalytic fees, and a rough standard prevails in most communities. It is the departure from these standards, necessitated by exceptional cases, that will tax the skill of the young analyst. For the purposes of this text, which has to do with theory rather than the practice of analysis, it is sufficient to emphasize a few basic principles.

The analysis will not go well if the patient is paying less than he can reasonably afford to pay. It should be a definite sacrifice for him, for *him* and not for someone else. Sometimes it is inevitable that someone else will have to make a sacrifice too, such as a wife or parent, in order for the treatment to be paid for, but innumerable complications arise if a patient pays for analysis with the largesse of a relative, a friend, or a Foundation to whom (or which) he has no effective responsibility for repayment.

On the other hand, complications also arise if the patient pays more than he can afford. In an effort to please the analyst or to make a good impression, some patients will agree to a higher fee at the beginning of an analysis than they are able to continue paying as the analysis runs on longer and longer. Some analysts take the position, and I am inclined to agree with them, that usually, if money is a serious problem, psychoanalysis is not the treatment of choice. The patient should not expect to pay for his analysis out of his current earnings (although some do); it is a capital investment, not a mere expense. Furthermore, all sorts of things—the unexpected illness of a wife, the loss of a job, and so forth—make this very hazardous. The point may come when the patient cannot pay anything, and the analyst will then have to decide whether he can afford to continue treatment without compensation or whether he can afford, for reasons of professional obligation and human concern, to do otherwise. This is not just a question of the therapist's generosity, because a free treatment is apt to be a very prolonged treatment and may even then be an unsuccessful treatment.

It is generally agreed to be undesirable for the patient to be permitted to run into debt to the analyst. Mounting indebtedness puts the patient under obligation to the therapist, and this is always a handicap and can be disastrous. It should be understood from the outset that bills will be rendered monthly and paid monthly. There is no need to go into a long discussion of this with the patient but it should be made clear to him that it is one of the "rules" of the treatment. To give all the reasons would necessitate long discussion which the patient will not understand, anyway.

The analyst should at some time explain that psychoanalytic appointments cannot be cancelled, that telephoning a prospective nonappearance does not imply the cancellation of the fee for that particular hour. This may come as a surprise to some patients.

Dr. Nils Haak [74] has discussed the question of fees so ably that I should like to quote from his recent statement:

> An important aspect of the analytical situation, perhaps a little neglected in the analytical literature, is the question of the patient's payment of the analyst for consultations. There are two schools of thought among Swedish analysts: on the one hand a stricter line, which I myself now support, on the other a more conciliatory, "human" line, represented in literature by Fromm-Reichmann [63] and implying that if the patient can prove "valid reasons" for not attending consultations previously agreed upon, he need not pay for them. I myself earlier belonged to this school of thought. I wish to recall Freud's attitude (p. 346): "I adhere rigidly to the principle of leasing a definite hour. A certain hour of my available workingday is appointed to each patient; it is his, and he is liable for it, even if he does not make use of it. . . . No other way is practicable." [48] Kubie [88] says: "If the patient were not charged for appointments which he missed, the analyst would in effect be offering him a financial inducement to escape painful sessions, since he could go off and enjoy himself and save money as well."

Kubie considers that there must be a strong, restraining factor which deters the patient from the natural temptation to avoid analytical sessions, as soon as things become difficult.

My own view on the question of fees is that during the three years in which I have applied the same strict rules, I have only had therapeutically favourable experiences of them, and I consider it to be an essential and dynamically important factor in the analytical process.

Below are some of the reasons which have persuaded me to a rigorous system of payment.

(i) The patient regards the analyst as a reliable, integrated person who dares to accept the aggressions which the patient releases against this strict system of payment. The patient learns that the analyst, unlike his parents, does not become frightened by threats of being scandalized. Thus the analyst becomes a good object of identification. It appears that candidates, who themselves have had to follow these rules as analysands, find it easy to apply them to their patients, and the opposite is true of those who are accustomed to something different.

(ii) Furthermore, the patient experiences the analyst as an honest, upright person who dares to defy the general hypocrisy regarding money, which is a relief for the patient. That the analyst dares to take payment, indeed good payment, for all his appointments is regarded by the patient as a sign of healthy self-esteem and appreciation of his own time and qualifications. This becomes a good and realistic ego-ideal for the patient in contrast to his own neurotic one.

(iii) Uncompromising financial demands are among those measures which, for certain patients, are necessary to overcome in the analysis the defence against the patient's repressed, passive-masochistic tendencies. I have had several examples of this state of affairs in my practice. Previously, when I adopted milder

measures, I had difficulty in dissolving defence attitudes against such tendencies. The patient was then more easily able to retain a feeling that the analyst was dependent on him, which was an unnecessary link in his defence. The patient now experiences that he has entrusted himself to a strong person who knows what he wants, who will not allow himself to be directed or frightened, who will stand up to various kinds of provocations and testing attempts to which the patient exposes him in this connexion, who lives as he teaches. All this also counteracts the patient's illusion of being in a privileged position—the favourite child.

(iv) By a strict system of payment, the patient is not tempted to test the analyst's patience or to castrate him, or to be absent so as to avoid difficult material, which was Freud's experience, or to remain in bed and be childishly looked after by his family for the slightest cold. I know a patient who finished with one analyst with a mild system of payment because it was far too easy to telephone his cancellations. The patient totally lost respect for this kind and reasonable analyst.

(v) The analysis must involve a sacrifice, otherwise it becomes a matter of indifference in the patient's life. It is deeply rooted in the human mind that what is cheap is of little value and what is dear is valuable. On one occasion, I treated a patient for whose analysis the social services paid, and I cannot recall a worse analytic case. There was no progress whatsoever after two years of analysis. We may well ask what will happen to our patients if the National Health Service should pay the greater part of their fees. (Since 1 January, 1955, there has been in Sweden a compulsory sickness insurance system which awards patients three-quarters of certain maximum medical fees [about £2]. It has not yet been decided whether compensation will be paid for psycho-analytical treatment.)

Alexander has somewhere written of a patient who could not be treated for a low fee. The patient violently abused his new, expensive analyst, but nevertheless became healthy.

(vi) A sufficiently high fee makes it more difficult for the patient to relax into a passively dependent, infantile, help-seeking attitude. Naturally a strict system of payment can be masochistically misused by the patient, just like everything else. Patients with such tendencies, however, have as a rule previously used their money in a much worse and more destructive manner than for analysis. It can also occur that a high fee provides an outlet for the patient's otherwise destructive, masochistic tendencies. I have had a case which indicates this.

To succeed in talking the analyst into granting certain favours in respect of the fee can be and, by certain patients, has been experienced as having fooled the analyst.

(vii) A sufficiently high fee, punctually paid, is necessary to counteract the patient's guilt feelings for his aggressions against and demands on the analyst. The patient then has no chance of getting into any kind of humiliating debt of gratitude to the analyst, as he has often been to his parents. A financial favour would give cause for gratitude which binds and fetters the patient. When the analysis is over the patient can be entirely independent of his analyst without feeling a debt of gratitude. The patient also dares to be aggressive during the analysis. "Kind analysts" help to inhibit the patient's aggressions.

(viii) It is important for the analyst's own counter-transference situation that he should not, perhaps hesitatingly, agree to a low fee or accept a loss of income during his normal working hours. If this happens there is reason to ask if there does not exist an unsettled counter-transference attitude on the part of the analyst, for instance that he has guilt feelings; that he is masochistic; that he is in love with his patient; that he wants to bribe his patient to love him; that he is afraid of his patient; that he is afraid of being considered greedy. Furthermore it can be repressed aggressions against the patient which make the analyst "kind." He can also play the part of the good, orally generous mother. All this is of great detriment to the analyst's ability to analyse his patient. I have seen examples of how such uncontrolled counter-transference attitudes have had destructive effects on analyses.

(ix) It is not least important that the analyst be compensated for the suffering to which his patients expose him. Too low a fee or too great generosity may easily give cause for aggression against the patients which reduces the analyst's possibilities of analysing them.

The same thing applies to vacation times sought by the patient which do not correspond to vacation times of the analyst. Psychoanalytic treatment must be considered by the patient one of the most important things in his life, and there is no such thing as a vacation from it, as a rule. There are, however, interruptions of treatment involved in the analyst's necessary absences.

RELATIVES

Among the problems in the initiation of an analysis is the relationship of the analyst to spouses, relatives, and close friends of the patient. Naturally, in order to protect the precious and special patient-therapist relationship, the analyst will avoid as much as possible nonanalytic contacts with the patient. But the question will arise whether the analyst should see the wife or the husband or the mother who are very often worried and eager to meet the doctor. All the young analyst has to remember about this is that such meetings may impair or complicate the patient-therapist relationship, but to omit them may impair the relationship worse. It seems to me absurd to stand on the principle that one has nothing to say to anyone but the patient. My impression is that it is often out of laziness, or lack of self-confidence, that many analysts refuse to see close relatives, thereby handicapping their efforts with the patient.

Some analysts make it a routine practice to see the husband or wife once and explain to the patient the reasons for this. It gives them an opportunity to see what the spouse is like (which is often very different from the impression given by the patient), and to warn him against premature reactions to the patient's behavior during the treatment. This often gives great reassurance, especially to insecure, apprehensive, and troubled relatives. But it is only fair to add that sometimes it "contaminates the field," as Greenacre [73] puts it, impairing the surgical asepsis which is our ideal. My own practice has been to see the relative, at the patient's request and usually in his hour and to report the interview to the patient afterwards. Usually I tell the patient beforehand what I intend to say or not say.

I think we must remember that psychoanalysis may involve considerable sacrifice and suffering to the relatives of the patient, over and beyond the burden to the family treasury. Sometimes, as Henri Ellenberger puts it, they experience an unpleasant "one-way-vision-room" effect; that is, they feel themselves seen, perhaps in a distorted way, by a psychoanalyst whom they cannot see. Then there are always the "acting out" episodes in which the patient takes out on the relatives what he should talk out to the psychoanalyst, and it cannot be expected that relatives unfamiliar with the theories of psychoanalysis can be as tolerant or understanding of such acts as is the analyst. Finally, there is always some envy of the opportunity which the patient is having to be listened to, to be understood, to be helped. Must one get "sick" to have this boon?

FREQUENCY OF TREATMENT SESSIONS

Another initial question is that of how frequently the analytic session should occur. This has undergone much discussion of recent years, partly because of the greatly increased numbers of patients seeking psychoanalytic treatment, partly because of the (American) trend to shorten the work week, and partly because of certain theoretical propositions made by one group of analysts who hold that the frequency of visits should be variable at the discretion of the analyst. Originally patients were seen six times a week. Five times a week is now perhaps the prevalent standard in this country, and four times a week a minimum.

Dr. Phyllis Greenacre has stated precisely what most of us believe about the frequency of treatment sessions and stated it so clearly and well that I would like to quote the passage in full:

It is well to have analytic sessions spaced sufficiently close together that a sense of continuity of relationship (between analyst and analysand) and of content of material produced may be sustained. It would seem then that as nearly as possible a daily contact avoiding frequent or long gaps in treatment is desirable. In the setting of the organization of most lives, the analysis takes its place in the work of the week and accordingly five or six sessions are allocated to it. Later in many analyses it may be desirable to reduce the number of sessions, after the relationship between analyst and analysand has been consolidated, and the analyst has been able to determine the analysand's reactions to interruptions, first apparent in the reactions to week ends. If the analysand carries over a day's interruption well, without the relationship cooling off too much or the content being lost sight of, then it may be possible to carry the analysis on a three- or four-session-a-week basis, keeping a good rhythm of work with the patient. The desirability of this, however, can only be determined after the analyst has had a chance to gauge the patient's natural tempo and needs and the character of his important defenses; and this must vary from patient to patient. This initial period is generally at least a year, and more often longer.

There are three additional unfavorable factors here, however, which are seldom mentioned: (1) The actual prolongation of the treatment by spreading or infrequent spacing of sessions, in analytic work as well as in other psychotherapeutic approaches. If this prolongation is great, there is that much longer impact on other arrangements of the patient's life. "Brief psychotherapies" are sometimes paradoxically extended over very long times indeed, being repeatedly ended and reopened, because little was consolidated in the treatment and all sorts of extraneous and unnecessary interferences entered. (2) The larger the number of analytic patients possible at any given time when sessions per patient are less frequent, the greater the tax on the analyst in keeping at his mental fingertips the full range of facts and reactions belonging to each patient. The monetary recompense may, however, be greatly increased. Here again the feasibility of spacing must depend on some factors belonging to the analyst's special equipment and demands, combined with the patient's ability to "carry over," and there will inevitably be considerable variability in these. (3) The less frequent the therapeutic sessions the greater may be the risk of inadequate analysis of the negative transference. Especially with those patients where hours are made less frequent because the patient is thought by the analyst to be "wasting the hour" by what appears as unproductive talk or by silence, or where the analyst fears that the patient is feeling guilty over his silences, it has sometimes been recommended that the patient be given a vacation from treatment or that sessions be made less frequent. From my experience in the reanalysis of a number of patients, it has seemed to me rather that many of these periods are due to the patient's difficulty in expressing hostile or erotic feelings. It is about these feelings, rather than about his silence, that he feels guilty. Too often if he is given a rest or hours are made infrequent, these emotional attitudes are never brought out to be analyzed, and appear later on in disturbing forms. I am further impressed with the fact that those analysts who talk most about the dangers of dependence seem rarely to consider the reciprocal relationship between tenacious dependency and unanalyzed negative transference. In so far as negative attitudes toward the analyst are not analyzed or even expressed, the need of the patient to be reassured of the love and protection of the analyst becomes enormously increased and demanding. The analyst may see only this side of the picture and erroneously attempt to deal with it by greater spacing of contacts.

The length of the hour is, as a matter of practice, generally maintained at forty-five to sixty minutes. Certainly it is desirable that a sufficient span of time be permitted for a kind of natural organic pattern of productivity to occur during many of the sessions. The hour is our time unit in general use, perhaps because it does involve some kind of natural span of this kind, and is a feasible unit fitting into the working day. While there have been many experiments of speeding up analytic sessions to two a day or increasing the length to two hours at one session, no such practice has generally taken hold. It is my belief, however, that a regular allotment of time—the same duration and so far as possible on a prearranged and constant week-by-week schedule (in contrast to varying spans of time in sessions at irregular periods not expected in advance)—generally aids in the rhythm and continuity of the work and minimizes utilization of external situations as resistance by the patients.[73]

For reasons that will become increasingly clear as we go on, the psychoanalyst must *try* (and it is not easy) to remain neutral and "aseptic." This means that one doesn't *chat* with patients, touch them (*e.g.,* shake hands) unnecessarily, ask favors of them or accept favors or gifts from them,* attend small social engagements where they will be, or discuss their "material" with numerous other colleagues. I mention the latter point because it is particularly tempting to young analysts to do this. I shall only mention more serious transgressions of the rule against physical contact as sometimes occurring, but as representing *prima facie* evidence of the incompetence or criminal ruthlessness of the analyst.

OTHER DETAILS

An important detail in practice relates to necessary interruption of treatment by the analyst. These are of several kinds. A brief absence, unless it occurs at a very critical period, can be explained to the patient as it arises (at the end † of an hour several days before

---

* Comments my associate, Dr. H. G. van der Waals:

"I think every analyst in Europe, at least every analyst I know, shakes hands with his patient at the beginning and the end of the hour. It gives valuable information about the mood of the patient, his reaction to the hour, etc. In Europe it would be a technical error not to do this; patients would think it very queer."

"As a general rule an analyst should not accept gifts, but he should also know when to make an exception. When a patient who has great difficulty in giving anything is able in the course of his treatment to make the analyst a small present, it would be a serious mistake not to accept the gift."

† The analyst who "begins" a patient's hour by an announcement violates his own statement of wanting to hear the spontaneous free association material of the patient's mind. It is bad manners, and it is a technical error. The exception to this is the situation developing when the patient consistently suppresses or represses his reactions to "end-of-the-hour" events, such as receiving his bill. This makes it necessary for the analyst to take it up, artificially, in subsequent sessions.

the analyst is leaving). Longer absences, such as vacations, the patient will half expect. But no patient should be abandoned for a month a few weeks after beginning an analysis. If this is unavoidable, as in the case of emergency, the analyst should recognize that he is breaking the terms of the contract, and make the best compromise he can in reparation. Sometimes this involves finding another analyst for the patient. Sometimes it involves taking the patient with him. Sometimes it involves keeping in nonanalytic contact with the patient during the absence. Analysts who get married or divorced during the course of the analysis of a patient can expect plenty of trouble. It is impossible to keep knowledge of these things from the patient, and they always cause serious, sometimes devastating, reactions.

The psychoanalyst is a psychotherapist, and the fact that he is usually also a psychiatrist and a physician is for our purposes here of academic interest. *As far as this patient is concerned,* the psychoanalyst is a specialist and not a general medical practitioner. He has not contracted, and should not undertake, to either diagnose or treat intercurrent physical affections. The patient is justified in expecting him to have medical knowledge and to answer some types of relevant questions within his competence; but if the patient needs much medical information or examination or treatment of physical diseases, he should be referred to a colleague.

There are a few other matters of importance in connection with the sealing of the original contract. The patient does not know exactly what the treatment is like. He may believe that he will be immediately and progressively better and wiser. He should be warned, therefore, that this is not necessarily true, that analysis is an upsetting and *then* a restorative process, and that important moves and decisions in the life program should be deferred until the analysis is complete. This applies to such things as marriage or divorce, change of occupation, and so on.

In spite of all the preparatory instruction, which should be minimal, and in spite of the (now) widespread popular familiarity with some features of the treatment, the patient who contracts with a therapist for psychoanalytic therapy does not really know what he is letting himself in for. To be sure, the same might be said of various surgical operations and other technical procedures in modern medicine. But the very nature of psychoanalysis, in opening a way for the direct expressions of previously unconscious material, makes it peculiarly exotic, strange, and unimaginable. That of which the patient is unconscious he naturally does not know, by definition. In theory he understands this, but only *after* he has had the experience of being psychoanalyzed does he fully appreciate the depth and power of the forces and mechanisms of the unconscious.

The patient who submits himself for psychoanalytic therapy begins with a certain blind faith in the psychoanalyst, regardless of the disclaimers he may profess. He begins, too, with various hopes and expectations, regardless of the skepticism he may express. As we shall see, these are actually far more specific than he realizes, and may have little to do with "getting" or "being" well in the conventional sense of the words. And finally, he has some fears, most of which are unrealistic to be sure, but disturbing nonetheless.

But his faith is not entirely blind, if he has been well advised. For the psychoanalyst has certain scientific and ethical obligations. The patient does not know just what will happen, but he should have reason to believe that he may advantageously enter into a contract with this fellow human being and expect professional integrity and competence. The patient's fears thus tend to return to his own inadequacies, his own incompetence to fulfill a contract. And he may be right. It is the task of the analysis to forestall this failure if possible, to defeat this defeatism, or—in the occasional sad instance—to recognize that it is invincible and gently redirect the seeker toward more attainable goals.

III

THE REGRESSION

The Reaction of the Party of the First Part
to the Psychoanalytic Treatment Situation

THIS CHAPTER DEALS WITH THE COMPLEX NATURE OF THE REGRESSION
induced in and by the analytic situation. Given the privilege to say
whatever one is thinking to a listener who refrains from excessive or
discouraging interruption, an individual seeking therapeutic help
will experience both a gratification and a growing frustration, which
lead to the denudation of the original wish to be cured and its replacement with more primitive, buried wishes and the employment of
techniques that once applied to expectations of other kinds from
other persons for whom the therapist is substituted. With this regressive trend go fluctuations and variations in the "I" concept, or self-
estimate, including body image and ego-ideal. This regression
proceeds in waves and cycles of alternating attitudes, with frequent
"surfacing" and realigning. By maintaining a steady position of non-
reaction and an optimum degree of frustration, the therapist assists
the process of self-visualization, objectification, and stabilization
which represent aspects of the self-knowledge enabling an abandon-

ment of the regressive position and progressive return to "health."

Whoever undergoes psychoanalysis soon realizes that he has become involved in a most extraordinary and unique process. For many of us it is so familiar and "routine" that we forget how remarkable this situation is. A patient who has come to a doctor for relief from his pain is invited to lie down and to talk about it, or about anything else he chooses! He may talk about himself, he may talk about his neighbors, he may talk about his wife. He may talk about the past, about the present, or about the future. He does not have to be fair; he does not have to be considerate, he does not have to be objective. Everything is to be considered "tentative"—an opinion as of this moment only. The main object of the procedure, as it has been explained to him, is that he present his thoughts and feelings to the joint observation of himself and his unseen listener. Thus he may—indeed *must*—say anything that comes into his mind, which is something he cannot do in *any other existing human circumstances* or in any other social situation.

It is little wonder that few patients can take full advantage of such an opportunity immediately. The uniqueness of the situation is more apt to be only preconsciously or subliminally perceived, so that the first few sentences spoken by a patient after the psychoanalyst has seated himself and announced his attentiveness often give important clues as to the nature of the deepest problem. But after the introductory phase, the patient's "natural" resistance is aroused and he only gradually feels his way into this unparalleled situation of "free thought" and "free speech." With more or less difficulty, sometimes with eagerness and sometimes with trepidation, he starts talking.

For one hour he pours out his thoughts—helter-skelter—into the ears of the physician. To all of it the physician listens, but makes little response except to indicate his close attention. He makes no suggestion. He gives no comfort. He makes no criticism. He gives no diagnostic opinion. He only listens.*

Grateful for the attention and audience and intrigued by the new experience, the patient pays his money (in credit †) and takes his

---

* It is not quite correct to say he "only" listens or to imply that he is as stiff and silent as a statue. I will clarify this later; here I am schematizing the relationship.
† Sometimes in cash. See discussion by Fingert.[37]

leave; one unit of the transaction is completed. On the following day the patient returns, reclines, recites. Once more he gives, and gives, and gives. He tries his best to do as he thinks the doctor wants him to. He submits his "free associations," his memories, his reflections, his confidences, his intimate thoughts, his gravest fears. Again the physician listens and is silent (and does *not* "give"). Again the patient pays and leaves.

This process of free association in the sense of verbalizing one's random thinking is really a most extraordinary phenomenon with a long history. Something like it appears to have been used by the Greeks, if we may judge by the sample reported in Aristophanes' comedy, *The Clouds*. They even used a couch! *

According to Freud himself,[51] Friedrich Schiller in his correspondence with Koerner in 1788 recommended that anyone who desired to be productive should adopt this method. Freud[51] also mentions Ludwig Boerne's article entitled, "The Art of Becoming an Original Writer in Three Days," written in 1823, which pretty much described free association. Freud also referred to Havelock Ellis' discovery of the publication by a Dr. J. J. Garth Wilkinson in 1857 of "A New Method" of writing poetry, which was essentially free association. William Lecky,† the English historian, specifically described

---

* The story is that Strepsiades, an unhappily married, stupid, and dishonest farmer, comes to Athens to consult Socrates as to how one can successfully cheat his creditors. Socrates directs him to lie down and give free associations, which he tries to do, in spite of bedbugs, and other interruptions, while Socrates points out inconsistencies and inferences. The play thus ridiculed the teaching of Socrates. See the Benjamin Rogers translation in *Fifteen Greek Plays*.[137]

† In *Rationalism in Europe,* Vol. II, 1865, quoted by Oberndorf [118] as follows:

"That certain facts remain hidden in the mind, that it is only by a strong act of volition they can be recalled to recollection, is a fact of daily experience, but it is now fully established that a multitude of events which are so completely forgotten that no effort of will can revive them, and that their statement calls up no reminiscence, may nevertheless be, so to speak, embedded in the memory, and may be reproduced with intense vividness under certain physical conditions.

"But not only are facts retained in the memory of which we are unconscious, the mind itself is also perpetually acting—pursuing trains of thought automatically, of which we have no consciousness. Thus it has been often observed that a subject which at night appears tangled and confused, acquires a perfect clearness and arrangement during sleep.

". . . In the course of recollection, two things will often rise in succession which appear to have no connection whatever; but a careful investigation will prove that there is some forgotten link of association which the mind had pursued, the existence of unconscious connections between thoughts in 1865. However, Plotinus [121] (204–270 A.D.) and Leibniz [90] (1646–1716) both explicitly pointed out the existence of unconscious mental connections.

Hobbes in his *Leviathan* (1651), according to Macalpine and Hunter,[101] described that

> TRAYN of thoughts [by which], I understand that succession of one Thought to another, which is called . . . *Mental Discourse*. When a man thinketh on any thing whatsoever, His next Thought after, is not altogether so casual as it seems to be. Not every Thought to every Thought succeeds indifferently. . . . Only this is certain, it shall be something that succeeded the same before, at one time or another. This Trayn of Thoughts, or Mental Discourse, is of two sorts. The first is *Unguided, without Design,* and inconstant. . . . In which case the thoughts are said to wander, and seem impertinent one to another, as in a Dream. . . . And yet in this wild ranging of the mind, a man may oft-times perceive the way of it, and the dependance of one thought upon another.

Immanuel Kant published a pamphlet, "The Power of the Mind, Through Simple Determination, to become Master over Morbid Ideas," in which he relates that while suffering with gout he performed an experiment on himself:

> In order that my sleep should not be interfered with, I at once seized upon my stoical remedy, that of directing with effort, my thoughts towards some chosen indifferent object, for example, towards the many associated ideas brought up by the word Cicero. In this way I led my attention away from every other idea. Thus these became quickly blunted so that sleepiness could overcome them. And this I am always able to repeat in attacks of this kind with a good result. That I had not dealt with imaginary pain was clearly evident the following morning when I found the toes of my left foot swollen and red.[14, 84]

---

but of which we are entirely unconscious. It is in connection with these facts that we should view that reappearance of opinions, modes of thought, and emotions belonging to a former stage of our intellectual history. It is especially common (at least especially manifest) in languor, in disease, and above all, in sleep."

Freud apparently never consciously discovered the report of Francis Galton, published in *Brain* in 1879 as "Psychometric Experiments," which Gregory Zilboorg [162, 163] has so vividly brought to our attention. Galton recorded his having become interested in what passed through his mind when he looked at certain objects or thought of certain words. He called these "associated ideas." He wrote them down and noted their number and the time it took him to register them.

> The associated ideas arise of their own accord, and we cannot, except in indirect and unperfected ways, compel them to come. My object is to show how the whole of these associated ideas, though they are for the most part exceedingly fleeting and obscure and barely cross the thresholds of our consciousness, may be seized, dragged into daylight and recorded. . . . The results well repaid the trouble. They gave me an interesting and unexpected view of the number of the operations of the mind, and of the obscure depths in which they took place, of which I had been little conscious before. . . . I was sure that samples of my whole life had passed before me, that many bygone incidents which I never suspected to have formed part of my stock of thoughts had been glanced at as objects too familiar to awaken attention.[163]

Freud discovered that this process goes on much more easily when there is a listener. But then other complications develop. For as this consciously undirected process of thinking and talking goes on with a minimum of participation by the listener except occasional indications of his attentive presence, the talker begins to develop expectations. "Perhaps," he thinks, "the doctor is accumulating sufficient information to enable him to say something to me that will solve everything." For a time the patient is sustained in this one-sided transaction by such assumptions as this. Having poured out his "soul," as the expression goes, and thus enriched the physician's knowledge about his "case," he expects from the physician the "magic word," the oracular pronouncement.

In such generalizations as we are making, it should be remembered that different patients *begin* the course of treatment at various levels of maladjustment—*i.e.*, degrees of regression or, more frequently, lags in development of the normal pattern of adjustment. They may be desperate; they may be only sorely troubled; they may be perplexed and uncertain; or they may be calmly resolute in the direction of improving certain self-observed deficiencies. Whichever it be, each patient will have endeavored to present to the world in everyday life a certain front. Upon beginning psychoanalytic treatment, even though it be in the privacy of the consultation office, he tends to present this habitual front to the doctor in spite of the "permission" to do otherwise. Rado [124] has described successive levels of this initial "front." There is the relatively mature individual, who takes the position: "I am (consciously) delighted to cooperate with the doctor and to utilize this opportunity to discover how to make better use of my potentials." At a somewhat lower level is the attitude: "I have troubles which I have not been able to solve myself, and I am willing to cooperate with the doctor in order to learn how to do this." At a still lower level is the patient who would say, "I don't know what to do. I want to find out. Perhaps by this method I can get relief from my torture." At a still lower level there is greater helplessness: "In my desperation I turn to the doctor for the help he can give me, the relief he offers me." And, finally, at the lowest level there is almost hopelessness but with the magic-craving expectation of a miracle.

SUCCESSIVE LEVELS OF REGRESSION IN THE COURSE OF TREATMENT

Treatment of various kinds—including psychoanalysis—can be applied at any of these various levels. All of these levels appear in the course of any psychoanalysis. In our presentation of the theory of psychoanalytic treatment we shall assume that the patient comes in at the highest level, which of course he rarely does. And we shall remember that, even at this level, something is wrong or the patient would not be seeking treatment. Increasingly, in the course of the treatment, he will tend to "regress" to the lower levels; he will become more and more childlike in his attitudes and in his emotional dependency upon the physician. He will become a child again, and be reborn, so to speak.* Then he will grow up again, grow up better than he did before, guided by his now more mature intelligence and the warnings and lessons of his unhappy experiences now better understood.

This is the general thesis of psychoanalytic treatment. It involves the induction (or occurrence) of a regression,† over and beyond that partial regression or developmental lag present at the start, representing the illness for which the treatment was undertaken. Psychoanalytic treatment is a little like removing an embedded fishhook which has to be pushed farther and the barb removed before the hook can be extracted. Freud hinted at this when he spoke of neurotic illness as expressing the suffering from *reminiscences* which can neither be fully repressed nor fully recalled. In psychoanalytic treatment they are, first, more completely recollected and then more fully repressed (or discarded).

Psychoanalysis is not alone in making use of regression in order to favor a new development. It was recommended by Jesus to Nicodemus, who was astounded by the recommendation that he be born

* This metaphorical language can be helpful in grasping the general principle of regression, but it will be confusing if one pushes it too far. Of course, the patient cannot actually become a child, in one sense, but in another sense he does become a child. He acts like one and he sees that he has always acted like one to some extent, and he can compare how he has actually acted with how he has often wanted to act and couldn't, especially when he was a child. An occasional patient will carry the regression back to an enactment of infantilism which is disturbing and undesirable; the prognosis is better if the extreme infantilism is merely glimpsed.

† The term regression is one of the more ambiguous concepts of psychoanalytic theory. It refers to many phenomena that can be viewed from dynamic, economic, topographic and adaptive aspects. Kris [87] suggested an intriguing addendum to the theory of regression; the integrative functions of the ego may include self-regulated regression. Perhaps this is the regressive quality that is most apparent in most successful psychoanalytic treatment.

Some of my colleagues take issue with my model of regression. They hold that what appears to be an increasing regression in the analysis describes rather the increasing accuracy of the patient's awareness of himself, of the infantile nature of his intentions, wishes, needs, moods and so forth. They think regression does not properly describe the increasing knowledge acquired by the observing part of the ego, which is (therefore) constantly progressing, in one sense. Other colleagues object to my use of the word *induction* as attributing too much power to the analyst and implying that he can determine the form of the regression. Of course I don't mean it in this way. The regression occurs; it develops; it is induced by the total situation, as explained above. The analyst should not develop fantasies that it is *he* as a person who has induced it. Cf. D. W. Winnicott.[161]

again and really grow up. The same idea appears in other (especially Oriental) religions.[112] In a technical sense hypnosis and the insulin therapy routine depend upon this device.* Indeed, it occurs to some degree in all hospitalization, whether for psychiatric illnesses or for medical and surgical illnesses, and in anaesthesia, shock therapies, insulin treatment, etc.†

But in psychoanalytic treatment, *for one hour a day*, the regression is there, to be heard and seen and utilized and ultimately resolved. It is sometimes called the "transference neurosis," but whatever it is called, this phenomenon of regression and its technical exploitation are of the very essence of psychoanalytic treatment. (See contributions of Fisher, [38] Gill,[65] MacAlpine,[100] and Nunberg.[117])

Freud made eminently clear, time after time, that what he meant by psychoanalysis as a treatment method involved the development of transference neurosis, implying and including this kind of regression. There are a few contemporaries who are skeptical in regard to the desirability of permitting or favoring a further degree of regression in psychoanalytic treatment.[1, 83, 123] The experiments of these workers in the exploration of the unconscious and the use of insight without the induction of regression are interesting and suggest methods of psychotherapy valuable for some conditions, but these methods are not properly called psychoanalysis. In this book we shall consider the regression incident to psychoanalytic treatment as an essential element. In the material that is to follow we shall offer a theoretical framework within which to explain why the regression occurs, the way in which it usually occurs, its therapeutic derivatives, and its ultimate recession and disappearance.

What we call regression in the psychoanalytic treatment situation refers to a very considerable retrograde process of personality development. There is a regression to earlier and more primitive

---

* Patients awakening from electroshock therapy frequently describe themselves as having been reborn.

† The recent reports by scientific observers of various indoctrination programs by communist governments suggest that an important psychological principle has been employed in the induction of cognitive changes that vary in extent and duration. Such reports describe extraordinary phenomena that may be conceptualized as processes of regression.[64, 93, 141]

ways of perceiving and conceptualizing and behaving. There is a constriction in the field of attention, a preoccupation with the self, and a simplification or reduction in the structural complexity of psychological functioning. Primary processes emerge and secondary processes diminish in importance or disappear.[6, 66] As we shall see, the process can be described from various standpoints.

Why does the regression occur? This topic has been long and much discussed. We must most certainly try to avoid the fallacious causality explanation. No one thing "causes" * the regression but it results from numerous factors. The partial regression already present which represents the patient's illness has been already mentioned. Coming to the physician is a further step backward, in a sense—a step backward in order to make a better "run" forward. But coming to the physician makes it possible to lay aside the façade or pretense of normality, so that the already existing degree of regression covered by the façade becomes immediately apparent.

Entering upon psychoanalytic treatment means the taking of not just *one* more step, but many more steps, backward. During the analytic hour (and sometimes outside of it) he is definitely "worse" or "sicker" than was apparent before the treatment. From one point of view this is only apparent; he and the analyst are able to see how sick he really was, but he can cover it up. But in another sense it is real in that his pretense at being normal is diminished, made more difficult.

Freud called these phenomena to our attention. In his 1914 paper, "Recollection, Repetition and Working Through," he stated:

> He [the patient] also repeats during the treatment all his symptoms and now we see that our special insistence upon the compulsion to repeat has not yielded any new fact but is only a more comprehensive point of view. We are only making it clear

---

* For the Aristotelian theory of complex causation, the "formal cause" of the regression might be ascribed to the basic rule, the permissiveness of the analysis, the very nature of the therapeutic situation. The "material cause" would then be the very existence of the neurosis, the need of the patient for help, the already present tendencies toward regression. The "efficient cause" would be the frustration in the therapy to which I have referred. Then the "final cause" would be the assumed capacity of the patient for ultimate reintegration, resumption of growth and "cure."

to ourselves that the patient's condition of illness does not cease when the analysis begins, that we have to treat his illness as an actual force, active at the moment, and not as an event in his past life. . . . Transference thus forms a kind of intermediary realm between illness and real life, through which the journey from the one to the other must be made. The new state of mind has absorbed all the features of the illness; it represents, however, an artificial illness which is at every point accessible to our interventions. It is at the same time a piece of real life, but adapted to our purposes by specially favorable conditions, and it is of a provisional character.[57]

We must remember that it is precisely this more honest, even if more disturbing, behavior that the therapist must learn about in order to offer help. He has invited the patient to let himself go, to let himself be as childish as he wishes, to say whatever comes to his mind regardless of the consequences that would ensue were this not a special situation. Thus, the patient is not only permitted but encouraged to abandon those very devices which he has spent a lifetime in acquiring with respect to what he might say to and about another human being. *In this situation* there is no need to be polite, no need to be considerate, no need to be fair, no need to be practical, no need to be realistic. It is only necessary to follow the original instruction: "Try only to be honest. Think whatever you wish and say whatever you think. It may be only tentative. At any rate I promise there will be no retaliation, no passing of judgment, not even a definite conclusion."

Such an invitation from the therapist for the patient to become more self-preoccupied may not be needed; for many patients the urge to regress in this direction is only too strong. It occurs even outside the analytic hour. Regression is greatly favored not only by the "permissiveness" of the analyst's attitude but by the physical features of the analytic situation—the reclining posture, the invisible physician, the quietness of the chamber, the relative silence of the therapist. Gill mentions "The general atmosphere of timelessness . . . the disregard of symptoms . . . and the frequency of visits, which, metaphorically speaking, we may regard as the constant irritation necessary to keep open the wounds into the unconscious. . . ."[65] The diminution of external sensory stimuli furthers this; Hebb and his associates of the University of Montreal have shown that a considerable degree of regression can be induced by this device alone.[12, 78] *

In the opinion of one of our most thoughtful writers, Bertram Lewin,[91] the regression in psychoanalytic therapy is comparable to that which occurs in sleep, the psychoanalytic situation having indeed arisen from a kind of sleep therapy (hypnosis) from which subsequently, by a bargain with the patient, so to speak, actual sleep was excluded from the manifest picture. Lewin has developed the idea that traces of sleep insinuate themselves into the manifest picture. The wish to be put to sleep becomes supplanted by the wish to associate freely, and the patient lies down, not to sleep, but to associate. But in associating he tends to regress and to dream. The analyst, as Lewin has pointed out in another paper,[92] contributes to a magical effect which operates either to waken the patient somewhat or to put him to sleep a little deeper, to soothe or to arouse.

THE CONTROLLED FRUSTRATION

The sense of frustration experienced by the patient in the analytic situation is partially a reflection of the reality situation, but it can and must be regulated by the analyst. Actually, of course, the patient is not denied anything except that which he should not have —like a child who sees a shiny, loaded revolver. But the sense of frustration *experienced* by the patient is directly attributed by him (even against his better judgment) to what the analyst does and does not do—or say. Knowing this, the analyst must indeed do or not do that which is necessary to control the rapidity of the retrograde process and the depth of the regression. Therapy is defeated by too rapid or

* From the recent studies in experimental isolation which followed the early study by Hebb (for example, by Lilly,[94] by Macalpine,[100] and by Solomon, Leiderman, Mendelson, and Wexler,[145]) we are beginning to realize more and more how great the role of external stimulus impact is on ego functioning. In the light of these isolation experiments and accumulating data regarding solitary sailors, polar explorers, prisoners, and the deaf and blind, it is increasingly apparent that the autonomy of ego is maintained only by a balanced dependency on both the id and the external world. (See Rapaport.[126])

too slow a regression or by too deep a regression too early in the treatment. We cannot go back on our original invitation and promise; that would be a breach of contract. But we did not promise to give him anything except audience and "help." And we must decide what kind of help to give and when to give it. The analyst must learn to withhold, but he must also learn to give and to give at the right time.*

Our theory holds that a patient's illness reflects a growth, impeded in its original, natural development by deflections incident to faulty responses to early crises. Dammed up emotions, chiefly rage, have followed unmanageable, unendurable situations. Hence, the release for better direction of long repressed rage is, in a narrow sense, an *immediate* object of the treatment. This must be not only a temporary drainage but an elimination of the basic or typical provocations of the rage in order that the energy required for this inflammation and blockage can be more expediently invested. This should never blind the analyst to the *ultimate constructive* objectives of the treatment as defined above.

Thus the patient undergoing psychoanalysis can be expected to display—after a while—inappropriate and futile anger. He may not *feel* it as anger; he may want to call it resentment or depression or

* One of my colleagues, Dr. Herbert J. Schlesinger, makes the sage observation that "the analyst cannot, of course, fulfill the patient's anachronistic wishes even if he were to want to. While he might accede to a patient's specific requests, for instance, to speak to him more often, his action would only be such as to encourage the patient to continue to express his regressive wishes in pseudo-mature forms. I don't believe that the analyst has to think of himself as frustrating the patient's regressive demands; the frustration is built in to the fact that this is a transference neurosis, a re-enactment rather than a primary experience. I think that the sense of frustration experienced by the patient is a very real phenomenon but, like the regression, it should be thought of as part of the patient's psychology, not the analyst's. I recall you saying something to some of us that is relevant here. When the analyst finally 'gives' something to the patient (an interpretation) it is something much more and different from what the patient wanted and, like a drouth-breaking cloudburst, it brings a measure of relief but also problems of its own. It is necessary to emphasize that the analyst's giving and withholding are not conceptually coordinate with, and are certainly not intended to fulfill the needs expressed by the patient. Although the analyst learns to intervene judiciously so that the patient is not unnecessarily helped to feel constantly that he gets too much or too little (a common resistance pattern that serves to reduce the analyst's comments to a common denominator of so many quantities of verbiage), the analyst must avoid becoming preoccupied with "dosing" the patient with his offerings. To do so would be merely to meet the patient's transference expectation with a complementary countertransference attitude.

righteous indignation or discouragement. But whatever he calls it, he will display it, and in displaying it rather than masking or "controlling" it, he will regress still further. His sense of frustration affords a continuing provocation to resentment. For, as the days go by, there develops in the patient a growing suspicion that there exists between him and his therapist what an economist would call "an unfavorable trade balance." The patient has "cooperated," he has obeyed the instructions, he has given himself. He has contributed information, exposing his very heart, and in addition to all this he has paid money for the sessions in which he did it! And what in return has he gotten from the physician? Attention, audience, toleration, yes—but no response. No "reaction." No advice. No explanation. No solution. No help. No love.

This is not quite right, of course, because there have been some responses and reactions on the part of the therapist. But they have not been what the patient expected. There was certainly no magic word. There was a minimum of reassurance. There was no indication, for the most part, that the therapist took a position in anything. The therapist was told about the enormity of the patient's wife's behavior —but he said nothing. He was told a good joke—but he didn't laugh. He was given a full account of an incident with a traffic officer—and he asked only how the *officer* felt about it! He interrupted the recounting of a most important episode to ask a most irrelevant question—something about the day of the week on which it occurred.

These unpredictable responses from the therapist are disconcerting and cannot be dealt with in ordinary "secondary process" (logical) ways. Combined with his general nonresponsiveness and silence, they favor a growing sense of frustration. This is increased by the fact that, in the course of relinquishing his self-censure and his long-used conventional habits of verbal restraint, the patient has become increasingly concerned about being approved of by the therapist. Gradually the sense of having contributed in vain, of having failed to please or satisfy or even provoke the therapist, begins to weigh upon the patient, first as mild uneasiness, then as anxiousness, and finally as frank frustration and resentment. Phyllis McGinley probably wasn't thinking of psychoanalysis when she wrote, very aptly:

> Sticks and stones are hard on bones
> Aimed with angry art
> Words can sting like anything
> But silence breaks the heart.[102]

Frustration of and in itself is certainly not an effective form of treatment. If it were, many simpler ways could be found in which a patient could be frustrated than by the use of the psychoanalytic couch. Indeed, it is just because of other frustrations that many patients are ill. No, frustration itself is not treatment, although it is sometimes employed as if it were. It is properly a condition whereby the real dynamics of psychoanalytic treatment become effective. This we shall examine more minutely.

These principles stem from Freud's second "fundamental rule" of psychoanalysis:

> *Analytic treatment should be carried through, as far as is possible, under privation—in a state of abstinence.* By abstinence, however, is not to be understood doing without any and every satisfaction—that would of course not be practicable; nor do we mean what it popularly connotes, refraining from sexual intercourse; it means something else which has far more to do with the dynamics of illness and recovery.
>
> You will remember that it was a *frustration* that made the patient ill, and that his symptoms serve him as substitutive gratifications. . . . The patient looks for his substitutive gratification above all in the treatment itself, in his transference-relationship with the physician, and he may even strive to compensate himself through this means for all the other privations laid upon him. A certain amount must of course be permitted to him, more or less according to the nature of the case and the patient's individuality. But it is not good to let it become too much. Any analyst who out of the fullness of his heart and the readiness to help perhaps extends to the patient all that one human being may hope to receive from another, commits the same economic error which our non-analytic institutions for nervous patients are guilty of. They exert themselves only to make everything as pleasant as possible for the patient, so that he may feel well there and gladly take flight back there again away from the trials of life. In so doing they entirely forego making him stronger for life and more capable of carrying out the actual tasks of his life. In analytic treatment all such cosseting must be avoided. As far

as his relations with the physician are concerned, the patient must have unfulfilled wishes in abundance. It is expedient to deny him precisely those satisfactions which he desires most intensely and expresses most importunately.[60]

The state of abstinence, then, refers to the activity of both patient and analyst: the analyst must abstain from responding to the patient's pleas, charges, maneuvers, requests, and demands in the way he would ordinarily respond were this a social relationship, *and* the patient must experience the denied satisfaction. For so far we have come upon no better method for allowing the patient to discover his style of, and his conditions for, loving and hating. It is this controlled frustration in analysis that highlights the patient's typical methods of relating himself to the significant people in his life. This self-discovery is crucial for the process of recovery.

STEPS IN THE REGRESSION

Obviously the mounting sense of deprivation and frustration described above cannot go on indefinitely. It provokes in the patient certain reactions of various kinds and degrees, and the desired effect can be obtained only if the frustration tension is held within a certain optimum range. Technical skill consists in knowing at what time and in what degree and in what form the patient's need for response from the analyst should be ministered to in order to maintain the optimal degree of frustration, or, to put it another way, in order to keep him from becoming completely demoralized from an excessive feeling of frustration.

We can answer this, in theory, by examining closely just what the patient really expects or wants from the therapist at a particular time. To be sure, he wants relief from something uncomfortable. He wants to be "cured" of some affliction, or at least to have it ameliorated. This is his conscious avowal in having undertaken treatment and in the making of the two-party contract. But we soon discover that considerably more and different expectations underlie this conscious motivation.

If one listens without comment to the free associations of a patient for a series of thirty or fifty or a hundred hours and then condenses the essence of the material to the simplest possible schematic form, it would often appear something like this:

1. I am suffering (and have suffered) in this way and that way, thus and thus and thus.

2. I don't want to suffer thus and thus and thus. (*Analyst inquires.*)

3. I want the analyst, by fully understanding my suffering, to cure me or relieve me. (*Analyst says nothing.*)

4. (*Patient goes on.*) In order that he may do so, I will explain more fully how I have long suffered in this way and sometimes in that way, formerly in that way and now in this way. (*Analyst listens.*)

5. By now surely the analyst understands me and could, if he would, counsel and advise me and prevent my having to suffer in these ways. (*The analyst remains essentially silent.*)

6. I have told him everything, now—well, nearly everything— he is omnipotent and omniscient—and he could probably take away my suffering almost by magic.

7. Surely he realizes how I suffer, surely he knows how much I want his help. But he is silent. Why? When is he going to help me? Why doesn't he? (*Analyst still silent.*)

8. I may as well confess. Of course I knew I would have to tell him at last. He knew I had done such things; he must have known. He was waiting for me to tell it all; now I have done so. I feel ashamed, but relieved.

9. He does not scold me, nor seem shocked. He makes no comments. Is he perhaps angry? Is he laughing? (*Analyst asks one or two questions.*)

10. I am getting nowhere, in spite of my confession. I still suffer this way and that way. Yet he is so good to listen, so patient, so calm, so *understanding*.

11. If he could only accept me, believe me, pity me—helpless, weak and guilty as I am. But how can he?

12. I wish he would talk to me—scold me, praise me, tell me I'm not impossible, or even say he liked me a little. I've tried so hard to please him in the ways I have always thought worked best. But I don't seem to. (*Analyst comments briefly.*)

13. Regardless of his coldness, I do like him, I love him anyway. But how can he love me—or even like me? No one does, no one can. No one really ever did. I must go on, I guess.

14. I don't like this fellow at all; he is crude and rude, he is un-

sympathetic, he is indifferent, he is impossible to please. He doesn't understand me. He is stupid, a fraud, a quack, an ignoramus. I will tell him so. (*Analyst is silent.*) *

This is as far as we shall take the schema now. Of course, the progression is never precisely this, and rarely so clear and simple as I have diagrammatically represented it. There are always various furbelows, digressions, interruptions, and minor complications. But in general it is quite "typical," as I can guarantee, and from it several significant things can be deduced.

First, the patient's sense of frustration which we were describing derives not alone from the mere unresponsiveness or unpredictableness of the party-of-the-second-part, baffling and disconcerting (and frustrating) as this may be. It is clear from even this short sample that the patient is seeking something not explicit in the original contract. He is seeking to get something (from the analyst) without being quite sure what it is. We see, too, that in the pursuit of this desideratum he uses successively various approaches, various devices or techniques to try to obtain it. In this process, too, he is able to see that it is not the analyst who frustrates, but he, the patient, who frustrates himself; that all his life he has adopted maneuvers that had "informed against" him, as it were. He begins to feel that it is his own responsibility to take charge of his life, and not the analyst's function.

Thus, we can condense the schema to an even shorter formula:

1. I will *give* to the doctor what he asks; then I shall *expect* something † *from* him.
2. I have given, but I do not get. I will expect.
3. I still do not get; to do so, I will try the techniques I have always used—or once used.
4. I have tried these in vain. Are the techniques wrong? Is the doctor wrong? Am I wrong? Surely something is wrong!
5. How do I get what I want? I will back up and start over. I will give more, and then—

---

* By these comments, I do not, of course, mean that the analyst is literally silent. I intend these remarks to indicate the state of the analyst's abstention discussed above.
† What this "something" turns out to be, we shall see later.

Techniques of getting what one wants from the environment were learned, as we know, in childhood and developed as our bodies and minds developed. In all adults they have been *somewhat* modified by experience. In the "normal" adult they have been greatly modified, in realistic directions. In the "neurotic" adult they have been less completely metamorphosed. Hence, under frustration the "normal" adult may "regress" to the use of "neurotic" techniques, as we see when people get angry or frightened. And in analysis the "neurotic" patient will use first his customary, semi-mature techniques and then regress to those still more infantile ones used earlier in his life.

He usually begins by wanting the physician to be sympathetic— *i.e.,* to recognize that he is really suffering—and he may interpret the physician's audience and silence to be sympathy. Encouraged by this, he tells more about himself, including sooner or later some things of which he is ashamed. He will often interpret the physician's silence as forgiveness. But soon he begins to wonder if the physician is—after all—just indifferent or perhaps bored or even disgusted. But, again encouraged, or desperate, he soon goes ahead with his revelations. For a time he (again) appreciates the therapist's attentive silence but gradually succumbs again to misgivings. "Why doesn't he say something? Am I not doing just as he told me to do? Am I not trying? Am I not producing? Why doesn't he at least commend me, even—God forgive me—praise me a little? I'm trying so hard to please him. Am I failing?"

The function of analysis is not, of course, to have the doctor "pleased" or the patient praised. Nevertheless the patient will, like most other human beings, do his best to be as pleasing as possible in his particular way because this is an early learned technique which daily experience of later life confirms. He will keep hoping that he has in some measure succeeded. The analyst's continued silence, however, is ultimately interpreted as an indication that this technique has failed. The patient may even come out quite frankly and ask, "When are you going to say something, Doctor? I have come here hour after hour now, for quite a while. I've paid my money and I've spoken my piece. I have done what you told me to and what am I getting? I don't hear a word out of you. Isn't it about time that you woke up and said something?"

The young analyst, no matter how much he has prepared himself by reading, is certain to be startled when he first encounters this astonishing phenomenon—the frank "admission" by the patient that he is not in treatment for the sake of getting better. I recall the dismay of a candidate in connection with his analysis of an intelligent scientist who complained at length of loneliness because his wife had gone on a brief vacation. He spoke of the way in which he looked forward to his analytic hour as an opportunity for both companionship and sympathy. He began to describe himself as having been "abandoned" by his wife. Apparently disappointed that his analyst made no comment in regard to this self-pity, he mumbled grudgingly that perhaps he wasn't doing what the analyst expected of him. To this the analyst remarked that his only expectations were that the patient say what came to his mind and try to analyze the meaning of his thoughts. The patient (to the analyst's astonishment) burst out in anger. It was, he said, a most injurious, destructive, devastating remark. It left him helpless and hopeless. It expressed clearly the analyst's attitude, which was one of complete rejection, of utter indifference toward the patient and his suffering. Sympathy, companionship, friendship—these were what he needed, not interpretations and snide remarks.

Rado [124] has schematized this progressive shift in the patient's attitude from the ingratiating and seductive to the expiatory, resentful, and vindictive in the following schematic way which is only slightly different from mine but may help to convey the feeling.

1. I am courting your favor, doing everything you wish; be nice to me.
2. It's time for you to cure me (by magic).
3. Meanwhile, make love to me (the magic of your love will cure me).
4. Your aloofness fills me with guilty fear. I should like to expiate for my disobedience and I promise to be obedient—please forgive me.
5. When I was a child, my parents never let me have my way. You said yourself that's how they started my intimidation and illness. It's *your* job to undo the wrong they did me. You urge me 'to get it off my chest,' but you hold me in your clutches just the same. You can't fool me.

6. Now I am really furious. Stop this double talk and cure me.

7. I shall get even with you . . . I never wish to see you again.

Similar sentiments are expressed in an untraced poem by one Tom Prideaux:

> With half a laugh of hearty zest
> I strip me off my coat and vest.
>
> Then heeding not the frigid air
> I fling away my underwear.
>
> So having nothing else to doff,
> I rip my epidermis off.
>
> More secrets to acquaint you with
> I pare my bones to strips of pith.
>
> And when the exposé is done
> I hang, a cobweb skeleton.
>
> While you sit there aloof, remote,
> And will not shed your overcoat.

UPS AND DOWNS IN THE PROGRESSIVE RECESSION

Not all the time does the patient feel frustrated. There are waves of gratitude for being listened to and understood, surprised joy in the achievement of new insights and progress, relief from oppressive guilt feelings, dawning hope for new possibilities. I have been emphasizing the patient's negative feelings because I feel that they tend to be neglected in psychoanalytic writing and teaching. But to avoid a similar blunder of one-sidedness, let me stress here the fact that psychoanalysis is a series of ups and downs, of ebbs and flows, of little gratifications and then disappointments. I have sometimes imagined the analytic hour to be like a magnifying mirror reflecting an imaginary beam of light emanating from the oscillations of the patient's moods from day to day, as determined by all of the external and internal stimuli bearing upon him. As a practical matter I have always taken occasion at one time or another in the analysis to follow the advice of one of my teachers, who said it was well to warn patients against being depressed over the fact that they are depressed, because when one feels the worst may be the time when he is making the most progress.

It is well to keep in mind the model of a customer seeking to obtain something in an exchange. The patient really wants something; he has paid for it (or will) and he will seek in his way to get it. He may avoid asking for it explicitly, endeavoring to be agreeable, at first, and suppressing plaintive and complaintive thoughts. He may express these covertly in dreams or by various roundabout maneuvers. He may ask to be reassured or to have certain dreams interpreted, thinking that this will both please the analyst and obtain some assistance. Other patients, or the same patient at other times, will grieve and stew and worry, trying different methods to please the analyst, to bribe him, or to provoke him, whimpering, pouting, sulking, storming, sobbing—in short, using all the methods of a frustrated child, and particularly those used by this particular patient as a child. Sometimes the latter have succeeded, in times past; sometimes they have failed. But in this new and baffling situation the patient is impelled to try everything.

In good time, the origin and meaning of these techniques will be pointed out to him, if he does not recognize them himself. But first he must *experience* them, see and feel the ways in which he tries to get what he wants. He will ultimately realize that certain methods, constantly unsuccessful, nevertheless were retained by him, whereas better ones were abandoned because under certain circumstances— one particularly painful time, maybe—they didn't work. This cyclic, repetitious factor in attempts at mastery is an important feature of psychoanalytic theory, and one sees it clearly in the psychoanalytic treatment process. The neutrality of the therapist, later on his confrontations and interpretations, enable the "observing" portion of the ego to get a panoramic view of what hitherto was only felt intensely and uncomprehendingly.

Of course, the therapist does break his silence, *his* abstinence— occasionally. He too is experiencing these abortive techniques as used by the patient; he too is surveying this panorama. In helping the observing ego to see it more clearly or more comprehensively, he may also gratify the regressing portion of the ego by this indication of interest and approval. The momentary abandonment of his role of detachment for the purpose of a comment may be interpreted as a mark of approval or even as a reward.

The patient in turn will often then respond with appreciation, euphoria, encouragement, and renewed hope. The young therapist is sometimes misled by this wave of "improvement." For, if the analysis goes as it should, frustration will mount again and the cycle will be repeated over and over. But each time the perspective will have been enlarged, the area of exploration widened, the penetration into the hidden part deepened.

I have often attempted to construct drawings which would indicate this oscillation of the course of analysis diagrammatically. I have never been satisfied with any that I have made, nor wholly satisfied with some of the better ones which some of my students have made, to indicate how each succeeding frustration and regression takes the patient deeper or further back, but how, with each recovery, each capturing of insight, he reconstitutes himself at a higher level, as it were. Perhaps it is a little like a mountain climber who discovers that the path which he is following will never take him to the top but may bring him to a rise from which he sees how he must go down again in order to get on a path which will take him higher.

There is a classical experiment in gestalt psychology used to test certain forms of animal learning in which an ape is placed in a cage with an opening to the rear and a banana outside the cage to the front. The animal must bring himself to surrender for a moment the exciting view of the banana, detaching himself from the stimulus of its proximity and making a direct move away from it, in order to get effectively to its actual capture.

This is comparable to the regression induced by the treatment, which is over and beyond that degree of regression—already present at the time the treatment began—represented by the patient's "illness." It is a "progressive regression"! It is a repetitious going-back to look and to remember and then coming forward to compare and in a sense correct.

I shall call attention to four aspects of this regression, regression in regard to the nature and substance of the thing wanted from the therapist, regression in respect to the techniques for getting the thing wanted, regression in respect to the source or indirect object of the patient's expectations, and regression in respect to the nature and character of the seeker himself. This can be made a little bit more clear if we diagram the sentence: I, the patient, want from the doctor cure (of my illness). (See Figure 6.)

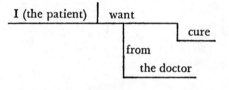

REGRESSION IN THE OBJECT

Let us first examine the regression in regard to the thing wanted. When the patient first comes to the doctor, there is no question about it. He wants help, relief, cure. At least that is what he *says* he wants. But very soon he comes to realize that he wants *more* than this. Even before he gets relief, often, he wants sympathy. And in the process of getting relief he gives evidence of wanting all those signals from one's fellowman which other human beings want—approval, acceptance, and even praise. In short, he wants to be liked. He wants to be thought of as having some intrinsic likableness, in spite of his symptoms, his failures, his complaints.

Gradually the patient comes to realize that his "wants" do not stop at this. Over and beyond sympathy and help and praise and being admired, he wants to be loved. He wants to have tokens of, or proofs of, love. Slowly and painfully he proceeds to this main stream underlying the persistent quest for some attainment in the treatment contract.

We can show this progressive substitution of a more primitive *object* of the patient's seeking as it develops in the regression by successively substituting for the *object* in our diagrammed sentence thus (see Figure 7).

Figure 7

Someone might ask why the search for love is considered characteristic of a regressed state. The confusion lies in the many ways in which the word "love" is used in our vocabulary. Love in the sense it is experienced by the patient when this type of regression has occurred is ultimately recognized by him to be comparable to the yearnings of a nursing baby at the breast or of a child first experiencing pleasurable skin sensations or excitement. This love is something given by someone else almost concretely, like milk or a caress—not not as it is expressed (given) in a mature way. It is something almost magical in its powers, as essential and restorative and pleasure-giving as a mother's milk. There is a little echo of this magic feeling in the ecstasy of adolescent romance when it seems appropriate to say such things as "Love me and the world is mine."

During the analysis of certain patients, this yearning for something he calls love from the analyst becomes strikingly intense. It is a simple matter for the analyst to defend himself against the impact of these passions by discounting the patient's love as "not real." We should not forget, however, Freud's warning that "One has no right to dispute the genuine nature of the love which makes its appearance in the course of analytic treatment. However lacking in normality it may seem to be, this quality is sufficiently explained when we remember that the condition of being in love in ordinary life outside analysis is also more like abnormal than normal mental phenomena. . . . It is precisely these departures from the norm that make up the essential element in the condition of being in love." [52]

We have to remember that such infantile experiences, intense and idyllic as they were, cease to be clung to by the normally developing person because of the number and breadth of adult substitute satisfactions with the maturing of the love capacity. We never abandon the wish to be loved in this magic way, but it loses its poignancy for most of us. But the patient who comes to analysis has not found these substitutes and has not experienced this development, and for him the early experiences thus have a greater relevance. Once the patient reaches the stage of "I want (from the therapist) *love* (but don't get it sufficiently)," he begins to elaborate on the expectation. It is as if he were to say: "If you *do* love me, you will prove it. You will *give* me symbolic tokens of it, you will *do* things for me and to me."

Hence it develops that the formula "I want *love* from the therapist" undergoes metamorphosis into "I want *proofs of love* from the therapist." These tend to become specific according to the specific needs, real or imagined, of the patient either in a past situation or in his present reality situation. Typical examples are represented in this diagram (Figure 8):

FIGURE 8

Likewise the patient will fantasy and finally announce, progressively, his wish for the physical *expressions* of love from the analyst, thus (Figure 9):

FIGURE 9

REGRESSION IN THE VERB

Let us now return to our diagrammed sentence, "I (the patient) want cure from the doctor."

Having spoken of the aspect of the regression referring to the object, let us turn our attention to regression in respect to the verb of the formula (see Figure 6). We have seen what the patient wants, craves, and feels he needs. We have already mentioned the fact that his techniques for gratifying this need also tend to regress to lower levels of sophistication, but we want to discuss this further.

In beginning the treatment and tacitly agreeing to comply with the basic rule, the patient feels at first that he is merely performing as directed in his own best interests to obtain that which he seeks. Gradually, however, his compliance in this respect comes to mean for him obedience which, in childhood, was the price of parental help. The patient begins to use his verbalized self-examination (free associations) as a medium of exchange, a *quid pro quo*. He attempts to use his analysis as he once used various communications to or deeds for his parents, teachers, and others—*i.e.*, to get a certain desired return. Along with obedience may go a pleasant manner or a surly one, laughter or tears, joking or whining. All sorts of counterfeits may be tried out. "Obedience" may be prompt or lagging, perfunctory or enthusiastic.

Sooner or later the cumulative frustration in the analytic situation will arouse sufficient anger to make good manners (suppression) and fear (repression) no longer able to contain it. It is an illusion that the anger appears suddenly; it was there from the very beginning. It was not only suppressed because of good manners and discreet tactics; it was *repressed,* covered up, as the consequence of earlier conditioning experiences which made the betrayal of one's real feelings too great a danger. To oversimplify it somewhat, one could say that every patient is sick just because of his long present but inexpressible anger. Something happened in the patient's life which has crippled his devices for handling his own instinctual pressures; he could (can) only control his raging aggressiveness by devices which cost him too much and make him sick. The very symptoms of which he complains exist partly for the purpose of controlling that anger, suppressing it or keeping it out of consciousness by repression, and partly for the purpose of expressing it. Every one of his symptoms may be considered to be an expression of anger in which he does not feel or recognize the original emotion.

Bear in mind that the patient doesn't immediately get angry. It is unnecessary to do so; it is ill-mannered. It is even dangerous. Before he gets angry, he will have tried all sorts of things. Besides, there are many satisfactions in the regression despite the "frustration." He will have attempted to bribe the analyst, arouse his pity, tease him, trap him. No analyst is proof against being caught off guard in some of these respects. But this only makes matters worse, for the analyst will recover himself and the patient's frustration continues. He is not getting what he wants, and sooner or later he says so, and he is likely to say so the sooner just because of the extra surcharge of poorly controlled anger which he has carried around from childhood.

When, therefore, we say that anger appears in the psychoanalytic situation, we mean that the patient becomes conscious *again* of an anger that once arose in him and, unexpressed, has made him "sick." But the provocation is now not the whipping his mother once gave him or the embarrassment his father once caused him or the victory his brother once gained over him; the provocation now is his feeling that the *analyst* is disappointing him, punishing him, neglecting him. Suddenly then, the formula of "I want to please the analyst in order to insure his loving me" is changed into "I *don't* want to please the analyst. I want to *hurt* the analyst."

One might say that on this general basis come all sorts of variations and in a sense further regressions in the verb of the formula. "I want to win love by pleasing" becomes transformed into "I want to pay him back and I want to get whatever I can get from him by irritating and hurting him as he has hurt me. I want to cheat him. I want to embarrass him. I will pretend to comply with his wishes but only to make fun of him. I will try to exasperate him. I will discourage him. I will argue with him. I will baffle him. I want to humiliate him and show him up. I want to tell people lies about him. I will slander him. I will try to insult him." Or, in another direction, the formula may go, "I will seduce the analyst. I will find his weakness and prey upon it. I will destroy his power. I will castrate him. I will kill him."

All this behavior is an echo, a re-enactment, a contemporized recollection of situations and events of long ago. But it is met by a reception different from that which the patient once found so cruel and hurtful. The analyst reminds himself and, if need be, the patient, that in the analytic situation all statements are tentative and are to be taken only in the perspective of *all* the material. The patient comes to see how he defeats himself, how his rage at not getting prevents him from getting. He doesn't see this immediately; he is apt to be blinded by his own angry tears.

Sooner or later, of course, there come the reactions to the fury and helplessness represented by outbursts of rage directed toward the analyst. On the one hand, the patient identifies them more or less accurately as belonging somewhere else, somewhere in the long ago. On the other hand, the influence of the conscience and of the recognition of the injustices of some of his accusations leads him to penitence and remorse. He may offer apology (which, of course, the analyst should not accept any more than he accepts the accusations). He may undertake self-imposed penance. He may redouble his efforts in whatever he thinks the analyst wants him to do, or he may swing over completely to the masochistic position of "I want the analyst to scold me for what I have done, to punish me, to attack me, to humiliate me, to assault me sexually, to castrate me, even to kill me!"

REGRESSION IN THE
INDIRECT OBJECT (DISPLACEMENT)

All the while the analyst remains (or attempts to remain!) in a detached, unchanging, stable position, so that whether the patient is up or down, whether the patient is provocative or seductive, whether he is angry or gay or flippant or sad, the analyst remains as he was. This constancy on the part of the analyst is unhuman, to be sure. It constantly surprises the patient because in ordinary life people respond to the behavior of others by corresponding changes. It is reassuring and encouraging to find someone who is both interested in and yet unaffected by one's mood swing and one's confessions. To some extent this is the antidote or "healthy sequel" to the sense of frustration first experienced. This constancy in the analyst tends to stabilize the patient and enable him to orient himself in spite of his oscillations, so that gradually these oscillations diminish in frequency and latitude of excursion.*

Let us go back again to Figure 6. Thus far we have discussed aspects of the patient's regression represented by successive changes in the form of the object and of the verb. We have yet to consider the metamorphosis in the subject, I, and in the indirect object, the therapist. We shall take up the latter first.

* Candor compels me to append here a comment from Dr. Herbert J. Schlesinger: "How, in your theory, does the constancy of the analyst stabilize the patient? Is this a matter of imitation, identification, a prod to his own reality testing? I think this is an important idea and ought not to be left simply as an assertion."

But I have to leave it as an assertion because I don't know the answer precisely. I think that I have always felt that it was based on that complex combination of factors which are represented by our selection of ideals, norms, aspirations, and the like which are too easily lumped into the term of identification. The analyst as a person certainly becomes a point of reference for the patient. The very fact that so few aspects of the analyst's personality are available to the patient's scrutiny and judgment perhaps make them more diagrammatic and heuristic.

It must be remembered that the progressive denudations of the primitive human wish to get something from someone or to have something pleasant done to one take place under the peculiar circumstances that the self-denuding patient is talking to a listener he does not see or know. He is talking in the presence of this person in a way in which he would not speak in the presence of any other human being. This unseen person is acting in a completely unexpected way in that he is not responding as any ordinary human being would to these very earnest appeals. It is just because this person who is listening cannot be seen and is rarely heard that it is possible for the patient to indulge his tendency to distort in fantasy the actual character, attitude, intentions, and even appearance of the analyst.

Hence, just as the nature of the thing desired and also the techniques of obtaining it change, so the image or prototype of the person from whom it is to be obtained also changes. It is as if the patient by mere repetition of the experience was enabled to regress back through the years so that instead of saying, "Doctor, I want relief from my headache, from my fears," the patient says, "Mother, I want to be taken into your arms." *

This phenomenon of displacement is perhaps the most familiar of all unconscious psychologic mechanisms. The veriest layman knows about kicking the dog or telling it to the chaplain or marrying on the rebound. But in the psychoanalytic situation there is more to it than mere displacement of affect and substitution of objects. There is a series of such displacements and a rainbow of affects which extend way back toward the earliest interpersonal relationships. This forms one of the most important aspects of the psychoanalytic treatment, perhaps the most important, and we shall devote a whole chapter to it later under the general heading of "transference."

---

* Dr. Earl Bond, in a lecture to the Fellows of the Menninger School of Psychiatry, March 1957, described a patient afflicted with a severe mental illness of lengthy duration in the course of which she expressed overtly many sexual wishes. One day her physician in an experimental mood picked her up and held her in his arms, thrusting the nipple of a nursing bottle between her lips. She drank the milk avidly, expressing great satisfaction. "This," she said, "is what I have always wanted, this nonsexual love." This episode marked the beginning of a rapid return to recovery. Cf. also the work of Marguerite A. Sechehaye.[142]

REGRESSION IN THE SUBJECT

For the present we have yet to discuss the fourth aspect of regression—regression in respect to the *subject* of the formula of Figure 6.

We should remember, first of all, the extraordinary and unique feature of psychoanalysis that not only the doctor but also *the patient himself* observes the phenomena of the patient's illness and of his regression in treatment. Thus, while he is making this progressive cyclic retreat into the behavior and attitudes and memories of his childhood, which we have reviewed schematically here, the patient is observing it, too, along with the therapist. He observes it—we hope—with the more adult or healthy part of his mind, his present-day conscious intelligence. Hence, a precondition for the therapeutic use of psychoanalysis is a certain relative or partial intactness of the patient's ego, a part which can ally itself with the analyst, as Freud pointed out long ago.

In other words, we assume that the patient's perceptions, memory and reality testing capacity are sufficiently intact to enable him to cooperate in this strange contract we have been describing. Sterba [147] put it that this alliance between the healthy part of the ego and the analyst enabled the patient to overcome his resistances in the treatment! Indeed, resistance might be described as the urge for the observing part of the ego to give up its brave aloofness and join the regressing ego. (*Cf.* Loewenstein.[96, 97])

The discrepancy between the feelings experienced by the patient, on the one hand, and the reality situation as he knows it to be, on the other, is increasingly apparent to him. However, the significance and usefulness of this discrepancy may easily be lost unless a certain kind of orientation to reality is maintained for the patient by the analyst. As Macalpine neatly puts it, "While the analysand has to experience the past and observe the present, the analyst has to experience the present and observe the past; he must resist any regressive trend within himself. If he fall victim to his own technique, and experience the past instead of observing it, he is subject to counter-resistance. The phenomenon of countertransference may be best described by paraphrasing Fenichel: 'The analyst misunderstands the past in terms of the present.' " [100]

It is natural, therefore, that the patient often becomes confused even regarding his identity. He sometimes doesn't know which of the various "I's" that comprise his total or essential self is now speaking. Is this the infantile "I" that is complaining, or is this the objective, adult "I"? Is this the four-year-old boy complaining to his mother or the eight-year-old boy reproaching his father or the twenty-five-year-old man scolding his doctor? He tries to distinguish and identify these, but one of the essential tasks of the analyst is to help the patient to obtain and maintain his orientation and to become aware of these many identities and the way in which and the conditions under which he employs them. This help is often best given not by official pronouncements or clever rejoinders or sharp queries but by the proper dosage of interference with or interpretation of the autistic process of the analysis. A few words of concurrence, or an indication of understanding by a chuckle or a casual comment or an expression of doubt about some "fact"—any of these may serve at one time or another to reorient the patient and start him on his way again in the further exploration.

It may have seemed thus far as if nothing but blind rambling and futile frustration occurred in an analysis but, of course, psychoanalysis is not a matter of perpetual silence on the part of the analyst. From time to time the silence is broken and the patient is helped in the direction of continuing the process by certain responses which both clarify and gratify.*

We shall have more to say about the analyst's facilitation of the treatment later, under "Interpretations." For the present we must go further in schematizing the natural history of the "transference neurosis," as it has been called traditionally, by which is meant the regression in point of subject, verb, direct object, and indirect object of the sentence, "I want help from the doctor."

* "At this point I want to introduce a new term for the reaction of the analyst to the communications, words, gestures, pauses, and so forth, of the analyzed person. I call the sum of this reaction, which includes all kinds of impressions, *response.* The analytic response is thus the emotional and intellectual reply to the speech, behavior, and appearance of the patient, and includes awareness of the inner voices of the analyst. Every interpretation, all that the analyst says, the

THE REVERSAL OF THE REGRESSION

Having gone back to the beginnings of all his misunderstanding and misinterpretations and mismanagements, having conceded his errors and forgiven those of others, having recognized the unrealistic nature of some of his cherished expectations and love objects and methods of procedure, the patient gradually begins to put away childish things. The "I" begins to grow up. He gradually "works through," as we used to say; he works his way back to reality, abandoning his inexpedient goals and techniques and attitudes for more appropriate ones, more adult expectations from more suitable love objects obtained in more effective ways. In this process of working through, the more infantile aims and goals lose much of their compulsive force; the patient is then free to choose or to develop new techniques, aims, and goals that are more adaptive and gratifying.

In this *reversal phase* of the regressive process, the psychoanalyst who has been all sorts of people in the fantasies of the patient gradually becomes increasingly a kind, friendly, incorruptible person who has stood by the patient, withstood his attacks and reactions and fulfilled the contract realistically. This objectification of the analyst characterizes the final stage of the treatment; its success is a good criterion of the patient's progress toward "health," but not the only one. We shall discuss this at greater length in the chapter on termination.

Just how it comes about that the regression suddenly turns around and becomes a progression, surely a most important and critical event, remains something of a mystery. Perhaps it would be better to say that as yet I am unable to extend my theory to the point of an adequate explanation of this occurrence. I presume that there is some balancing of forces in the way that any conflictual process becomes

---

form of his explanation and exposition, are all preceded, and to a great extent determined, by this response. The response is, so to speak, the inside experience of that which the analyst perceives, feels, senses, regarding the patient. It is clear from the preceding chapters that the main part of that response is in its nature unconscious or, to put it otherwise, that only a small part of it becomes conscious. The response is thus the dark soil in which our understanding of psychical processes is rooted. Out of these roots, which are hidden deep in the earth, emerges our intellectual, logical grasp of the problems. Out of these concealed roots grows the tree of psychoanalytic knowledge." (Theodor Reik [132]) stabilized, but I feel as if we ought to be more explicit about it. Certainly some therapeutic regressions do not seem to have regressed far enough; the turning point occurs too soon, and the patient turns back in what has been called a flight into health. On the other hand, perhaps all recovery could be described as a move toward normality, which is certainly a commendable direction. The optimum depth of the regression and the circumstances related to the optimum excavation are part and parcel of the difference in viewpoint between those (for example in England) who think in terms of psychoanalysis as a five- to seven-year process and those who think of it in the terms of a two- to four-year process. I am under the impression, however, that similar practical problems often face the surgeon and occur perhaps in many fields—medicine, education, religion.

An existentialist concept, *kairos,* may apply here. It means crisis, in the special sense of a dramatic moment, full of emotional charge, a particularly "right time" with various possibilities. It is a moment of heightened choice in that the individual is called upon to add his weight to the tenuous balance of forces, personally helping to determine the direction in which he will go. This Greek word, it will be recalled, was used in Hippocratic medicine to designate that moment at which an acute illness changed its course for the better or for the worse. It was believed that certain critical symptoms pointed to this moment and indicated the new direction, recognizable by the proficient physician. This time-honored concept has been revived in the theological field by Paul Tillich [152] and reintroduced into psychotherapy by Arthur Kielholz.[85] The implication is that such moments occur not only in the process of psychoanalytic treatment but in the process of any other deviations from a previous course of life and way of living.[27]

IV

TRANSFERENCE AND
COUNTERTRANSFERENCE

The Involuntary Participation of the
Second Party in the Treatment Process

THIS CHAPTER WILL BE DEVOTED TO AN AMPLIFICATION OF ONE PHASE
or aspect of the regression described in the preceding chapter; namely,
the successive alterations in the indirect object of the conscious-
unconscious wish "I want help from the doctor" which becomes "I
want something from someone." As we saw in Chapter III, the therapist becomes various someones—a husband, wife, mother, brother,
sister, father, grandmother, etc., in the fantasies and unconscious
formulations of the psychoanalytic patient. Although this is only one
aspect of the therapeutic regression as I conceive of it, many psychoanalysts speak, write, and even think of transference as characterizing the whole process and refer to the total regression as the "transference neurosis." There are historical and rational explanations for
this, all dependent upon the fact that of the four features of the
regression occurring in the treatment situation, transference is undoubtedly the most important or at least the best understood.

For centuries, physicians and others have observed the childishness which characterizes the sick and dependent person in point of techniques and objectives. Some regression accompanies almost any illness, and this is furthered by the importuning of help from the doctor. Some physicians almost consciously play the role of the "grand" father or of the jocular uncle. But rare, indeed, the doctor who perceives that he is unintentionally filling the role of a sister, a mother, or a hated employer! This is equally unrealized by the patient, and Freud himself was astonished at the discovery. Later he recognized its existence in all therapeutic relationships, but he always considered the phenomenon and its correct management to be one of the essential and distinguishing features of psychoanalysis. As Greenacre beautifully puts it:

> Human beings do not thrive well in isolation, being sustained then mostly by memories and hopes, even to the point of hallucination, or by reaching out to nonhuman living things (like Mendel and the beans). This need for sensory contact, basically the contact of warm touch of another body but secondarily experienced in the other senses as well (even the word "contact" is significant), probably comes from the long period of care which the human infant must have before he is able to sustain himself. Lonely infants fed and cared for regularly and with sterile impersonal efficiency do not live to childhood.
>
> Even if the periods of repeated contact between two individuals do not comprise a major part of their time, still such an emotional bond develops and does so more quickly and more sensitively if the two persons are *alone* together; *i.e.*, the more the spontaneous currents and emanations of feeling must be concentrated the one upon the other and not shared, divided, or reflected among members of a group. I have already indicated that I believe the matrix of this *is* a veritable matrix; *i.e.*, comes largely from the original mother-infant quasi union of the first months of life. This I consider the basic transference; or one might call it the primary transference, or some part of primitive social instinct.
>
> Now if both people are adults but one is troubled and the other is versed in the ways of trouble and will endeavor to put the torchlight of his understanding at the disposal of the troubled one, to lend it to him that he may find his way more expeditiously, the situation more nearly approximates that of the ana-

lytic relationship. The analyst acts then like an extra function, or set of functions, which is lent to the analysand for the latter's temporary use and benefit.

Since this relationship may, in its most primitive aspects, be based on the mother-child relationship and since the patient is a troubled person seeking help, one can see at once that the relationship will not be one of equal warming, but that there will be a tendency for the patient to develop an attitude of expectant dependent receptiveness toward the physician. It is the aim of treatment, however, to increase the patient's maturity, to realize his capacity for self-direction, his "self-possession" (in the deeper sense of the word); and *not* to augment his state of helplessness and dependence, with which he in his neurotic suffering is already burdened.[73]

Freud had been struck from the first by the curious behavior of patients in hypnosis, in that they accepted the authority of the hypnotist as if he were a far more powerful individual than he actually was. Freud sought an explanation for this, both as an observer of Charcot and in the course of his own subsequent treatment of patients with and without hypnosis. He called this curious tendency for the patient to respond to the therapist as if the latter were *someone else* "transference." In attempting to explain it, he invoked the mechanism of displacement and the principle of the repetition compulsion, but confused the issue by referring to it as suggestion.*

It is understandable that Freud should have been puzzled by transference and that he later modified his earlier explanations of it.

---

* Freud's first allusion [59] to what later became his concept of transference was made in 1895 in the comment that one of his patients made a "false connection" to the analyst when an affect became conscious which related to memories still unconscious. In 1905,[47] discussing the sexual nature of the impulses felt toward the physician, he asked: "What are transferences? They are new editions or facsimiles of the tendencies and fantasies which are aroused and made conscious during the progress of the analysis . . ." In 1912,[46] he emphasized the repetitive character of transference, and in *Beyond the Pleasure Principle* [44] he indicated this to be the very origin of transference. Infantile sexual experience is a painful injury to the child's narcissism; its repression conforms to the pleasure principle; its repetition (transference) is contrary to the pleasure principle and derives therefor from the repetition compulsion. Freud raised objections to this himself and to some extent returned later to his earlier notion of transference merely as an opportunity for a previously unsatisfied need. See Daniel Lagache.[89]

In his earlier writings Freud repeatedly equated transference and suggestion. See Ida Macalpine,[100] for five instances.

We know now that certain transferences permit—indeed, greatly enhance the effect of—suggestion, but constitute something quite different in essence. There has been an increasingly clear recognition of the fact that the displacement, introjection, projection, and repetition associated with the (partial) misidentification of the analyst and the use of various attitudes and techniques toward him are all part and parcel of the total regressive process described in the preceding chapters of this book. In the years since Freud's discovery of the *phenomenon,* the *word* transference has been applied with confusing variability. For some it means merely an attitude toward other persons; others use the word to describe any unrealistic attitude toward another person, especially an unrealistic attitude toward a therapist. Commonly but incorrectly it is used to describe a consciously positive feeling toward a therapist.*

To cite some additional authoritative definitions, Anna Freud defines transference as "all those impulses experienced by the patient in his relation with the analyst which are not newly created by the objective analytic situation but have their source in early . . . object relations and are now merely revived under the influence of the repetition compulsion." [41] Glover [68, 69] defines it as the "capacity . . . to repeat in current situations . . . attitudes developed in early family life," which, in my opinion, is too narrow. Fenichel [32] equated transference with resistance (which in my opinion is also too narrow). Lagache [89] has defined transference as "a repetition in present-day life, and particularly in the relationship to the analyst, of unconscious emotional attitudes developed during childhood within the family group and especially toward the parents." Macalpine's definition is broad: "Analytic transference may thus be defined as a person's gradual adaptation by regression to the infantile analytic setting." In other words, she includes all forms of the regression under the term *transference.*

The analysand brings, in varying degrees, an inherent capacity, a readiness to form transferences, and this readiness is met by something which converts it into an actuality. In hypnosis the

* For a brief, lucid statement, see Waelder's "Introduction to the Discussion [of] Problems of Transference." [159]

patient's inherent capacity to be hypnotized is induced by the command of the hypnotist, and the patient submits instantly. In psychoanalysis it is neither achieved in one session nor is it a matter of obeying. Psychoanalytic technique creates an infantile setting, of which the "neutrality" of the analyst is but one feature among others. . . . In their aggregate, these factors, . . . amount to a reduction of the analysand's object world and denial of object relations in the analytic room.[100]

I define transference in a much more limited way as *the unrealistic roles or identities unconsciously ascribed to a therapist by a patient in the regression of the psychoanalytic treatment and the patient's reactions to this representation derived from earlier experience.* In other words, it is the aspect of the regression which relates to the indirect object of the patient's expectations and constitutes an involuntary participation of the therapist in the treatment situation. It is, as Silverberg[144] says, always irrational and to a considerable degree disagreeable to the patient. It is especially facilitated and furthered by the total psychoanalytic treatment set-up, a point which has been emphasized by Macalpine.[100] It is not the result of suggestion on the part of the analyst, although the characteristic natural behavior of the analyst inevitably assists in determining aspects of it.

My definition, given above, endeavors to describe transference as a phenomenon usually occurring in association with the regression in the psychoanalytic treatment situation called the transference neurosis. Transference, as I have defined it, eliminates (I hope) such presumptuous and mischievous notions as "manipulating" the transference. One can, to be sure, behave in certain ways that affect the frustration tension. This will, in turn, affect the depth of the regression which will be reflected in the transference manifestations.

On the basis of my definition, also, there are no such things as "positive transference" and "negative transference," terms which we hear used to mean all sorts of unrelated things. One may speak of positive and negative attitudes in the transference; one can say that the transference is at the moment such as to present a positive or a negative feeling toward the analyst. My definition places emphasis upon the fact emphasized earlier; namely, that the analyst and the analysand are engaged in a two-party contractual relationship in which the patient makes his payment and expects a return. He gets a return, but not in the form in which he expects it. What he actually gets that is valuable and "worth the money," so to speak, in this two-party process, is the *result* of his disappointment in not immediately getting what he originally expected! In the course of his experience he relives many phases and incidents of his life in relation to a neutral figure to whom he ascribes many roles or as-if identities.

A fairly typical illustration of this can be cited. An unmarried male laboratory technician of thirty underwent psychoanalysis for the relief of his lifelong loneliness and general dissatisfaction with himself and what he was getting out of existence. Early in the process he described his father's reserve and aloofness. Later, however, he made similar observations about one of his teachers and then about his employer. Ultimately, of course, it was the analyst who seemed reserved, cold and aloof. A little later, however, he recalled certain earlier experiences with a girl cousin whose warmth was a sharp contrast to the chill formalities in his own home. He felt guilty, however, because of certain of his responses to her advances and feared particularly what his father's reaction might be. Something similar was repeated with a young woman he met in college. The analyst was not surprised, accordingly, when some months later the patient dreamed of the analyst in the form of a seductress, which evoked reproach that the analyst was expecting too much of him and encouraging him in forbidden directions. Next, it developed that there had been in his childhood a particularly stern aunt whose judgments were feared by all the relatives and, indeed, by the entire neighborhood. She evidently represented to him, then, what law and order, the police court and purgatory came to represent to him later. This began to appear in the transference when the analyst, who had previously been accused both of coldness and of seductiveness, became a stern figure of retribution from whom the patient expected punishment and dismissal.

In all of these aspects of transference one sees the irrational roles in which the analyst is cast, the ways in which the earlier models are used. The little details of identification—inflections of the voice and irrelevant coincidences such as the color of a necktie worn—are always striking. Even more impressive is the way in which the patient takes advantage of subtle situations and even creates opportunities for some apparent actualization of the role. In this, of course, unintentional countertransferences in the analyst may unwittingly cooperate, as we shall see later.

Near the end of an analysis the analysand becomes merely a recovering patient, talking to a soon-no-longer-necessary physician; all fantasy assignments to the analyst are abandoned.* It is in this sense that one can say the transference is ultimately dissipated (although there may be continuing displacements).

This chapter was introduced with a subtitle of "The Involuntary Participation of the Second Party. . . ." This was to imply that the analyst does participate in the contract by more than his presence and the rent of his office, so to speak. He does give something to the patient beyond audience. By his noncritical attention to what the patient is saying and doing, the analyst is doing something. He is gratifying the patient as well as frustrating him. But certainly the frustration exceeds the gratification, and this is related to the patient's progressive regression, if we may use such contradiction in terms, the tendency to regress further and further. Freud ascribed this regression to the frustration alone (see Lagache [89]), knowing that some frustration is always involved in learning; but psychoanalysis is not like the regression of the Buddhist holy man, for there is constantly some correction not only from the analyst but from the hours spent outside the analysis.

As we shall see later, in the chapter on interpretation, the patient gradually becomes aware of the fact that he has responded to the therapist as if he were mother or father or someone else, and when this is clearly perceived consciously, the former value of the myth is lost. The patient "corrects" for (*i.e.*, in line with) reality, and although he may "forget" (repress) and verbalize the father "image," he usually moves on to another phase or period of his life with other personae. Korzybski [86] made a vivid contribution to our understanding of this mechanism with his insistence on distinguishing the identity of any particular person or thing by precise statement of time,

---

* Lagache [89] has elaborated this interacting of regression and projection in an extension of some ideas put forward originally by Pierre Janet in regard to the dual character of all social behavior.

place, and circumstances, graphically insisting that M' (the mother of, say, the 6-year-old Tom Jones) is *not* M'' or M''' or M^x, meaning that same woman as related to Tom Jones at the age of twelve or thirty or other successive periods. Dr. van der Waals tells me he often says to his patients, "You see your analyst not as he really is, but as he appears through the colored glasses put on your nose in childhood."

COUNTERTRANSFERENCE

We may not forget that the psychoanalyst himself has an unconscious, and that he, too, has a persistent temptation to indulge in infantile techniques and objectives, magical thinking, and the like. But whereas the patient has many encouragements to indulge in these things, the analyst has many reasons for not doing so and much support for the resistance of his temptations. Although it is true that he, the analyst, is involved in the analytic situation with the patient, he is not subject to the same frustrations and—theoretically—is not involved in a "transference neurosis" (regression). Nevertheless, his reactions to the patient may contain strong irrational and unconscious elements. This empirical fact must be discussed in connection with the corresponding misidentifications made by the patient. Countertransference is often linked in discussions with transference, although, since the analyst is not receiving treatment, *his* unconsciously determined reactions to the patient cannot and should not be described as if they were his therapeutic reactions to the patient's therapeutic intentions. But they *are* adventitious, unintentional, and involuntary participations by the party of the second part in the contract and they are always there and always important.

Having made the great discovery of the tendency of patients to make a displacement upon the therapist of the emotions and feelings experienced in childhood toward his parents and other (significant) persons, Freud made the secondary and allied discovery, five years later, of what he named countertransference, "which arises in the physician as the result of the patient's influence on his [the analyst's] unconscious feelings. . . . We have noticed that every analyst's achievement is limited by what his own complexes and resistances permit. . . ." [49] *

At first, this was regarded as a troublesome and interfering phenomenon, for which allowance and correction had to be made lest it "blur the transference picture." [32] Freud's recommendation of emotional aloofness and coldness, like a surgeon "who puts aside all his own feelings, including that of human sympathy, and concentrates his mind on one single purpose, that of performing the operation as skillfully as possible," [58] set an ideal which analysts, for a time, strove to achieve. Later, of course, it was realized that the analyst must not only be this surgeon, but he must also be the warm, human, friendly, helpful physician. He must be both. Freud's advice to analysts on the role of warmth and sympathy in the analytic process is rarely quoted in full. True, he urged restraint; but he also urged tact and eschewed cold rejection of his patients' confessions of their love for him. He advised against both ignoring "the transference love" and responding to it. Only in this context can the patient's conditions for loving come to light.

But regardless of what he tries, consciously, to be and do, the analyst will *tend* to react to unconscious roles he ascribes to the patient. In the words of Annie Reich, "Counter-transference is [not only an inevitable feature but also] a necessary prerequisite of analysis. If it does not exist, the necessary talent and interest is lacking. But it has to remain shadowy and in the background." [127] It is a part of the interrelationship.

More and more it is recognized that psychoanalysis is not something which happens to one person under the observing eye and with the occasional help of a second person, but that it is a two-party transactional relationship. This is what I have attempted to emphasize

---

* Thereafter, Ferenczi contributed a classical paper on the subject [34] and there were increasingly frequent references to it in the literature, with, more recently, quite a number of serious studies devoted to it. Curiously enough, most of these have been by women colleagues—Alice Balint,[5] Therese Benedek,[8] Frieda Fromm-Reichmann,[61] Paula Heiman,[79] Phyllis Greenacre,[71] Margaret Little,[95] and Annie Reich.[127] However, the contributions of Fenichel,[32] Berman,[11] Fliess,[39] Gitelson,[67] and Winnicott [160] are also important. Recent contributions to the significance of countertransference have come from Szasz,[150] Tower,[154] Spitz,[146] and Racker [122] to whom readers are also strongly commended.

throughout this manual. Sullivan,[148, 149] Lagache,[89] and Fromm-Reichmann [62, 63] have also emphasized this. We become so preoccupied with describing the reactions of the patient, and particularly the predetermined character of his reactions, that we forget that the analyst is also a person, that he, too, is a party to the contract, that he, too, is reacting, even though his predominate, overt reaction is one of silent listening. One has to remind oneself over and over that it is never accurate to say that a certain reaction is that of person *A* to person *B*. The reaction is always a fluid process in which *A* is also reacting to the way in which *B* reacts to *A* and, to be still more accurate, *A*'s reaction is modified by the way *B* reacts to the way *A* reacts to the way *B* reacts, and so on. And likewise *B* is reacting to *A*'s reactions to the way *B* reacts to *A* and so on. One could summarize it by saying that *A* and *B* interact with each other.

On the other hand, the relationship between a psychoanalyst and a patient is not that of two participants in a fencing match who have to make constant mutual adjustments to each other's moves. The analyst is a relatively fixed point. By reasons of training, dedication, interest, experience, tradition, and other factors, he has great authority. The patient, on the other hand, has great potential freedom of motion, but relatively little power. The only thing the patient can be authoritative about is the way he feels, and he is not always very sure about this.

Now, in any adjustment between two individuals, there are—for both—certain gratifications and certain frustrations. The gratifications tend toward a closer union of the two, toward integration, toward contact, toward love; the frustrations tend toward hostile attitudes and separation. These gratifications and frustrations are, as we know, both conscious and unconscious. In our everyday life they have crystallized in habitual preferences and aversions and friendship patterns.

In a psychoanalytic treatment contract, we ask one of the two parties that he examine day after day his own reactions to a situation in which there are both gratifications and increasing frustration. The other individual is presumed to be under less frustration and of him we may seem to make no such demand; it is not a part of the didactics of psychoanalysis. Theoretically, he has merely to observe the effect of the role he plays as a silent listener and apparent frustrator upon the suppliant party. They are *both* participants in this process, and notwithstanding the fact that the patient is consciously and undeniably frustrated in the analytic situation whereas the analyst is theoretically not frustrated, what we all realize is that to some extent the patient *is* gratified and to some extent the analyst *is* frustrated. Correspondingly, the analyst, as a human being, reacts to his frustrations and makes use of various of his "defense" measures, particularly identification and projection. He, too, undergoes waves of temporary regression, including temporary misidentifications of his patient. His patient momentarily becomes his mother, his father, a pupil, a colleague, another patient, or even a projection of the analyst's own self.

It seems scarcely necessary to illustrate countertransference with clinical examples, because they are so abundantly available in every training center. But if we may revert for a moment to the case cited earlier in this chapter of the laboratory technician who made his analyst into a father, a cousin, and an aunt successively, we can show how the countertransference appeared there. The analyst was actually a rather warmhearted fellow, and by the accusations of coldness he was only somewhat amused. The accusation that he was like a female seductress, however, he found a trifle disturbing. "Does the patient realize how irrational such accusations are?" he thought. A little later, when he was cast into the role of a stern female judge, he was less annoyed at being made a woman than at being regarded as a moralist. (Actually he *was* somewhat moralistic—more so than he realized.)

But he asked himself, "Why is the patient annoying me? Why would it occur to me to say, 'Find yourself another analyst, Mr. Fellow!' Of course, I won't, but. . . ." And then he reflected that the patient wasn't soliciting affection and being rejective so much as attempting to create a situation in which he would be rejected and thus given justification for releasing the anger so long pent up against these original figures. In so doing he would sacrifice what little companionship he had had and suffer again the loneliness of complete rejection. This illustration does not contradict the previous statement that countertransference is an unconscious reaction. The manifestations of countertransference may be conscious although the intrapsychic conditions resulting in its appearance are unconscious.

THE DETECTION AND CORRECTION
OF COUNTERTRANSFERENCE

Some of the common ways in which countertransference makes its appearance—*i.e.,* becomes an interference—may be worth listing for their didactic value. The following are some I have jotted down at various times during seminars and control sessions in which they appeared: I think that I have myself been guilty of practically all of them.

Inability to understand certain kinds of material which touch on the analyst's own personal problems.

Depressed or uneasy feelings during or after analytic hours with certain patients.

Carelessness in regard to arrangements—forgetting the patient's appointment, being late for it, letting the patient's hours run overtime for no special reason.

Persistent drowsiness (of the analyst) during the analytic hour.

Over- or under-assiduousness in financial arrangements with the patient, for example, letting him become considerably indebted without analyzing it, or trying to "help" him to get a loan.

Repeatedly experiencing erotic or affectionate feelings toward a patient.

Permitting and even encouraging resistance in the form of acting-out.

Security seeking, narcissistic devices such as trying to impress the patient in various ways, or to impress colleagues with the importance of one's patient.

Cultivating the patient's continued dependence in various ways, especially by unnecessary reassurances.

The urge to engage in professional gossip concerning a patient.

Sadistic, unnecessary sharpness in formulation of comments and interpretations, and the reverse.

Feeling that the patient must get well for the sake of the doctor's reputation and prestige.

"Hugging the case to one's bosom," *i.e.*, being too afraid of losing the patient.

Getting conscious satisfaction from the patient's praise, appreciation, and evidences of affection, and so forth.

Becoming disturbed by the patient's persistent reproaches and accusations.

Arguing with the patient.

Premature reassurances against the development of anxiety in the patient or, more accurately, finding oneself unable to gauge the point of optimum frustration tension.

Trying to help the patient in extra-analytic ways, for example, in making certain financial arrangements, or housing arrangements.

A compulsive tendency to "hammer away" at certain points.

Recurrent impulses to ask favors of the patient.

Sudden increase or decrease of interest in a certain case.

Dreaming about the patient. *asks analyst to be non-human?*

A personal analysis, no matter how long or thorough, is never sufficient to eradicate all of one's blind spots or all of one's tendencies to find surreptitious satisfactions for infantile needs in other than realistic ways. Some of these lurk constantly as potential "neurotic" tendencies, as it were; others become organized into the personality structure. They are bound to determine certain attitudes and reactions of the analyst toward all of his patients. We have to assume that the more serious and more interfering neurotic persistences have been called to the analyst's attention by his teachers to the point that he is prepared to make the proper allowances for them in his clinical work. If not, there is nothing for it but more personal analysis.

But short of this, the conscientious young analyst may become greatly concerned over a realization of his involuntary participation, and his proper therapeutic "attitude" will be impaired by this over-concern. On the other hand, the less sensitive or less conscientious young analyst may tend to be oblivious of or indifferent to the ways in which he is deleteriously affecting his patient or impeding the patient's progress. Since countertransference is by definition an "unconscious" phenomenon, the question is how one may deal with something he doesn't know about. Some practical suggestions seem to be indicated even in a book dedicated to theory, and I have accordingly set down a few rules of thumb, each one of which deserves (and, in a teaching seminar, would receive) fuller discussion. Here they are:

One must be constantly alert to the existence of countertransference but not intimidated by it, recognizing both its pitfalls and its uses. It may alert the analyst to unverbalized themes and impulses in his patient. But although it may be useful and though it may be inevitable, let us not assume that the more of it the better. Think about it from time to time; reflect on it. In this one might well take a page out of the book of some religious orders. For countertransference is dangerous only when it is forgotten about.

Try to recognize those manifestations of a disturbing countertransference which enter into one's work generally and to analyze their meaning in the light of one's own personal self-knowledge. This refers both to those phases of countertransference which do not seem to interfere with the treatment of patients and to those which do. This is greatly facilitated by discussing the matter with a trusted colleague.

When you become aware of feelings of countertransference, especially if they are persistent, try to think through the analytic situation again and identify those features or acts or words of the patient which triggered off this reaction in you. "Why am I irritated? Why am I erotically aroused? Why does this come up now? What is the patient subtly trying to get me to do which I haven't seen clearly, maybe because I so much want to do it?"

But avoid becoming so introspective about your countertransference that the patient is forgotten; after all, it is the latter who is the primary object of the process.*

One might go so far as to say that one of the most important functions of psychoanalytic societies is a control of countertransference tendencies. Dr. Robert Waelder has emphasized this point. No analyst can see everything; each one's vision is limited by his personality. Members of a group are mutually self-corrective. As Waelder puts it, "Since we are all partially blind, the best we can do is to support each other so that the vision of one may make up for the myopia of the other, and vice versa." [160]

---

* A recent physiological study of the tensions manifested by therapist and patient in their psychotherapeutic relationships has thrown some light on countertransference from an unexpected angle. The authors conclude that there was a tendency for the therapist's heart rate and lability to follow a pattern similar to that of the patient. But in phases of antagonism on the part of the patient, his heart rather tended to slow down whereas the therapist's tended to speed up. [19]

THE CHARACTER OF THE THERAPIST

We have described now how in the regression induced by the psychoanalytic treatment situation the patient reacts to the analyst in successively different ways: first, as a mysterious medical person who promises some kind of help; second, as a misidentified father, mother, brother, and so forth; third, as a human being with certain weaknesses; and, finally, as a human being with certain strengths. I believe it is important to say more about these strengths, and about the character of the psychoanalyst. Several colleagues have written thoughtful articles on this aspect of the treatment.

We cannot ignore the fact that what the psychoanalyst believes, what he lives for, what he loves, what he considers to be the purpose of life and the joy of life, what he considers to be good and what he considers to be evil, become known to the patient and influence him enormously not as "suggestion" but as inspiration. A degree of identification with the analyst is inevitable, although not necessarily permanent. However, for that longer or shorter post-analytic period during which identification with the analyst is operative, the patient shows forth the analyst—or at least some aspects of him—to the world. No matter how skillful the analyst in certain technical maneuvers, his ultimate product, like Galatea, will reflect not only his handicraft but his character. Waelder has well put it that although analysts are taught to discard the overestimates made of them by their patients, regarding them not as sound reflections of mature judgment but rather as the consequences of a situation of regression, there is always the possibility of forgetting this.

> No doubt all psychoanalysts withstand the danger of flattery for some time; but if flattery continues as a daily fare year in year out, there is a danger that some people may eventually be persuaded to accept part of it as a reality. It is a great danger to be trapped in self-overvaluation and complacency
>
> > for as you know securitie
> > is mortal's chiefest enemie.
>
> [Furthermore, he continues], psychoanalysis is an occupation in which practitioners work alone with nobody observing them and without any controls. If a surgeon operates on a patient, the

result is known immediately among many people in the hospital. What happens in a psychoanalytic situation remains between analyst and patient and reaches out from this closed situation only in instances of extreme emergency. In this way the analyst works without checks other than those imposed by his sense of responsibility. There is always a danger of deterioration in the work of people who do not have the benefit of comparison with the work of others and who are in no way supervised. I do not think of deterioration in the crude meaning of a blurring of the sense of responsibility—such instances, happily, are very rare—but in a more subtle sense. An analyst knows what he has seen in a patient but he cannot know what he has not seen but might have seen, and he may get an exaggerated idea of the completeness of his observations and the adequacy of his interpretations.[158]

Waelder made these observations in connection with demonstrating the usefulness of psychoanalytic societies, but in the same article he went on to speak of the pitfalls and dangers of psychoanalytic societies. It was inevitable that, in a young and growing science such as psychoanalysis has been, there would be great zeal and intensity and almost evangelistic defensiveness. It is difficult for the analysts of today to recognize the prejudice and suspicion with which those of us who are older, and those who are still older than we, were once surrounded. Freud ascribed this to the nature of the subject matter and the injury it inflicted upon our narcissism to realize that we are not quite so free or so masterful as we had assumed. But I suspect that it goes beyond this. The dissection of human bodies met with the same general aversion, as did numerous other medical innovations. The mysteriousness of psychoanalysis and the closed group principle have offended many scientists, who find it difficult to accept our explanations of why this is necessary. But perhaps to an extent larger than we realize some of us are guilty of just plain bad manners or, to speak more psychiatrically, of poor self-control and arrogant truculence. Some analysts seem to assume that having learned about the unconscious of a dozen patients, we now *understand* human nature—and understand it *our way.* It has been remarked by numerous observers how much more friendly and congenial the meetings of neurologists, internists, and other colleagues frequently seem as compared with meetings of psychoanalysts. However much more interesting we may believe ours to be, theirs are certainly less hectic. Do our preoccupations with the unconscious and our zeal in undertaking to clarify the unconscious of other people foster some pathological degree of narcissistic megalomania in us? The more necessary, then, our unceasing effort to maintain an appropriate humility.

Humility, modesty, and all those qualities opposite to arrogance are not only becoming in an analyst—they are more than necessary as a part of his therapeutic equipment. This is not to say that patients cannot be benefited, sometimes, by even the most ill-mannered assertions or the most condescending explanations. But the very spirit of psychoanalytic science is to help an afflicted ego to realize its *own* potentialities, to let a patient discover what he can really do—not because he is commanded to, not because it is diagrammed for him, but because he is acquiring a new view of himself.

NEUTRALITY AND ETHICS OF THE THERAPIST

Neutrality in the analyst is one of the essentials of psychoanalytic treatment. But neutrality does not mean wooden aloofness. It means, rather, a hovering attention to what the patient says, with a suspension of expressed moral judgment. The material presented is to be considered tentative and contemporative. No analyst should pretend that he takes no moral position in regard to what the patient may do. He will refrain from passing a moral judgment prematurely on what a patient mentions or fantasies or even contemplates doing. If it approaches enactment, and if it is dangerous to the patient's life or welfare or that of other people, the analyst will *of course* express disapproval. He will not announce a position of moral condemnation regarding what the patient has already done, but neither will he approve it nor condone it. It is probably something that the patient does not fully understand any more than the analyst, and both wish to try to understand why the particular act came about. As members of the same culture it is very likely that both the analyst and the patient know that what the patient did is socially disapproved, but this must not preclude, indeed may further stimulate, the search for the reasons for it. Freud spoke very definitely and frequently to the effect that "the analyst respects the patient's individuality and does not seek to remould him in accordance with his own—that is, according to the physician's—personal ideals; he is glad to avoid giving advice and instead to arouse the patient's power of initiative." [56]

What is important for the patient is the analyst's ethic, his consistent fairness, his intellectual and economic honesty, his genuineness, his concern for the patient's best interests.*

One of Dr. Maxwell Gitelson's patients (he tells me) paid him the high compliment of saying, "You have helped me with your virtues and not hurt me with your defects. I can now be myself, my own man." Of course, he might prove to be mistaken about his resolution, but at least he sees it as an ideal, he aspires to it, and he believes in himself.

A few years ago I participated in a seminar and panel discussion with some theologians, some professors of philosophy and of ethics, and some practicing psychoanalysts, who discussed the topic "Do the Psychiatrist's Moral Convictions Play a Significant Part in His Psychiatric Therapy?" (Gallahue Conference, Topeka, 1955). All of the speakers made definitely affirmative replies to the topical question. All of them felt that no psychiatrist would be able to avoid imparting his value system to his patients. But in spite of the unanimity of my colleagues, I felt that the conclusion represented more of a paradox than they realized. If we think of psychoanalytic treatment as a two-

---

* It is odd that so excellent a clinician as Otto Fenichel [32] could write "If we do not break off the analysis too soon and if we consistently show the patient his intrapsychic reality, he will recognize that clinging to inappropriate ideals and moralities [*i.e.*, those disavowed by the analyst—KAM] has a resistance function. . . . It has been said that religious people in analysis remain uninfluenced in their religious philosophies since analysis itself is supposed to be philosophically neutral. . . . Repeatedly I have seen that with analysis of the sexual anxieties and with the maturing of the personality, the attachment to religion has ended." *Of course*, Fenichel saw it (as a temporary phenomenon, at least). His personal preoccupation with and devotion to psychoanalysis were well known. And his patients strove to please. I have seen the *reverse* of Fenichel's observation, for *my* patients strive to please, too. In the long run the ex-patient finds his own attachments and commitments. I like what Ella Freeman Sharpe has said about the analyst and the analysand as persons and I recommend Chapters I and II of her book to all students. I also like the reflections offered to students of psychoanalysis in the article, prepared shortly before her death, entitled "The Psychoanalyst." All of these appear in her *Collected Papers on Psycho-Analysis*.[143]

party contract like that described in the first chapter, we realize consideration was given to this kind of intangible. If one drives into a filling station for gasoline, one does not expect to receive advice about the best make of car or the proper political party. I discussed this problem at the forum just mentioned in the following words:

' We have heard these eloquent and capable colleagues, representing various fields of human thought, give it as their opinion that no psychiatrist would be able to avoid imparting his value system to his patients in the course of therapy. It would seem from this to be quite obviously so. But this is a somewhat paradoxical fact and remarkable enough perhaps to be emphasized as indicative of an important change in the concept of treatment.

"Let me review certain aspects of the history of this matter. In the course of discovering and applying his new techniques of listening without reproach or censure or revulsion to the 'confessions' of patients regarding their fantasies and behavior, Freud was accused of encouraging socially improper behavior in the name of treatment. I and many others vigorously and explicitly refuted this, emphasizing that the whole philosophy of psychoanalysis was based on intelligent control of behavior and not wanton, profligate, and aggressive indulgence.

"Nevertheless the public still has a vague impression that there is some truth in the allegation, that in some way or other we psychoanalysts have a different moral code from the rest of society, a code that says that people may do anything they want to. Now do we?

"Remember that at the time when Freud began to discover what he did about human actions, certain kinds of behavior were not considered to be indicative of illness but rather of wickedness. I am speaking now not only of the viewpoint of society but of the viewpoint of physicians and of medical science. Anyone who would undertake to treat such a condition was *prima facie* guilty of abetting crime, like the surgeon who was imprisoned for years because he set the broken leg of the fleeing assassin who shot Lincoln. The attitude towards many psychiatric illnesses was: 'Those are not sick people, those are bad people.' Freud was publicly admonished that the case material he was presenting belonged in the police court, not in a scientific meeting!

"But Freud said in essence, 'Let us listen to what people have to tell us of their behavior and not take a position too quickly until we hear all the facts.' He had to say this with great emphasis because it was so customary for physicians to say, 'If *those* are your symptoms, I don't want to treat you.' Freud said: 'Let us treat psychiatric illnesses like medical and surgical illnesses. Let us not condemn the sinner, but try to remedy the symptom. It is something he does not want, either; that is why he comes to us. We may be able to help him to get rid of the necessity of repeating it. But we can't get the thorn out of his flesh if we chase him out of the door before we get hold of it!'

"It was in this spirit that great emphasis was put on the psychoanalyst's neutrality in the early days of the science, his refraining from moral judgment of the patient without resigning the hope that it would ultimately be possible for the patient to accept a different point of view and 'behave himself.' The early-day psychoanalysts hence put much stress on *not* telling the patient what the proper ideals of life should be.

"One of their reasons for this was the reaction against the prevalent medical attitude. They realized better than some of their colleagues how strongly value systems have been influenced by traditions, going back as far as Hammurabi, which are more vengeful and punitive than moral. They realized too that it is often from a very excess of such self-imposed morality that the patient is suffering. Bear in mind that the theory of psychoanalytic technique is that the analyst not advise the patient, not sympathize with him, not make decisions for him or try to make him happy. The psychoanalyst does not assume to remove the patient's conflicts. The charge that psychoanalysis 'fails to relieve the unresolved sense of guilt of sin' (I quote verbatim from a very vocative television clergyman) is, of course, totally absurd. It is also absurd (and almost as ungrammatical) to charge (as I think the clergyman meant to) that psychoanalysis *does* relieve an unresolved sense of guilt of sin.

"And so, in spite of the general agreement in this forum, it should be made clear that many colleagues do feel that there is a technical danger that the psychiatrist, the psychoanalyst, *will* exhibit a moral attitude and thus occlude the treatment, thereby hurting the patient instead of helping him. Therefore, psychoanalysts tend to lean over a little bit the other way. They do not deny that penalties follow error, whether the error be called sin or stupidity. But they do not regard themselves as responsible for inflicting an artificial penalty, a tailored punishment.

"In some psychoanalysts this attitude of nonjudgment becomes almost a religion. Such individuals get themselves into absurd and illogical predicaments in their zeal to supplant social vengeance with social understanding. But it is just as absurd to scold society and punish it for its stupidity as it is to scold a patient and punish him, and this attitude leads some analysts to espouse a *laissez faire* philosophy in regard to patients' 'outside' behavior which in practice is dangerous to their patients and dangerous to the good name of psychoanalysis. The most free-thinking and modern young mother would probably not leave a two-year-old child to do as it likes in an ammunition factory, and for some patients the everyday social community is more dangerous than an ammunition factory.

"A more rational position would be to concede the point of view of society and of the law and of religion—that 'sin' is alluring and that, if we yield to it, we have to pay for the 'fun.' But the psychiatrist's further assumption is that sin is not nearly as much fun as it is made out to be, that it is usually painful and in a large sense unwanted by the individual, and that there are better ways than punishment to influence people to avoid it.

"Perhaps all of this could be said in a much simpler way: There have been many attempts to explain the behavior of ourselves and other people which is not propitious or comfortable. Once it was all blamed on the devil; it was assumed that in some way or other we made pacts with the devil or yielded to his persuasions. Misbehavior was sin. Then for a while, in the days of enlightenment and even more recently, misbehavior was ignorance and required not a priest or a penance but a better education. Today both priests and educators are agreed that in some individuals, though they be both sinful and ignorant, the misbehavior can be seen also as evidence of a sickness—*i.e.*, a symptom.

"Now it is quite possible that it can be all three of these. But the practical problem is, which kind of help is most available and most effective with a particular sufferer or misbehaver? To some extent this is determined by the social and philosophical atmosphere of the place and the time and the people. We can only speak in the last analysis for the immediate environment in which we live and with which we are most familiar. I have no idea what position I would take on many questions that might arise were I attempting the psychoanalysis of an Eskimo woman in Alaska or of one of Socrates' disciples in ancient Greece. I have difficulty enough trying to keep my finger on the pulse of social thought and feeling among those people with whom I have grown up, who make up one country in a world in which we are all such small but interdependent parts."

V

RESISTANCE

The Paradoxical Tendencies Exhibited by
the Party of the First Part Toward Defeating
the Purpose of the Contract

IN THE PRECEDING CHAPTER WE DISCUSSED THE *involuntary* PARTICIPA-
tion of the therapist in the contract. It might seem logical to discuss
next his *voluntary* participation, the furtherance he gives to the process, intentionally and designedly. But from another standpoint it
would be more logical to complete the natural history or systematic
portrayal of the reactions of the patient, the party of the first part,
to the therapeutic situation. After all, the transference phenomena
just described as the involuntary participation of the therapist occur
in the *patient;* they are a part of his regression.

In our account of the process of "progressive regression" and the
"recessive recovery," we have spoken thus far as if the patient undergoing the process were "all for it," consistently eager to participate,
to "tell all," to observe his past with one eye and his present with the
other eye and compare the views. We may seem to have assumed that,
once started, he would easily and progressively put aside his natural

reluctance to communicate the unpleasant, the embarrassing, and the compromising data of his life, assuming, indeed, that such material ever "occurred" to him!

But of course, as everyone who tries it discovers, this is not what happens! Almost from the very start the patient realizes that telling one's mind, even though it relieves something, requires effort, and proceeds against certain counterpressures. Sometimes it seems irrelevant and scarcely worth the breath (and the costly time) to relate a passing thought; sometimes it might reflect on the appearance or skill of the analyst or on the reputation of some "innocent bystander" —or otherwise offend all canons of good taste. Sometimes it is just "too embarrassing."

This is true in spite of the extraordinary situation of psychoanalytic treatment, in which one person is permitted to say whatever comes into his mind to another person without suffering punitive consequences for having done so. The patient enters into the contract, as a rule, with misgivings, usually with considerable fear. But, at the same time, he welcomes the opportunity to talk about himself and to discharge a certain pressure of confession. In the early days of analysis this confession relief was spoken of figuratively as "catharsis" and the expression still persists in psychiatry. The implication of this term was that some kind of blocking of communication occurred comparable to constipation, so that pressure of an accumulation of unspoken emotionally charged ideas could be released by encouragement in a properly protected opportunity.

The phenomenon is not as simple to explain in psychological terms as the figure of speech would indicate. The pressure of talk in a two-party situation sometimes seems to stem largely from a sense of guilt and a wish to confess, but at other times it represents a compelling need to establish contact with someone who will "understand," meaning some one who will accept without rebuff a prickly, lonely individual who cannot expediently control his long accumulated resentments and bitterness. This tendency to relieve "pressure" verbally is a familiar phenomenon, whatever its full explanation, and facilitates the *beginning* of an analysis.

Sooner or later, however, the confessions and confidings of which the early flow of communications consists begin to include material which the patient had not been aware of any need to confess. He remembers the analyst's assurance, explicit or implicit, that no ill consequences will result from his communication of these confidences, that everything he says will be considered only tentative and completely confidential, and he tries to believe it. Indeed, he does come to believe it in time, but he soon gets into the position of "betraying" himself and implicating others. He finds himself telling tales out of school and admitting things which he has previously denied—perhaps even to himself. So, whereas at first he had been relieved by the diminished pressure of his confessions, now new pressures develop because of them. Not only guilty secrets but aggressive and perverse fantasies are voiced which carry in their wake fears of retaliation or punishment. This leads in turn to "clamming up."

Thus the patient seems to suffer simultaneously from a yearning to "get well" and a compulsion to defend himself against any change in his life adjustment (especially the intrapsychic adjustment), uncomfortable though it may be in many respects. He had found certain coping devices with which he "made do," after a fashion. Now, like Hamlet, he begins to wonder whether it is better to suffer the familiar pains and aches associated with these old methods or to face the dangerous possibilities of a new and *perhaps* better way of handling himself. He knows that *probably* what he fears in the new situation is less dangerous than he supposes, and the rewards better than he imagines. He knows (*i.e.,* reasons) that his fear is *probably* based on misapprehensions. Nevertheless, the fear is there, the doubt is there, the hesitation is there. And they remain for a long time.

Thus, from the very beginning of the psychoanalytic treatment, every patient, in spite of his cooperativeness and eagerness to "get better," is partially "on the defensive." He unintentionally but purposively obstructs the very process upon which he counts so heavily. He may obstruct it so effectively as to terminate it soon after it has begun. One of my early cases was very illuminating to me in this respect, and I have often used it as a teaching example. A young man had achieved a reputation for brave and dashing military exploits. For this, and because he was handsome and well-to-do, he was a romantic figure. But his physical relations with his wife were a disappointment to both him and her, and he began psychoanalytic treatment for this and some other symptoms. The early weeks of his analysis brought a sincere contrasting of the world's impression of him with his own realization of weakness. This encouraging phase was succeeded by a period of slowed up production culminating in a dream. He was exploring a house which looked very good on the outside. But as he went further through the halls of this interesting and handsome building he came to a corner of one room where he stopped short, horrified. For on the floor in that corner lay something dreadful, disgusting, terrible—"too awful to look at. Perhaps it was a decaying dog—a cur—a beast—something of mine." He did not dare to look at it but turned and fled from the building.

A few days later the patient wrote that he was feeling better and believed he would discontinue his analysis.

More often the resistance is less tornadolike, but develops in a certain rhythm or pattern which continues with fluctuations throughout the analysis. The psychoanalyst soon becomes familiar with its peculiar manifestations in each case. In a way the analysis of each patient is a kind of never-ending duel between the analyst and the patient's resistance. It is no wonder that resistance almost becomes personified for some analysts and that they tend to equate it with the disease process. Resistance is not something that crops up occasionally to "impede" the course of treatment; it is omnipresent. In Freud's words, "Every step of the treatment is accompanied by resistance; every single thought, every mental act of the patient's, must pay toll to the resistance, and represents a compromise between the forces urging towards the cure and those gathered to oppose it." [44] It is a fascinating, dramatic production, on a par with the creation of a dream, in that the patient's resistance makes use of his typical defenses and more stable character traits. Or, to turn it around, his defensive repertoire is used in the service of resistance.

Some analysts have become so intrigued with the phenomenon of resistance that they have based their entire rationale of interpretation—a topic which we shall take up later—on the principle of fighting the resistance with insight. This seems to many of us to be somewhat of an overemphasis upon one important aspect of the process.

There is also a tendency among some analysts to think of resistance as something "bad"—that is, something to be regarded as an obstacle. And Freud, too, in the early days felt this way. It is significant, however, that Freud received the strong impression even while he was at Bernheim's Clinic that resistances could not be ordered out of existence by the therapist. He recoiled at Bernheim's charge that the patient was "countersuggesting." It is to be reckoned as part of Freud's uncanny sensitivity to the dynamics of human behavior that he early recognized that the content of a wish is only one part of an intrapsychic conflict. In 1910 he wrote, "The idea that a neurotic is suffering from a sort of ignorance, and that if one removes the ignorance by telling him facts (about the causal connection of his illness with his life, about his experiences in childhood, and so on) he must recover, is an idea that has long been superseded, and one derived from superficial appearances. The pathological factor is not his ignorance in itself, but the root of this ignorance in his *inner resistances;* it was they that first called this ignorance into being, and they still maintain it now. In combatting these resistances lies the task of the therapy. Telling the patient what he does not know because he has repressed it, is only one of the necessary preliminaries in the therapy. If knowledge about his unconscious were as important for the patient as the inexperienced in psychoanalysis imagine, it would be sufficient to cure him for him to go to lectures or read books. Such measures, however, have as little effect on the symptom of nervous disease as distributing menu cards in time of famine has on people's hunger. The analogy goes even further than its obvious application, too; for describing his unconscious to the patient is regularly followed by an intensification of the conflict in him and exacerbation of his symptoms." [53] Analysis of the patient's resistances, then, allows the patient to realize the conditions that bring about his dilemmas and unhappiness.

The phenomenon of resistance is one of Freud's greatest discoveries, and by his own definitive statement is one of the two essential planks of psychoanalytic theory. But when we say that Freud "discovered" resistance we mean that he brought to the attention of physicians that in psychological medicine resistance is a factor which cannot be ignored and which can be dealt with in certain ways. Experienced clinicians have known for thousands of years that something in patients under treatment seems to impel them to work against the efforts of the physician to cure them. But the traditional attitude of medicine throughout the centuries has been to ignore this opposition, to treat it with equanimity, as Osler said in his classical essay. The dentist does not lose patience with a man whose tooth has stopped aching after an emergency appointment has been arranged. The (good) surgeon does not get angry with a screaming child who dreads the lance. But the reluctance of such patients to accept treatment is ascribed to fear, in the hands of which they are considered helpless. But Freud showed us that resistance is more than fear, that it is a force related perhaps to the inertia discovered by Newton to reside in all matter, a reluctance to change position. The suffering patient submitting himself to our profession at no mean expense in time, pain, and money seems to be demonstrating how much he wants to get well. But there are always indications that he is a man divided against himself and that he does not *wholly* want to get well! He also wants to stay sick! Freud's genius was reflected in his discovery that this paradox has deep meaning, that the conflict is of the essence and not a mere complicating nuisance, and that the intelligence is our best weapon against it.

Resistance as it is used in psychoanalytic theory may be defined as *the trend of forces within the patient which oppose the process of ameliorative change.* It is not the analyst who is being resisted; it is the process within the patient which the analyst is encouraging. Freud identified this with the process of making unconscious material conscious or of letting it become conscious. This makes it seem almost equivalent to repression, which is not correct because it is too restrictive.

Clinically, resistance can be seen in a myriad of forms. Sometimes it is a mere concealing of acts and facts, sometimes an increased forgetting instead of an increased remembering, sometimes a tardiness or an absence, sometimes a prolonged silence. Enacting the events of a memory which does not come to mind as such is a form of resistance called "acting-out"; indeed, some analysts feel that one criterion of the end of an analysis is when acting-out is entirely replaced by remembering in the ordinary sense. There are also the forms of intellectualization, of cataloging, of dawdling, of "emoting"

Enacting the events of a memory which does not come to mind

instead of thinking and talking. There is a resistance of erotization, of which we shall speak in more detail shortly. There is a resistance of new symptom formation, psychological or somatic, as if to proclaim that the analysis is increasing rather than diminishing the patient's afflictions. (Ferenczi called this *passagère* resistance.)

In the appendix of *Inhibitions, Symptoms and Anxiety,* under the heading of "Modifications of Earlier Views," Freud reformulated his concept of resistance as a defensive action undertaken by the ego to buttress the repression it maintains to protect itself and to protect this repressive function from the dissolving effect of "insight." Freud compares resistance to such things as pity, conscientiousness and cleanliness in obsessional neuroses where there is a reinforcement or exaggeration of an attitude opposite to that of the instinctual trend relative to the situation. Similarly, even when given the opportunity in the course of treatment, "It is hard for the ego to direct its attention to perceptions and ideas which it has up to now made a rule of avoiding, or to acknowledge as belonging to itself impulses that are the complete opposite of those which it has made its own." [50]

FIVE CLASSICAL TYPES OF RESISTANCE

In the essay just mentioned, Freud listed five types of resistance. The first of them he called *repression resistance,* which comes from the persistent, automatic, normative tendency of the ego to try to control dangerous tendencies by blocking them off. The ego has the habit, so to speak, of solving its problems in this way as far as possible, and it resists the process of "free thought" and ventilation of preconscious memories lest the change upset the homeostatic balance and permit the emergence of *dangerous* tendencies. It is the ego's lifelong "business" (in part) to hold back certain things from expression, and this is automatically extended to the analytic situation, especially when the expression of previously *repressed* impulses (as distinguished from *suppressed* material) becomes likely to occur.

The second of the types of resistance listed by Freud is *transference resistance.* I should prefer to call it *frustration resistance* or *revenge resistance.* It expresses the patient's resentment at not getting from the analyst (as a representation of an earlier figure) the expected response; it bespeaks the mounting frustration and anger of this disappointment. It is as if such a patient were sulking or, to put it more urbanely, as if he had become less eager to try to please the analyst, and almost too angry to want to tell him anything. We shall discuss it at some length presently.

Third, there is the *epinosic gain resistance,* which has to do with the reluctance of the ego to give up the advantages that have accrued to the patient as a whole as a result of an illness. These secondary gain resistances are related to the repression resistance just mentioned, but are more superficial; they are more recently acquired devices rather than lifelong habits of action and lie predominantly in the conscious and preconscious.

The fourth variety of resistance listed by Freud emanates, he believed, from the Id; he called it *repetition compulsion resistance.* It was the last to be discovered. As Freud put it, "We find that even after the ego has decided to relinquish its resistances, it still has difficulty in undoing the repressions," [50] despite the rewards and advantages we have (by inference) promised the ego if *it* will give up *its* resistances (the three types just listed). This period of strenuous effort which the ego makes following its decision to relinquish them is called *working-through.* This is carried on *against* the resistance of the repetition compulsion, "the attraction exerted by the unconscious prototypes upon the repressed instinctual process." [50] This form of resistance is related to the self-destructive principle which operates behind the ego, as Freud put it in *Beyond the Pleasure Principle.*

Fifth, there is the resistance which emanates from the superego, deriving from a need for punishment. This may be a socialized form of the preceding type, but one which is very characteristic of human beings in our culture and era. "I do not deserve to get well; it is fitting that I should suffer [*some*]." This is the inexpedient but partially effective way in which guilt feelings are atoned for and kept in a kind of spurious balance which resists change.

To summarize, Freud suggested that there is resistance derived from unconscious fear (repression resistance); there is resistance derived from disappointed expectations in the analysis (transference resistance); there is resistance derived from inertia, false prudence and short-sighted opportunism (secondary gain resistance); there is resistance derived from self-directed aggression on the basis of a deep biological pattern (repetition compulsion resistance); and there is resistance derived from the feeling that one should suffer (superego resistance).

Freud enlarged these ideas in his paper "Analysis Terminable and Interminable" (1937).[43] In this paper he distinguished resistances that reflect defensive operations of the ego, such as projection and displacement, from resistances that arise from the nature of the psychic apparatus and which are etiologically independent of conflict. These resistances that arise from the nature of the psychic apparatus include adhesiveness of libido, mobility of the libido, loss of plasticity (for example, in advancing age) and resistances from the sense of guilt (corresponding to the superego resistance mentioned in the "Problem of Anxiety"). Freud also mentioned the role of some nuclear conflicts in impeding the cure: penis envy in women and passivity conflict in men.

Resistance derived from any or several or all of these sources may appear in various clinical forms. We have already referred to such familiar expressions as silence, tardiness, evasion of the basic rule, etc. There are certain more comprehensive categories which deserve fuller treatment, especially *erotization* and *"acting out."*

Acting out is commonly understood to describe an extremely common phenomenon occurring to greater or lesser extent in all analyses. It is the tendency to substitute an act or series of acts for no very evident reason which turns out to represent enactments of forgotten episodes which the analysand cannot remember. In other words, the patient remembers not in words, but in behavior and thus repeats behavior. "He repeats it without, of course, knowing that he is repeating it." (Freud[57]) This is, of course, an extremely effective kind of resistance since, like a dream, it offers some discharge of tension. It is like charades played between the two parts of the ego.

This phenomenon has become of increasing importance in psychoanalysis since the inclusion as potentially analyzable of many of these individuals afflicted with various so-called "character disorders" (a most deplorable designation but one which will serve our immediate purposes). Fenichel [30] defined this form of resistance somewhat elaborately as "an acting which unconsciously relieves inner tension and brings partial discharge to ward off impulses (no matter whether these impulses express directly instinctual demands or are reactions to original instinctual demands, *e.g.*, guilt feelings); the present situation, somehow associatively connected with the repressed content, is used as an occasion for the discharge of repressed energies; the cathexis is displaced from the repressed memories to the present derivative, and the displacement makes this discharge possible."

Some patients are much more prone to this type of resistance than others, and numerous explanations for it have been suggested: strong oral phase disturbances and fixation; strong narcissistic needs; some kind of constitutional hyperactivity; special trends toward dramatization derived from exhibitionism; scotophilic impulses and a strong belief in the magic of action.

The latter two were suggested by Phyllis Greenacre [71] who carried her thinking about the matter further to the hypothesis that the common genetic situation which tends to produce such tendencies consists in a *distortion in the developmental relationship of speech and action.* Action may not always speak louder than words, but in most of us they do speak first. The essence of Greenacre's theory is that the patient who tends to "act out" chronically had inhibitions of speech in early life which encouraged relatively more motor discharge. It is as if the patient in the course of his therapeutic regression resumed those forms of expression with which he had originally felt most comfortable. Since this agrees with observations of my own, it appeals to me strongly as a rational explanation.

In practice there is a tendency on the part of some analysts to refer to any social misbehavior on the part of the patient during his treatment as "acting out." It would be better if some of this was differentiated as "acting up" or "acting in" or just "acting"! For certainly not all behavior that the analyst doesn't approve of can be put in the category of "acting out." Furthermore, as Fenichel suggested and as

how about too much speech & too little action

I can also confirm, some analysts provoke and enjoy or encourage dramatic acting out in their patients and even find reason to ascribe benefit to it. The patient, they say, is overcoming his inhibitions, he is getting courage to do what he should have done long ago. He is abreacting. To quote again from Greenacre:

> This seems quite occasionally the problem of young and inexperienced analysts, but may also occur among analysts who themselves tend to act out, either directly or in an inhibited form, and to enjoy this vicariously in their patients. This may be of greater frequency and importance than one might at first think. It occurs among analysts who display no overt acting out but who react as some severely restrained adults who enjoy and tacitly applaud the impulsive behavior of their children who dare to do what they themselves have not been permitted. This is seen strikingly in the parental attitudes which form the background of many impulse-ridden psychopaths. An attitude of overanxiety on the part of the analyst about the patient's acting out is frequently sensed and reacted to by the patient, who then unconsciously gratifies his sadism as well in the acting out and gets a spurious sense of power and independence through it. If the analyst behaves in either of these ways to any appreciable degree, acting out will continue no matter how much its specific content is interpreted.[71]

Aside from correcting the countertransference effect or the technical ignorance of the therapist, the standard attacks on this type of resistance consist in the interpretation of the behavior as resistance, the identification of the nature and meaning of the particular acts, and the forthright prohibition or at least deprecation of the acts. Meanwhile there is the hope that the patient will not get himself into too much trouble prior to such growth in the strength of the ego as is sufficient to control such impulses. But, as Greenacre says, "Since in its very nature acting out is ego-syntonic and the patient is not aware of its destructive nature, it comes to the attention of the analyst in most instances after its occurrence (if at all), and sometimes is not reported or only indirectly." [71, 72]

Some young analysts are reluctant to express their disapproval or their notion of the unwisdom of certain kinds of behavior lest they seem censorious and thus discourage their patient from communications. Others fear lest they become exploited by the patient and progressively forced into a position of giving continuous guidance. Many of them hesitate to discuss with the patient their mutual awareness that both of them are members of the same social order, have long institutionalized their disapproval of this kind of behavior or recognized its implicit dangers. Other analysts overlook and fail to deal with the patient's unconscious or dimly conscious wish to have the analyst interfere in his behavior.*

EROTIZATION RESISTANCE

We come now to the second of the two special forms of resistance requiring more particularization. There comes a day when the patient undergoing psychoanalysis, in spite of its expensiveness in time and money, in spite of its dreariness and the bitter tears and memories it evokes, realizes that in a curious way he enjoys it. This pleasure is quite apart from the symptomatic relief the treatment may have afforded him. It is a subtle, secret, pleasurable sensation. It may make both the patient and the analyst slightly uneasy lest it justify the accusations of unsympathetic outsiders who allege that what certain patients want is not cure but treatment and that what some psychoanalysts want to do is to treat rather than to cure. There is a germ of truth in this, of course, but there is much more to erotization than this.

Every patient's first and primary motive, we assume, is to be relieved of his symptoms. He is prepared to wait a while for this result, and he expects the treatment, like all medical treatment, to be more or less unpleasant. But like the man who submits to the dentist or to the surgeon or to any doctor, he tells himself that the ultimate gain will be worth the unpleasantness of the treatment.

But almost from the beginning of psychoanalytic treatment, de-

---

* One of my colleagues who carefully read this chapter feels that it should be made clear that not all acting out is physically or socially dangerous.

spite its unpleasant features, there is some conscious pleasure in the process. The opportunity to talk freely, to confess, to boast, to explain oneself, to be listened to sympathetically—this is no ordeal, but quite the contrary. The symptoms may abate or they may continue—for the present it doesn't matter. The narcissistic pleasure of contemplating and communicating oneself to an audience carries the process forward, and would continue it for a while even with no definite relief implied. This has been made amply clear by Roethlisberger,[136] Carl Rogers [138] and others. Gradually, however, and quite independent of the dawning of some of the misgivings and disappointment discussed earlier, there comes a time when we (analysts) begin to observe that the patient is talking on, telling us memories, fantasies, dreams, and experiences, not so much to please himself or for any other reason just mentioned as for the reason that he wishes to please *us!* As we saw in the previous chapter, this wish to please and to be found pleasing proceeds to great lengths or, better to say, depths. The patient is often aware of this motive and will acknowledge it frankly. It is almost invariably a repetition of an effort he has made with not one but various people in his life, beginning perhaps with one of his parents. The analyst has probably begun to represent some of these earlier objects.

But quite aside from the transference aspects, we should examine *the resistance feature* of these phenomena. Certainly, seeking to please others is no fault. The wish to please the analyst may indeed be a motive which facilitates the treatment at first, for no cases are more difficult to treat than those individuals who do *not* want to please the analyst even at the start. Nevertheless, it can develop into a form of resistance which becomes more and more apparent as such. Later on it will be replaced by the wish to *displease* the analyst, to hurt or provoke him, and this *too* is resistance. *Everything done for the sake of or for the effect upon the analyst* may be considered not only the illustration of a repetitive pattern but *prima facie* evidence of resistance. This is clear enough when such things take the form of attempts to bribe the analyst or seduce him or anger him, but it is also true in the more subtle forms. This does not mean that the material offered in this effort is worthless, but when pleasing or displeasing the analyst becomes preeminent as the motivation for the delivery of material, resistance is in control.

How is it that the wish to please the analyst is at the same time a motive power for the continuance of the analysis and a resistance? This is the explanation: For the patient to fasten upon the analyst as the object of his daily efforts is, of course, obviously irrational. The analyst is only a means to an end, and not an end (object) in himself. Now, of course, the phenomenon of transference demonstrates that the analyst always represents someone he is not. And that "someone" the analyst is *not* cannot be affected by the patient's efforts to please or displease the analyst. Furthermore, it is as if the patient were saying, "I want you to want me to get well, and to make me well; therefore I will try to please you, in order that you will do so." The patient forgets that the reality is that he pays for the analyst's help with money and not with good behavior or with psychoanalytic material, which assist, but do not reward, the analyst. The object of the treatment is the patient, not the doctor, who requires no special "pleasing." A surgeon cannot operate on a patient intent upon paying him compliments or kissing his hand. The surgeon will only be embarrassed and annoyed; the analyst must be neither, but he must see through the conscious to the unconscious meaning.

In a sense this is perhaps all a question of appropriateness of behavior. The purpose of analytic therapy is to bring buried, unconscious trends into consciousness, and in order to do this we encourage a "regression" in the several respects described in the preceding chapter. This regression regularly leads to increasing inappropriateness of "reactions" and fantasy behavior on the part of the patient. We expect it. In the regression the patient "wants" certain *inappropriate* things and seeks to obtain those things in various ways. We, his therapists, want him only to *see* that he wants them, to see that he once wanted them and failed to get them, to see why he failed, to see what better he could do. But instead of just "seeing" this, he *feels* it—and tends to express his feelings *not* merely in words, not merely in description of his sensations, dreams, and symptoms, but by gestures, symbolic acts, attitudes, and general *programs* of action modified, of course, to some extent by the healthy residuum of his ego.

The feeling on the part of the patient that he is doing something to please the analyst ordinarily enlarges to a feeling that the analyst gets pleasure out of the patient. To give pleasure affords pleasure, and the patient begins to enjoy pleasing, a pleasurable emotion, which is quite aside from the relief of his tension. Feelings of gratitude to the physician for listening, for showing interest in his problem, for protecting him in a way, for being kind to him in spite of his disagreeableness, are now added to by his feeling that he, the patient, is now gratifying the analyst.

Thus, from various sources in the analytic experience, in spite of its uncomfortable aspects, there springs a certain "illegitimate" pleasure for the patient. This pleasure may be felt only as a vague "spiritual" satisfaction, but it often becomes something definitely physical; the soma begins to become involved in the process. This involvement of the body may be reflected in physical symptoms and physical changes.

In this form, such resistance has been known classically as the *erotization of the analytic situation*. The patient unconsciously tends to convert the analysis into an erotic experience, which is, of course, one of his deeply buried infantile wishes in respect to his relations with the parent. It is seen typically in connection with fantasies involving the analyst which are repetitious of actual or fantasied experiences with some earlier person in the patient's life.

Let me give an example. A woman patient had developed an enormously strong feeling of dependency and helplessness, together with fantasies that the analyst could—were she sufficiently in his favor—perform a miracle and reconstruct her anatomically, psychologically, socially, and otherwise. She was sure that he was greatly pleased to learn that she had discontinued her relations with a lover and also that she had ceased to gratify herself sexually by manual manipulation. She began to hint, with some embarrassment, that her present satisfactions (*i.e.*, with the analyst) were preferable and sufficient for her—indeed, a little more than sufficient. She found it difficult to speak, she said; she much preferred to listen to *him* speak. The very material that she communicated to him, whether or not it pertained to sexual matters, seemed to her only an offering to him, as if she were offering her body. Whether she spoke or whether she listened to his brief comments, the sensations of mounting eroticism were consciously experienced. She would arrive at a point at which she would almost plead to have the analyst speak to her—to say anything, just so she could hear and enjoy his voice.

Fantasies of and expressed wishes for sexual gratification from the analyst are frequent, but sometimes the patient will go beyond these to vivid sensations of its occurrence from which, as in the example cited by Freud, the *patient* may run away in a panic (*e.g.,* Dora), if, indeed, the *analyst* doesn't! (*e.g.,* Anna O.).

The case cited above, like Freud's, was an unusual and extreme one, and the situation should have been detected by the analyst before it had reached that degree of development and, by interpretation, controlled. This is not always possible, as Freud himself reported. Freud believed that erotization resistance always indicates some need for interpretation. It results from the patient interpreting (misinterpreting) the invitation to think and say "anything" to be a seduction by the analyst. "You tempt me—then frustrate me," he thinks (and often says). Thus the frankly sexual dream often means, "You are not interpreting (*i.e.,* exposing) my resistance fast enough. You are letting me get away with something."

And in nearly every analysis there is some degree of this erotization resistance, with physical sensations experienced always with a degree of shame and guilt feelings. Hence there is usually at the same time a struggle to suppress them. The struggle is not entirely conscious; the whole process of talking about the experience has a general tendency to diminish both kinds of feeling, since one object of analysis is to translate physical sensations and physical urges into words and images.

More subtle forms of this resistance are very common indeed. The experience of pleasure may not be so definitely phallic. It can be observed in the early stages of analysis, for example, in oral forms; and in the middle stages of analysis in oral, anal, and even cutaneous modalities. It is proper to say, I think, that the analytic process may be sexualized or eroticized in all of the ways in which the patient as a developing child experienced physical pleasure: anally, orally, and so on. I have suggested that we can say that the analytic process is at various times *oralized, analized, phallicized,* and *genitalized.*

Oral erotization of the analysis, for example, is observable in some patients for whom talking—whether they do the talking themselves or merely drink in the words of someone else—has a high "libidinal value," as we used to call it. For some patients every word of the analyst is a pearl; for others, their own words are spoken as if they were minting gold coins with their lips. Pleasure from aggressive oral tendencies is sometimes clearly, although unpleasantly, detectable in the spitting or biting nature of the content or delivery of the patient's material.

Similarly, erotization of the analysis according to *anal* modalities results in a variety of phenomena derived from childhood experiences and emotional constellations developed during them. On the one hand, there may be a great overestimation of giving and receiving gifts, attempts to bribe the analyst, attempts to get special privileges from him. On the other hand, a typical (verbal) constipation syndrome may develop, with or without the equivalent of flatus production. It is often obvious that a patient is repeating on the couch the type of performance characteristic of him on the chamber-pot many years previously—straining, groaning, and making much effort to demonstrate to the analyst that he is trying very hard, but all in vain, or with a pitifully meager production. This may be preceded or even followed by the equivalent of a diarrhea and the sort of material that can be interpreted as defecation *for* or *upon* the analyst. A patient may act as if to say, "I will not move my bowels for you—unless, etc."; or "See, I move my bowels for you," or "I would if I only could . . . please help me," or "Help me get started," or "Please give me an enema." *

This enema phenomenon may be changing a little in these days now that the children subjected to forcible enemata are fewer. And perhaps the designation of the phenomenon should be changed to the soapstick or the suppository syndrome. But whatever it be called, it is very common and quite unmistakable. Some patients will not begin talking until the analyst has made a remark or questioned the silence or something of that kind. Then the patient will talk freely. Other patients will protest that they cannot go on or cannot get started

---

* In a study of anal erotism, my brother William Menninger [110] collected many illustrations of this symbolic language.

ess the analyst says something or, as the patients often put it, with .. hly overdetermined meaning, until the analyst *does* something.

Another aspect of anal erotization of analysis as a resistance mode is the use of particularly foul language, overvivid descriptions of offensive scenes and experiences, vulgar and disagreeable words and pictures. Material of this kind is sometimes "discharged" with particular reference to parental prohibitions and defiance. Young psychoanalysts sometimes find satisfaction in hearing such material in a way somewhat comparable to that of the satisfaction evinced by a surgeon whose incision is followed by a flow of foul-smelling pus. But the surgeon's satisfactions do not prevent him from recognizing its offensiveness and neither should the psychoanalyst's! Incidentally, the psychoanalyst who is under the impression that he facilitates an analysis by using vulgar language which the patient is "more likely to understand" is doubly deceived. The patient will correctly understand that the psychoanalyst is lowering himself or condescending to the patient's level instead of maintaining a standard to which he, the patient, may aspire to reach. Because the patient discharges psychological flatus is no reason the psychoanalyst should do so.

In the *phallic* erotization of the analysis the patient's behavior and material illustrates the dominance of his fantasies and thinking by the adolescent thesis that the genital organ and sensations connected with it are the totality of existence. For such patients the analyst's penis or vagina are made to seem the most important, indeed the primary, object of the patient's desires. Obtaining this genital organ for himself becomes a central fantasy; he becomes preoccupied with fantasies of seducing, inspecting, peeking at, or castrating the analyst. His behavior may carry out reflections of this phallic preoccupation in promiscuity, masturbation, and otherwise.

Evidence of what might be called a *genital* erotization of the analysis is represented by more mature, less narcissistic, even though unrealistic, fantasies of marrying the analyst or of having a child with him or her.

Any of these erotizations may involve more or less somatic compliance; *e.g.*, somatic "punishment" may appear in the form of sore throat, constipation, colitis, or dyspepsia. Genitourinary system complications of many kinds are frequent, such as polyuria, urinary retention, impotence, urethritis, dysmenorrhea, amenorrhea, etc. I have reported several instances of this. In one, a very severe coryza and other symptoms of a "bad cold" were a part of a total oralization of the analytic procedure.[106] In some other cases, urinary and uterine involvement were recognizable.[104, 108, 109] Indeed, our earliest clear insights into psychosomatic involvements were derived from the observation of these resistance phenomena in the course of psychoanalytic treatment.

One cannot expect an orderly development of these erotization techniques of resistance; however, the patient will often use first the one he has used habitually or characteristically. But even the most "oral" character will sooner or later try the effect of "anal-izing" the analysis, and later of phallicizing it. And, as explained above, erotization of the analysis, whether done symbolically, verbally, or somatically, is always resistance, because it substitutes the means for the end. It always says, "I want you" or "I want this." It says, vividly: "For your sake I try but I don't want to be changed. I want treatment that gratifies, not improvement that requires renunciation."

One final point about this erotization resistance: The analyst should never forget the aggressive component involved in it. Indeed, he should realize that the erotic wish and display act as a disguise for the hidden aggression underlying them. The analysand is asking for something improper and—by our standards—immoral. It is immoral in the same sense that giving morphine to an addict would be immoral. The thing wanted is self-destructive, and hence to yield to the importunity, no matter how urgent, is to assist in *hurting*, not helping the patient; and the patient *knows* this. Hence all erotization is an attempted distraction and seduction, a wish to remain ill and to hurt the analyst in revenge (for his alleged seduction of the patient) as well as himself (the analysand) in propitiation.

This is the place to mention what it would be better if we did not have to mention; namely, the fact that patients sometimes report that they were given physical gratification (or manipulation) by a previous therapist. He may or may not have been a psychoanalyst. He may or may not have regarded his behavior as an irresistible consequence of countertransference. But however he saw it, and whether or not he realized it then, he probably damaged the patient irreperably by this violation of the Hippocratic oath. Certainly such patients are thereafter very poor subjects for psychoanalytic treatment. They spend endless hours trying to work through the problem, "Can this doctor also be seduced?" or, as they may put it, "Will this doctor also betray his trust?"

The young psychoanalyst should never forget, however, that he has no real evidence that what the patient described ever happened. A patient's fantasies can be very vivid. We know that. And we like to assume that probably it was all in the patient's imagination. At any rate, it can never be mentioned and had best be forgotten. Yet as psychoanalysts we are obliged to listen to it sympathetically, open-mindedly. We have to assume for the moment that it may have been true, at least it seemed to the patient to have been true. We can be sorrowful that one of our colleagues betrayed his oath, but we must also remember that this could only have happened if the patient unconsciously wanted it to happen, and we must help him or her to see this and to take his responsibility for what he is now trying to reenact with us in a new situation. It is all the more important for us to be doubly faithful to the ideal and doubly aware of the aggression and resistance represented by the phenomenon of the attempted seduction via the appeal for help.*

In the psychoanalysis of some men one not infrequently encounters the fantasy which is referred to in vulgar jocularity as the wish to make all the girls happy. This we know stems from a childhood feeling of wanting to please mother, of wanting to do more for mother than father did or could do, and for various reasons extending this wish to other women who seemed to be lonely or sad or desirous. For some individuals this becomes translated into purely phallic terms, as if to propose that sexual pleasure is the sole aim or desideratum of life. This is, of course, a kind of unrecognized male prostitution.†

---

* I recall a patient who regarded herself as a *femme fatale;* she maintained that two physicians, a psychotherapist of world renown, and a priest had successively turned professional situations into sexual affairs with her. She denied to the end (of the interview) any responsibility for these affairs.

† In the latter form, the element of hostility for the woman is more evident. See L. L. Robbins.[135-A]

OTHER FORMS OF RESISTANCE

I have gone to some pains to illustrate these two common clinical forms of resistance, acting out and erotization, but I would like to remind the reader that prior to this I mentioned the existence of many other forms. Resistance might be divided into consciously felt opposition and opposition occurring with the best intentions, so to speak. For some patients it is necessary to pretend to be skeptical or independent. Others will consider it only their temperamental makeup that leads them to dawdle and delay. Some patients will insist that they never could talk spontaneously and use this as an excuse for not communicating thoughts, dreams, and reports of behavior. Sometimes resistance will take the form of lying, sometimes simply of not telling. These things have been mentioned. But they are all details. The important thing to see is that resistance exists, that it opposes treatment, that it is aggressive, and that it is self-destructive.

Some colleagues—*e.g.,* Kaiser [83] following Reich [129]—equate aggression with resistance, holding that if a patient's attention is called to how he is avoiding a communication which he wants to make, how he is behaving in order to *avoid* communicating—in short, how he is resisting—then it is not necessary for the analyst to expend any effort on specific interpretations of the content of the material behind the resistance. The patient is expected in the analytic situation to acknowledge and describe many suppressed or repressed impulses—not to yield to them. It is as if the analyst said, "These impulses are acceptable, insofar as they are verbalized, if they can be translated into speech." But the patient has difficulty in translating all of them into speech—he feels constantly impelled to put some of them into action or else to hold them back. But he does communicate some of them—by words, by gestures, by postures, and by acts. The words that he communicates are not always in the form of logical statements of feeling or statements of intention. They may begin this way, or they may begin as descriptions of sensations. But gradually to these statements and descriptions are added descriptions of fantasies and then accounts of dreams which are of course equivalent to unconscious fantasies, more direct in certain ways but also distorted in different ways. Finally, too, there are memories which the patient recalls, sometimes accurately, sometimes inaccurately. All of these statements, memories, fantasies, dreams, postures, physical symptoms, and so forth are to be considered communications. From them the analyst attempts to detect the type of injury which gives the repressed impulses their peculiar slant.

Now it is Dr. Kaiser's position that it is only necessary to point out the difficulties and inaccuracies of the communication. This is done either by describing to the patient precisely what he is doing as resistance—*i.e.*, in what way he is avoiding communication—or by giving the evidences of distortion in the communication. An experienced listener can recognize when there has been a substituted idea or substituted form in the communication. By this I am referring to the familiar phenomenon that when certain impulses attached to certain ideas meet with the repressive barrier of the ego, there is a tendency for the impulse to split off from the idea and attach itself to a more acceptable, substitute idea which is, in a sense, a counterfeit. This quality of counterfeitness or phoniness can be detected sometimes by the excess energy, the excessive or inappropriate quantity of energy with which a relatively prosaic idea is submitted, or by the bizarreness, isolatedness, irrelevancy, so to speak, of the idea with the rest of the known content of consciousness.

If this "phoniness," either of behavior or of idea, is pointed out to the patient, he becomes alerted and, so to speak, "goes into action." He attempts to explain it, and although this explanation will no doubt be chiefly rationalization, it will be closer to the original idea. In this way, by constantly pointing out the artificiality, the ungenuineness of the material, the analyst assists the patient to come closer and closer to telling the truth, the whole truth, and nothing but the truth—at least in regard to the impulses.

It is true that there is a strong urge for the repressed material to come out and that to dispel resistance is all that is necessary to permit this. But the deficiencies of this one-sided attack have been pointed out carefully by Fenichel [29] and others. I agree with Fenichel, although in some types of cases Kaiser's technique has considerable usefulness.

DIAGRAMMATIC RECAPITULATION OF RESISTANCE

The forces working against the process of recovery in psychoanalytic therapy may be paired at various levels with the positive efforts which they oppose, thus:

The patient wants to get help from the analyst	*but*	it is costly, time-consuming, strange, somewhat frightening, etc.
The patient wants to co-operate, follow instructions, "tell all," etc.,	*but*	it causes humiliation, shame, embarrassment, etc.
The patient wants love from the analyst, whomever he represents,	*but*	obtaining love is dangerous, uncertain, and costly.
The patient feels resentful toward the analyst for his silence and passivity and would like to tell him so,	*but*	the consequences might be unpleasant and even dangerous.
The patient responds to the encouragement of the analyst and the analytic situation to let himself go to some extent,	*but*	this offends his self-esteem, "seems so silly," unbecoming, indecorous, "and probably futile."
The patient is tempted to reveal repressed memories and suppressed fantasies,	*but*	"Surely, that can't be so," "It cannot have been I!"

The patient tries to get a clearer picture of his long buried unconscious strivings,	*but*	"It may be too horrible! I can't look. . . ."

The patient finally sees glimpses of how he has been misled by illusions and hatreds; he sees "The Better Way," or at least *a* better way, a more intelligent and realistic choice,	*but*	"I'm so used to my muddlings and misery; dare I make a shift? Do I really want to give it up? And how can I be sure?"

The patient gradually gives up his dependence upon analysis and the analyst and his unrealistic expectations of them; he is almost able to handle his life problems alone, and more expediently,	*but*	"Am I really ready? Might I not fail? Might I not relapse?"

These sample paradigms at various stages of the analysis are typical rationalizations at the various levels of the regression (but, of course, by no means *all* of them). They reflect the eternally conflictual nature of the moving, progressive process involved in psychoanalytic treatment.

Resistance to the treatment effect can be viewed as inertia, reaction, defense, self-directed aggression, analyst-diverted aggression, repetition compulsion, habit, psychological rigidity, fear of change, fear of the unknown. Not any one but *all* of these aspects describe and characterize it. *The process of recovery is always an other-sided view of the disease process:* and this applies to the artificial induction of a therapeutic illness, which is what the regression of "transference neurosis" really is. The psychoanalytic patient must get "worse" in order to get "better," and both changes require effort against opposition. It is the manifest, manifold expression of this opposition to the striven-for change that is correctly called *resistance*.

VI

INTERPRETATION AND OTHER INTERVENTION

The Voluntary Participation of the Second Party

TO RECAPITULATE, THERAPEUTIC PSYCHOANALYSIS HAS BEEN PRESENTED as a two-party contractual relationship in which one party engages another for assistance in changing himself; the party of the second part responds by setting up a situation in which he can listen uncritically and relatively silently to the free communications of the party of the first part. The latter then carries out (a part of) his obligation by making a continuous communication of his thoughts, fantasies, memories, impulses, and emotional reactions. First a little frightened, then progressively relieved and grateful for the opportunity of communicating to a sympathetic listener the nature and details of his suffering, the patient takes increasing advantage of the privilege. As he proceeds, however, there develop on the one hand certain reservations and on the other a mounting expectation that, as a result of the information he has so freely communicated to the therapist, the latter will respond with explanations, prohibitions, instructions, consolations, or other verbal magic which will resolve difficulties and relieve suffering and disability. The therapist does not make this expected response, and an effect of his abstemiousness and continued silence is a gradually increasing dissatisfaction and uncertainty for the patient which induces him to revert to less and less disguised forms of the techniques and objectives characteristic of his childhood.

After a time, however, against resistance manifested in many ways, including the exhibition of hostile feelings, fantasies, and even acts toward the therapist, the patient finally admits into consciousness certain "new" facts, new understanding, and, correspondingly, new attitudes. With these the process of regression is reversed, the patient begins to grow up again.

We should ask ourselves at this point theoretically why it is that the turn in the course of the regression comes about in just this way. Is it to be ascribed to new insights and new courage? Is it a reaction to something the patient discovers or to a kind of action of the law of diminishing returns, a super-surfeiting so to speak, with the meager satisfactions of reinstituted infantile behavior? Sometimes the model comes to mind of an archeologist digging in a pit for the relics of a vanished civilization; there comes a time when more and more digging recovers less and less material.

Or is it something like sleep, from which we seem to awaken in spite of the fact that it is pleasant and requires no effort to remain asleep? The hypnotized patient similarly seems to show a spontaneous tendency to return to his own habitual states of mind and ways of behavior. Acute episodes of psychiatric illness which tend to disappear promptly may serve the purpose of enabling normal patterns of adjustment to be resumed more comfortably.* Is the psychoanalytic regression something like these?

We may as well confess right away that we do not know. We only know that usually—not always—the direction of the regressive tendency does ultimately cease, the trend reverses and the psychological material produced by the patient assumes a more and more adult

---

* I have elsewhere expanded this idea that regressive and explosive discharge may serve constructive purposes of the ego by forestalling more extensive personality disintegration. (See Menninger and Mayman.[103])

form. The infantile objectives are given up for more realistic and mature ones and the techniques likewise undergo a progressive modification in the direction of maturity.

In the early days it was assumed that this came about because of something the analysand discovered. The analyst assisted the patient through the critical sticking point responsible for the *neurotic* regression, around and beneath which the *treatment* regression was assumed to have taken him. There was a conviction that the clear and full recollection of half-remembered traumatic experiences freed the patient from haunting and crippling derivatives of them (Breuer). Then the credit began to be ascribed to the explosive release of pockets of unhealthy emotion in the form known as "abreaction." This was regarded as some kind of riddance of an irritating substance from the psychological system. Next the therapeutic effect was attributed to the psychological disciplining involved in the so-called working-through process, about which we shall have something to say later. After this, insight became king for a short time, followed by the theory of cure through elimination of the superego.

There were other explanations, or perhaps we should say emphases. Freud's dictum, "Where Id was, there shall Ego be," was variously interpreted to mean the making conscious of significant, unconscious material; extending the "boundaries" or domain of the (observing) ego; abandoning the fixation points of immature development; and no doubt many other things, depending upon the conceptual model of the personality and the psychoanalytic process held by the interpreter.

Along with all of these went the tacit assumption that a deconditioning process occurred, for which Alexander[1] later coined the phrase "corrective emotional experience," implying that, with analytic enlightenment, the mature ego became able effectively to rearrange the distribution and investment of instinctual energies which had been so *dis*advantageously made by an immature ego. The unsolved dilemmas of childhood are not so unsolvable to the more sophisticated and experienced ego which can handle them when helped merely to look at them and see them more realistically.

It is likely that all of these things occur during the course of an analysis. We might view the matter somewhat comprehensively if we returned to the model of the partly sick, partly regressive ego. We have assumed that the relatively normal, healthier part of the ego could in a sense detach itself and observe the various stages through which the more mobile regressing ego successively passes. We assume that this alter ego is, like the saving remnant of the house of Israel, the steadfast portion or core of the personality which has been overwhelmed and defeated by what *another part* of the personality, another part of the ego, has felt it necessary to do. In the expression "necessary to do" I mean to include all of those emergency and compensatory maneuvers which seem to be necessary to preserve its integrity and also those peculiar *ad hoc* variations and gyrations which were connected with the psychoanalytic treatment process as such. This healthy part of the ego is the ally of the therapist and vice versa. It experiences vicariously and somewhat detachedly what the "unhealthy" part of the ego experiences directly.

Finally, we assume that the healthy part of the ego gradually gains strength at the expense of the afflicted ego. One can say that they tend thus to become united again or that the healthy part of the ego prevails and absorbs the other. Or one could imagine that the regressive ego tends to shrivel up and disappear.

THE THERAPIST'S INTERVENTION

With some such model in mind of the waxing and waning of the regression, we can approach the problem of what constitutes the actual and functional participation of the psychoanalyst. Where does he come in? Precisely what is *his* function in bringing about the "improvement" of the patient, the regression and the return from it? How does he establish a working partnership with the intact ego? To be sure, he sets up the remarkable situation in which the regression experience can occur, and we have seen that he has a very considerable involuntary participation as the silent center and subject of the patient's fantasies. But is this *all* he does? Has he no voluntary duties?

In theory, it *might* be possible to defend the thesis that, other factors being equal, the passive contributions of the therapist are sufficient to fulfill the contract. The patient contributes *his* function by following the basic rule, paying his money, supplying "material"; then, if we assume that the regression is the status *sine qua non* for a successful self-exploration, beyond getting the patient started in the right direction and giving him some assistance in acquiring the habit, so to speak, of free association, what reason is there for the analyst to make any verbal contributions?

It is helpful to discuss the possibility of a psychoanalytic therapy proceeding from beginning to end without the analyst ever having said a word. Of course, he would contribute to it by his consistency of appearance, attention, interest, and audience. But would not the patient, by virtue of the experience itself, gradually overcome his resistances enough to learn what the deeper meaning of his behavior was and decide how much of it he could relinquish, how much he could alter, and how much better off he would be to do so?

In *practice*, of course, it never happens. Even if it were theoretically possible, it would require an unjustifiably long time. The therapist, the second party of the contract, should, in the interests of economy of money, time, and suffering, shorten the process if it is possible and we believe it is. How?

We believe the process can be shortened in quite a number of ways. First of all, the realistic fact that time is money and the treatment costs both is in itself a facilitation. This is why some analysts prefer to hand the monthly or weekly statement of their charges to the patient in person. They consider it helpful to say, by this act, "This is reality. This is what it costs you." There is an implication here that the patient tends to linger in his regression, and about this we have been explicit in the chapter on resistance. We know that patients who pay less than an appropriate amount tend to make the analysis more expensive for themselves by various kinds of delay.

But the psychoanalyst expedites the process in other ways. He takes a hand in circumstances where the balance of forces in the conflict tend to bring about an impasse or an obsessional prolongation. He points to the existence or possible existence of connections and implications and meanings which tend to elude the patient. He reminds the patient of forgotten statements or he confronts him with a discrepancy or self-contradiction, a misrepresentation, an obvious but unrecognized omission.

In this way the patient is assisted more rapidly to objectify, visualize, and understand the meaning of the place of various bits of his behavior, emotion, memory, fantasy, and experience.

A few words from the therapist assist the patient to integrate new material about himself with the main body of his conscious self-knowledge. They enable him to see clearly what he could not see before and to feel things which he could not feel before by confirming or verbalizing his discoveries.

Interpretation is a rather presumptuous term, loosely applied by (some) analysts to every voluntary verbal participation made by the analyst in the psychoanalytic treatment process. I dislike the word because it gives young analysts the wrong idea about their main function. They need to be reminded that they are not oracles, not wizards, not linguists, not detectives, not great wise men who, like Joseph and Daniel, "interpret" dreams—but quiet observers, listeners, and occasionally commentators. Their participation in a two-party process is predominantly passive (and partly involuntary); their *occasional* active participation is better called intervention. It may or may not "interpret" something. It may or may not be an interruption. But whenever the analyst speaks he contributes to a process, a process which we described elaborately in an earlier chapter. (Of course, his silence contributes also and, of course, he *does* interpret dreams.)

In a contribution by Ekstein,[26] stress is similarly put not on a definition of interpretation but on the interpretive process, the patient's communication and the analyst's interventions. Ekstein relates our theory of technique to recent advances in ego psychology, developing a model of interpretation derived from Rapaport's model of thinking.[125] The baby's emergency cry is the precursor of communication, taking place at a stage when there are no true object relationships, and this quasi-communication is responded to by the mother's "interpretation," which meets the need of the infant and eases the tension state. This primitive communication and interpretation will later be replaced with symbolic communication, but the need for direct action and for direct gratification will continue to exist. The psychoanalytic patient, for example, may accept a specific interpretation but later express through a dream his feeling that the interpretation was a rebuke, or, perhaps, an oral gratification. The regression facilitates the patient's experiencing words not only on the level on which they are meant by the analyst but also on a different, more archaic level.

The extraordinary dependence of psychoanalytic therapy upon verbalization has given rise to renewed study of the functions of speech and of communication in general. Why is a memory made more vivid by recounting it? Why are emotions sometimes only recognized when they are described? Why is naming or characterizing something so effective in conceptualizing it? Why are connections between buried memories, symbols, events, and so on best "seen" when they are formulated in words? *

The cry, the gesture, the play of infancy and childhood have communication functions, relating no doubt chiefly to primary process needs. They are gradually (perhaps never completely) surrendered in favor of various symbols. In the course of the regression in psychoanalytic treatment, there are constant evidences of shifts from one to another level of communication in the psychoanalytic "dialogue."

It is for this reason that the analyst at times cannot use the classical form of interpretation but must use more primitive forms of intervention. An example of such primitive intervention is the method described by Madame Sechehaye [142] in which gratification and interpretation are joined. Even in classical analysis, Ekstein states, we speak frequently about the "giving" of interpretations, and it is suggested here and there that a patient "cannot swallow" or "does not want to stomach" an interpretation which we offer.

These different interventions are actually but precursors of interpretation proper. The author and Ekstein feel strongly identified with Bibring's [13] view concerning the hierarchy of therapeutic principles leading up to clarification and interpretation. Therapeutic interventions are justified and can be thought of as interpretive steps if they lead to interpretations of unconscious material, unconscious defensive operations, warded-off instinctual tendencies, hidden mean-

---

* Loewenstein,[98] Nunberg,[116] Cassirer,[16] Hartmann,[76] Sapir,[140] Kris,[87] Beres,[9] Ruesch [139] and others have made important contributions to this topic which students and interested readers should consult.

ings of behavior patterns and their unconscious interconnections. Technical interventions which prepare for such interpretations should be considered a part of interpretive action. If they do not prepare but constitute the final act itself, they cannot be considered interpretive in the analytic sense of the word.

From the beginning of an analysis, matters arise which require active participation from the analyst. The patient may not speak loudly enough to be understood. He may incompletely or obscurely describe a historical matter of some anamnestic importance about which fuller information is desirable. Or he may make obscure statements which the analyst does not understand at all and should not pretend that he does. Or he may be so overburdened by his fears, embarrassment, self-reproach, and so on that he bogs down completely and has to be helped out.

In the early stages of analysis, too, it is often important to ask questions occasionally about matters of fact touched upon in the material, to inquire as to the patient's feelings about such and such a matter, or to ask at appropriate points for an explanation of the purpose or meaning by a simple interrogation. The latter inquiry is apt to be overdone by young analysts who are impressed with the stimulating effect of asking the impossible—*i.e.*, "Why?" It can easily become a cheap and irritating "trick." But if it is not overworked, and if the analyst will remember that no one can ever honestly answer this question, that it serves rather to evoke chains of rationalizations and false reasoning which lead only indirectly to the truth, it has a valuable place. Another standard question is, "What occurs to you about that?"

There is often considerable value in indications on the part of the analyst that the communication offered by the analysand is being followed, and, without pressing the word too far, followed sympathetically. The interjection of such exclamations as "Really" (in the sense of mild astonishment), "Naturally!" (in the sense of a certain reaction being a very understandable one), a mild groan to indicate sympathetic deploring of a tragic situation, a chuckle at an appropriate time in connection with an amusing episode, and so on are often very useful especially early in the analytic treatment. They are useful because they convey to the patient the feeling that the analyst is there, is listening, is following, is participating in the sense of the communication, is trying to understand.

This is quite aside from the necessity for the analyst to cough or sneeze, to move in his chair, and, in short, to act like the living human being which he really is in spite of the fantasies entertained by the patient. Perceptible fragments of his behavior are bound to be seized upon by the patient and utilized either as evidences that the therapist is interested or that he is not.

As the analysis goes along and the patient begins to expect some material contribution, there begins what is actually a mutual testing. The analyst is testing the analysand's capacity for frustration, while the analysand is often testing the analyst's forbearance. The process passes out of the first stage, in which the frustration is minimal, into a second stage in which it gradually mounts. The analyst should remember that this mounting frustration must not—in the average patient—be permitted to go unchecked to the point of explosion. He should recognize that after the sense of frustration has begun to develop, the silence of the analyst is felt by the patient as unkind, essentially hostile. This quality of hostility must not develop too rapidly, and the frustration tension must be maintained at an optimal level—*i.e.*, a bearable and only *gradually* increasing level. Otherwise, it will be just as Freud hinted when he remarked, dryly, that one cannot analyze a patient who is no longer there.

Of course, on the other hand, were the contributions of the analyst as sufficient as the patient wants, there would be no frustration but a direct and ultimately disappointing gratification; there would be no progressive recall, the repressive barrier would not be penetrated, and unconscious material for the most part would not be reached.

What is probably meant by those who use the expression "handling the transference," which I consider to be a most reprehensible and improper phrase, is this tactical maneuver of maintaining the frustration at an optimum level. From it has arisen such jargon as "dosing the interpretations" and "giving the patient a little libido." These are clumsy and inelegant expressions, but the idea back of them is clear and it is sound. The patient continues to expect response from the analyst, despite the fact that numerous interventions have occurred during the earlier parts of analysis, and if this frustration tends to become too great (for him) to endure, this can be diminished by interventions on the part of the analyst. These do not necessarily "interpret" anything. They may be only in the nature of confirmations of something the patient has said, which is appreciated by the patient as a reassurance and hence a helpful participation. All he may have been needing, actually, is some indication that the analyst accepts him in a measure, accepts what he is saying, likes him a little bit in spite of his importunities and his infirmities.

TIMING

Interpretations and other interventions are most effective at that point when the frustration tension is mounting to what the analyst feels to be a too-painful degree, and must then be administered according to the principle of parsimony—*i.e.*, the least necessary quantity of help should be given the patient. To do otherwise tends to alter the desired optimum level of frustration tension in the opposite direction. It is, so to speak, too reassuring to the patient. It diminishes the internal incentive for him to plow forward. The analyst's participation, consequently, should be as simple, specific, accurate, and laconic as possible.

The question constantly arises in practice as to how the analyst can be sure when the optimum level of frustration tension is being threatened so as to use the best timing of his interventions. Practically, after some years of experience this comes intuitively. I know this is a discouraging comment for students, so I shall try to prepare some theoretical guidance. Freud said, "Psychoanalysis . . . prescribes that two conditions are to be fulfilled before it is done. First, by preparatory work, the repressed material must have come very near to the patient's thoughts; and secondly, he must be sufficiently firmly attached by an affective relationship to the physician [transference] to make it impossible for him to take fresh flight again" (*i.e.*, to repress again).[53, 58]

In line with the theory I have outlined, one looks for evidences of change in the nature of the patient's material in the direction of increasing negative features. It is difficult to put this in a simple way without oversimplifying it, but it is as if a patient, despairing of winning the approval of the analyst, is impelled almost to test or tempt his tolerance; he is actuated, too, by resentment which he is struggling to repress. He begins to let loose of, almost to fling from him, material which he has hitherto carefully guarded and concealed. But he has no sooner discharged this aggression than he recognizes certain implications in having done so. As his momentary penitence arises, it can be exploited by the obstetrical functioning of the analyst who assists him in delivering the larger body of the material. Furthermore, by inference the analyst commends the patient for what he expected to be punished for. It is helpful to some young analysts to have it put thus: One "tells" a patient what the patient *almost* sees for himself and one tells him in such a way that the patient—not the analyst—takes the "credit" for the discovery.

My position is in precise agreement with that of Gill[65] in his insistence that characteristic for psychoanalysis is the reduction of the regression or transference neurosis by techniques of interpretation alone. This means that we do *not* favor attempts to "handle" the transference by artificially assuming various roles or making artificial manipulations in the conditions of treatment, and so on. It is true, as Gill points out, that unceasing processes of affective, nonverbal communication go on between the analyst and the patient, but the ideal is to go on with the analyzing of the patient's material until the nonverbal interchanges have been converted into explicit verbalizations and have been understood by interpretation.

Perhaps in this connection we should say a word about what it is now customary to call parameters, after Eissler.[22] These are alternate or modified procedures, deviating somewhat from the basic model of psychoanalytic technique and from the rule that interpretation is our chief tool in the resolution of the regression. An example of a parameter would be a definite command or advice. Such additional or alternate devices are warranted if they fulfill certain conditions: They must be introduced only when the basic model technique really does not suffice; they must never exceed the least necessary intervention; they are used only when they finally lead to their self-elimination; and the effect of the parameter on the transference relationship must never be such that it cannot be abolished by interpretation.*

The distinction between psychoanalysis and psychoanalytically-oriented psychotherapy, with particular reference to this matter of interpretations, is clearly put by Merton Gill:

> [A psychotherapist] does not foster a regressive transference neurosis, since he does not employ the devices which would lead to this, but on the contrary actively discourages the development of such a transference by conducting the interview more like a social interchange of equals, by avoiding free association, by emphasizing reality rather than fantasy, by creating an atmosphere of temporariness and similar measures. He observes various elements of transference developing anyhow—which he correctly calls transferences rather than a transference neurosis—and he may or may not interpret these. If they become obtrusive and seem to be hindering the treatment, or if he sees an opportunity to make a valuable point by interpreting a piece of transference he will do so. But if the transference is reasonably positive and desirable and behavioral changes are occurring or if evidences of hostile transference seem too hot to handle, he will remain silent about it and permit the transference to persist unresolved.[65]

KINDS OF INTERPRETATION

For forty years there has been a running three-sided debate between proponents of *resistance* interpretation, proponents of *transference* interpretation and proponents of *content* interpretation. From one point of view this can be dismissed in a sentence: All three are necessary at different times.†

For what is it that we—we of the second part—want of the patient? We want him to see himself. We want him to see that as a result of his being a human being who came into contact (long ago) with other human beings who were not perfect, and as a result of misunderstanding certain things and being misunderstood by certain people, he experienced pain and fright from which he tried to protect himself by devices which he still continues to use not from present necessity

* For a discussion of the use of questioning as a parameter, see Olinick.[119]

† See the discussion of this in connection with resistance in general, pages 119-120.

but from a kind of habit. We want him to see that he persists in the same unprofitable formulae of adaptation. We want him to see that he expects the wrong things from the right people and the right things from the wrong people. And, finally, we want him to see that he doesn't want to see it, that he wants to get well—in a way—but is afraid to; that he wants to change, but fights against it.

Which of these things to point out to a patient at a particular time depends on which of them is most accessible to the patient's consciousness and to the analyst's consciousness at that time. The therapist hovers, in his attention, over the verbal productions of the patient observing his extending area of awareness and the direction of the trend of inquiry at the moment. And if he keeps "in tune" with the patient's unconscious, he *knows* when to speak.

One thing which we certainly *never* do—and by "we" I mean all of the analytic authorities in the world except a few whose recommendations have been generally discredited—is to tell the patient what is in his unconscious long before he has any capacity for grasping the significance of such oracular diagnostic incisions. Rather, interpretation begins by a kind of preparatory process. The patient will have communicated so much that he will have lost sight of the obvious connections—if indeed he ever saw them—between events and feelings and attitudes which will be apparent to the analyst if for no other reason than that he gets something of a bird's-eye view of the whole. However, he knows too that there are internal reasons for the patient not seeing these connections, and so just pointing them out acts correctively. Usually the patient is intrigued by this, surprised, pleased, and curious. Usually it is not necessary to impute some hopeful prospects to these early discoveries; the patient does so spontaneously (although Fenichel feels that we should take advantage of opportunities to "bribe" him to go further).[32]

Having identified some connections, or certain common elements, in a considerable number of events in the patient's life or items in the material presented, the next step is to further the preparation for real interpretation. Sooner or later, the therapist is in a position to say something like this: "This thing, then—(this trick, this experience, this defense, this defeat)—happens to you repeatedly; it seems to happen especially to you. You seem to have something to do with its happening. Perhaps it doesn't just *happen,* possibly you actually do it. You have done it before. Perhaps you have some hidden purpose behind it, a purpose which was once valid but which is no longer valid. This can be seen as what Fate does to you; but let us look at what you do with your Fate!"

Such an "interpretation" is always a "blow" (to one part of the ego, not to the observing part) even when it is enlightening and freeing. It seems to the patient like a stone, when he has asked—or hoped —for bread. It contains hope, but it often seems critical, and it is not comforting. It is as if the query, "If thy child asks for bread, wilt thou give him a stone?" were answered thus: "If my child asks for the moon, I'll give him a telescope."

The patient's indigenous and intrinsic negativism will seize upon any and all "justification" to delay and defeat the process of treatment and it is typical that, in such a moment of attempted clarification as we have described, the patient will block. He doesn't get it—or, it sounds pretty, but what does it mean? He forgets, theorizes, digresses, dawdles. He isn't quite able to accept (see) what he is now almost face to face with.

Instead of rubbing his nose in it, so to speak (which he will find his own ways to avoid), one proceeds then to the *interpretation of* the resistance. One says in substance "You do not want to see this for certain reasons." First, one points out that such resistance exists; then one points out how it manifests itself; then one points out its obvious purpose (and, of course, if one doesn't know what its obvious purpose is, then the patient's cooperation has to be enlisted in that search). In general, of course, the purpose is to avoid seeing the unpleasant truth. But it may be further obscured by various transference patterns and purposes; the patient may be bribing, defying, or seducing the analyst.

It is true that, having interpreted the resistance, we frequently behold the material behind it appearing spontaneously. But I feel in regard to this a good deal as a modern obstetrician feels in regard to the use of low forceps in deliveries. One can, to be sure, merely wait for a softening of the perineum, as it were, and the removal of any mechanical obstructions, and then wait for contractions of the uterus to force out the fetus. But one can save a great deal of time and suffering by assisting in the delivery by gentle traction. This is precisely what one can do in analysis, I believe. But one must remember to do it with gentleness. There is pain involved for the patient in these changes just as there is in an obstetrical delivery. The shattering of the narcissistic armor, as it has been called, can be exquisitely painful. The patient's capacity for pain tolerance is probably what is reflected in his frustration tolerance, or lack of it.

And this develops the necessity for what has been called "working through." For it is an empirical fact that the same general type of material and the same general type of resistance reappears in the analysis time after time, to the considerable dismay of the young analyst who feels that, having accepted everything, the patient has relinquished his insight for the same old illusions.

No analysis is carried on in a vacuum; patients being analyzed are still living out their lives. They encounter daily experiences which may or may not be of their own doing but some of which disturb their equilibrium again and again. Even without this, their resistance will often cover with the same obliviousness the repetition of the same old pattern, so that "all that was won by painstaking labor seems to be forgotten. . . . We have to begin [over and over] again from the beginning." [32] Sometimes reminding the patient of the previously identified resistance will effect a change; usually it is not sufficient. He will often resume his former state of resentment or depression or provocativeness or whatever.* One feels, as Fenichel says, as if everything had been in vain and had to be done over, and then over and over again. Some interpretations or explanations have to be repeated many times. Resistance never evaporates or flies away; it has to be consistently and persistently opposed throughout every analysis. It often appears as if the patient had never heard the analyst's previous interpretation. This necessity for "working through," for the analyst to repeat interpretations until they are taken hold of, is a reflection of the extension of the neurosis into many different aspects of or events of the patient's life. His defensive structure isolates these events from one another, so that he is not aware of the common tendency running through them. In the language of some

---

* A cartoon in *The New Yorker* some years ago by Kindl showed a middle-aged man on the couch saying to his doctor, "Don't you think, Doctor, in view of my marked improvement, I might resume my affection for my mother?"

learning theorists, the "transfer" or "spread of effect" of the insight from one situation to other situations is limited or blocked. In Freud's words,[57] "One must allow the patient time to get to know this resistance. . . ." Hence the necessity for repeating the interpretations as the patient repeats his neurotic behavior in different contexts.

In some patients more emphasis needs to be given to resistance interpretations, and in others more help is necessary in the reformulation, delivery, and integration of the material. Some analysts concentrate much of the analytic work on the destructive (*i.e.*, aggressive) elements in the patient's material. "Point out of the aggression," they advise, "and the healthy erotic expression and growth will follow naturally." True, perhaps, but complicated by the fact that all acts contain evidences of both positive ("erotic") and negative ("aggressive") elements, fused and/or defused in varying degrees. The "bound" and concealed aggression must sometimes be dissected and sometimes left alone.

I may seem to have neglected or at least postponed discussion of content interpretation. Have we forgotten, someone may ask, that the party of the second part has a responsibility for assisting the patient to gain insight? And by such a question it is implied that the analyst must at some point become a Joseph or a Daniel and tell the patient what certain things mean.

In the psychoanalytic literature of the past few decades there have been two extreme positions in regard to how this should be taught. On the one hand, Wilhelm Reich [129] believed that a systematic, highly structured program of interpretation could be outlined with procedures spelled out in a one-two-three order, just as one might plan an appendectomy. At the other extreme was Theodor Reik,[132, 133] who felt that psychoanalysts were handicapped by theorizing, reflecting and planning. He liked to put emphasis on the purely intuitive factors, and his books *Surprise and the Psychoanalyst* and *Listening with the Third Ear* contain excellent material to illustrate his thesis. They are good not only in content but in spirit. Just as one has to shut one's eyes to some of the strange digressions in Reich's book, so one must shut one's eyes to Reik's polemics against knowledge and thinking. Both authors are helpful in elaborating the details of technical practice.

Although I do not visualize or formulate the process quite as

Reich did, my didactic and written expositions are more in line with his thinking, whereas my practice, I suspect, is more in line with that of Reik, so eloquently described long before Reik by Ferenczi:

> One gradually becomes aware how immensely complicated the mental work demanded from the analyst is. He has to let the patient's free associations play upon him; simultaneously he lets his own fantasy get to work with the association material; from time to time he compares the new connexions that arise with earlier results of the analysis; and not for one moment must he relax the vigilance and criticism made necessary by his own subjective trends.
>
> One might say that his mind swings continuously between empathy, self-observation, and making judgements. The latter emerge spontaneously from time to time as mental signals, which at first, of course, have to be assessed only as such; only after the accumulation of further evidence is one entitled to make an interpretation.[33]

My own difficulty as a student was that with all the formulations and explanations and illustrations I never felt quite certain where my analysands were going or where they—and I—had been. This will sound strangely naïve to analysts who have acquired competence and self-confidence, who have learned how to fit pieces of new information in at the proper places in their own conceptualizations or reject them as unimportant. But the young candidate has the tender memory of his own recent tumultuous couch experiences, plus vast amounts of reading, plus various kinds of partially assimilated instruction. No wonder he is confused when his patient comes in day after day, piling Pelion on Ossa until all notion of the structure of the process is lost. To mix metaphors, one can well say that he cannot see the woods for the trees. In supervisory work in my practice from time to time I have the candidates review all the material from the beginning in order to get a grasp of the ebb and flow of trends, of the regression, the repetition, the general form of resistance, but more particularly to get a concept of the analytic process as a whole.

One reason for the difficulty encountered by the student is our lack of an adequate model or schema of psychoanalytic theory to which the student can attach his new ideas and experiences. Several such models have been proposed.

A GRAPHIC MODEL OF THE TREATMENT PROCESS

About twenty years ago, quite unfamiliar with Reich's ordering, I devised a conceptualization of the psychoanalytic treatment process which I found useful for myself and useful in teaching. Subsequent expressions of appreciation from former candidates encouraged me, so I shall record it here as best I can, although it is much easier to present it orally with the use of a blackboard and various colored chalks, so that a picture can be built up gradually and modified.*

I ask the students to try to think abstractly of the life-course of a child who is ultimately to become a psychoanalytic patient. I ask them to think of his birth (*B*) as a dot, his life course as a line. From the "dot" the line extends forward into the future. The influence of parents, siblings, circumstances, and events will combine with the constitutional and instinctual factors to determine the precise direction which the subsequent life course takes.

Were this to be a "normal" healthy, ideal life, perhaps the diagram of its subsequent course could be shown as it appears in Figure 10.

FIGURE 10

Or it might turn out that as his life developed his goals changed, but for the better. Assuming that G^2 represents an improvement of some kind, over and above an acceptable "normal" life objective (or series of objectives) represented by G^1, Figure 11 would indicate another schematic course of development.

* Incidentally, I would like to emphasize the value for teaching purposes, of requiring students to draw their own diagrams to schematize these concepts. There are two ways of doing this. One is to suggest that the students try to visualize the process before they have seen my diagrams. The other is to ask them, after they have seen some diagrams such as those which we are about to submit, to discuss, criticize, and improve them. A discussion of these differences can be helpful or confusing, depending upon the way in which the instructor handles it. Some individuals simply cannot construct a diagram or understand one constructed for them. Other individuals are greatly helped by seeing a diagram. Still others are most helped by constructing their own.

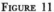

FIGURE 11

But the life that we are about to diagram is, by definition, that of an individual who was deflected from his goal—*i.e.*, an acceptable and approved goal—in a disappointing and unsatisfactory direction to a "false" goal (G^3).

We might diagram it as in Figure 12.

FIGURE 12

Our theory holds that such deflections toward an improper goal, or "false goal," come about through the early acquisition of wrong techniques of dealing with the opportunities and dangers of life. It holds, too, that these wrong techniques of living developed in response to handicaps, injuries, painful experiences, gross misunderstandings, and other "traumata" of the early formative period. On our diagram we can indicate these as X^1, X^2, X^3, and X^n (Figure 13).

FIGURE 13

Were this process of deflection to continue we would have a neurotic child, a psychotic child, or a criminal child. What happens, as we all know, is a split in the personality such that a partial return is made to the original "good" goal-seeking line or route. A part of the individual grows up and acts with social considerateness, if somewhat below the efficiency of his normal colleagues along the old G^1 line.

But another trend in his personality continues in the "bad" goal direction. A conflict between these two opposing tendencies within the same personality makes for tension and for the symptoms which ultimately impel the patient to seek treatment.

Now we shall introduce the *treatment* factor into our diagram. The conflict becomes unendurable. The struggling, baffled "victim" of fate, circumstance, and error reaches a point (the star in Figure 14) where he is impelled to seek help. Fortunately for our schema, he is brought into contact with a psychoanalyst and begins psychoanalytic treatment. This can be shown in the diagram by setting up a new sphere or area of activity quite distinct from the patient's past life or his contemporary life. The treatment is to bring a turning point into his life, but the turning point will not be visible immediately.

With the establishment of a relationship with a therapist, our subject as a "patient" begins to lead not a double life but a triple life. On the one hand, he continues relationships with his family, his friends, employers, employees, and all the other elements of his work-a-day world. This, as we know, is an incomplete, partial, "superficial" existence. Beneath it is a conflictual trend of existence, of which he is only vaguely conscious but which expresses itself in his life. But for one hour a day, in the mysterious memory-evoking chambers of the psychoanalyst, this unconscious, subterranean, perverse portion of his personality is given free range (for verbal expression). What he ultimately discovers, of course, is that this buried portion of his personality is a continuance of his infancy and represents an unjustifiably prolonged extension of the infantile period (or, more properly, of reactions to it). The old wounds and sorrows he supposed he had forgotten come back to him in the psychoanalytic situation, and as they come back to him there they disappear, so to speak, from within

him. For a time then the subversive "wrong" goal tendencies may
become worse. But at a certain point in the analysis they begin to
diminish and disappear.

In Figure 14 we have tried to show the next stage in the schema.
Psychoanalysis has begun (A) and the psychoanalytic situation in the
patient's life develops. Simultaneously a reality situation exists (R)
and beneath it is the pathological conflict extending forward from
the infancy situation, injuring and crippling the normative trend.

FIGURE 14

Day after day as the analytic treatment proceeds the analytic
situation enlarges, memories of days long gone by are recalled and
related to contemporary events, feelings, and emotional reactions
within the treatment situation. A parallel or reciprocal correspondence—not an exact one, to be sure, but a significant one—can be in-
ferred as existing between the "steps" of progress in the analysis, the
steps of demoralization or inhibition or fixation or whatever most
characterized the unhappy childhood, and the steps of improvement
in the contemporary adjustment. (For this and the subsequent discussion, see Figure 15.)

When the depth of the regression has been reached, the patient
tends to improve in his adjustments to life and more wholeheartedly

and concertedly to strive toward the "good" goal of comfortable and productive achievement.* Theoretically each step in the analysis brings the patient one step closer to reality and one step closer to the point when the analysis will no longer be necessary, as reflected in the patient's real life by steps toward improvement in relationships with others. Both the process of recovery and the process of psychoanalysis tend toward the same end point, although actually they will not terminate simultaneously. The area of the patient's life and interests represented by the analytic situation will grow smaller and smaller, ultimately to disappear, while the contemporary reality situation will enlarge and extend, in a greater freedom for object attachment and creativity.

In addition to this correspondence of steppage in the progressive changes (analytic situation and reality situation), there is an approximate parallelism between the steppage in the treatment process and the steppage representing the original development of the illness—*i.e.,* the sequence of deviant or *downward* steps in the original childhood or infantile situation. These are roughly images or replicas of one another, the one moving toward illness, the other toward recovery. I always point out *how easy it would be to assume* that the *first* recollections of an analysis are of the *earliest* (traumatic) experiences, followed by the recollection of the *second* traumatic experience (X^2) and then the third, and so on, to X^n. Of course, we all know that this is *not* the way it goes at all. Indeed, it is apt to be just the reverse of this, speaking very generally. It is the many, *more recent* disappointments, pains, and heartbreaks that are first recalled—and then the less recent and on back to the more remote. Thus as the

---

* This refers to the patient's *life* goal, not the treatment goal, although the latter is here assumed to be merely the achievement of the former. The goals of psychotherapy, including analysis, may not always be so simply stated, and actually vary considerably as Gill has recently reminded us eloquently.[65] The theoretical goals of psychoanalysis may be variously formulated; Freud [56] did so repeatedly, most clearly perhaps thus: "It may be laid down that the aim of the treatment is to remove the patient's resistances and to pass his repressions in review and thus to bring about the most far-reaching unification and strengthening of his ego, to enable him to save the mental energy which he is expending upon internal conflicts, to make the best of him that his inherited capacities will allow and so to make him as efficient and as capable of enjoyment as is possible. The removal of the symptoms of his illness is not specifically arrived at, but is achieved, as it were, as a by-product if the analysis is properly carried through."

C = *Childhood Situation*
A = *Analytic Situation*
R = *Reality Situation*
D = *Dream Connections*
RB = *Repression Barrier*

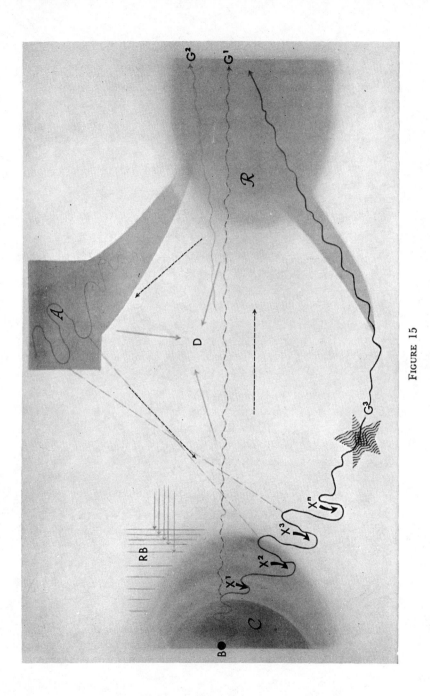

FIGURE 15

analysis goes further ahead, the recollection goes further back, but in a quite unpredictable order of recall.

These recollections of earlier events which correspond with contemporary experiences are not the patient's primary search. They merely "occur" to him in connection with experiences in the *two* contemporary situations—the analytic and the reality. They are like reference material in a library, which back up and explain the reflections of contemporary reality problems as the latter appear in the analytic situation. As we shall see, there is more orderliness and meaningfulness to this recollection of the genetic experiences than this implies.

But at first, as we all know, the patient tends to make the analytic situation reciprocal to his reality situation. The outside world has been unkind, and he expects from the analyst the opposite of unkindness. The outside world frightens him; from the analyst he wants reassurance. But gradually, of course, failing to find cooperation from the analyst in developing this reciprocality, the patient tends to deal with the analyst in the same way that he has disadvantageously dealt with people all of his life (from B to G^1).

But *now* there is a corrective element. We have indicated the tendency toward correction on the chart by steppage improvement away from the false to the true goal (G^3 toward G^1) but we haven't said what determined it. *What is the corrective factor?*

It will be recalled that we discussed in an earlier chapter the various theories put forward to explain the improvement resulting from psychoanalytic treatment. Every one agrees that something "happens," that changes in personality structure and function do occur, but we do not know why they do. We concede the importance of what we call *insight* in the process of recovery, but whether it be a product or a provocation of the change we cannot be sure. But just what *is* insight?

I define insight as the recognition by the patient (1) That this or that aspect of his feelings and attitudes, this or that technique of behavior, this or that role in which he casts other people, is *of a pattern;* (2) That this pattern, like the footprint of a bear which has lost certain toes in a trap, originated long ago and stamps itself on every step of his life journey; it is present in his contemporary reality situation relationships, and it is present in his analytic relationships; (3) That this pattern originated for a reason which was valid at the time, and persisted despite changes in some of the circumstances which originally determined it; (4) That this pattern contains elements which are offensive and injurious to others as well as expensive and troublesome to the patient.

Insight is not just seeing that something in the analytic situation is similar to something in childhood, or seeing that something in childhood is reflected in the activities of his contemporary situation, or seeing that something in his contemporary situation is a reflection of something in the analytic situation. In the proper sense of the word and in the useful sense for psychoanalytic technique, *insight is the simultaneous identification of the characteristic behavior pattern in all three of these situations, together with an understanding of why they were and are used as they were and are.*[*]

"The interest of analysis does not, as it is sometimes erroneously thought, focus on the past alone, but on the inter-relationship between past and present: the influence of the past upon the present and, paradoxical though it may sound, of the present upon the past. The paramount role which the analysis of transference plays in psychoanalytic technique is based on this particular inter-connection we find between the past and the present in human life." (Lowenstein [97])

I represent this on the diagram (Figure 15) by connecting the three areas—childhood, contemporary environmental reality, and psychoanalytic—to form a triangle, the triangle of insight. A fortuitous feature of this diagrammatic scheme is the fact that this triangle encloses an area which, for heuristic purposes, serves as a place to indicate the dream (D) as a packaged product of the timeless unconscious. Dreams become studyable and understandable in the analytic

---

[*] Richfield [134], [135] has remarked that the voice of the intelligence is not only soft, but speaks with two voices; that is, there are two kinds of insight, based on the fact that there are two kinds of knowledge, two different ways in which we can know things, illustrated by the ways in which we know alcohol and the way we know strychnine (Bertrand Russell). "What Reid and Finesinger [130] have called 'dynamic insight,' the 'intellectual *summum bonum* of analysis,' actually may be achieved by the effective timing of both fundamental kinds of insight in an appropriate order governed by the peculiarities of each case."

situation when the analyst receives them as gifts and code messages and disguised attacks and many other things. They are like the Rosetta stone, containing parallel columns, as it were, in terms derived from the analytic situation, the reality situation, and the childhood situation. Hence it is that the dream has been called the *via regia* to the understanding of the unconscious, and the passkey to the identification of the characteristic pattern-complex of the personality.

"Dreams, then, not only fulfill naked wishes of sexual licence, of unlimited dominance and of unrestricted destructiveness; where they work, they also lift the dreamer's isolation, appease his conscience, and preserve his identity, each in specific and instructive ways." [28] "As Erikson outlines it, the dream reflects the life cycle of the dreamer: his present phase and the related infantile phase, his psychosexual and psycho-aggressive fixations and arrests. It reflects the social process, the collective and ego identity, and defensive and integrative mechanisms of the ego organization." [23]

The importance of dream interpretation to psychoanalytic therapy was recognized by Freud from the very beginning, and it has not diminished with the passing of time and the accretion of experience. The theory of dream formation, recollection and interpretation is really the basic theory of technique, of which all these pages are but an elaboration. The seventh chapter of *The Interpretation of Dreams* is the Magna Carta of psychoanalysis.

This is the reason I have not discussed more specifically the theory of dream interpretation.* In practice I have always leaned heavily upon it and regard its evasion or neglect by young analysts as an indication of some incompleteness in their training. Dreams serve the psychoanalyst as core-drilling samples serve the geologist—except that our samples are spontaneous! They are coded communications from the unconscious which in that form can elude the repression barrier. When they are translatable, they—with the aid of association

---

* Thomas N. French [40-A] has undertaken an intensive examination of psychological processes in the light of psychoanalytic discoveries and conditioned reflex theory. The second of the five volumes in this study is devoted entirely to the theory of the dream and its interpretation in psychoanalytic treatment with special reference to recurring patterns and sequences in different dreams of the same person. He relates these patterns to behavior patterns of the patient.

—illuminate and clarify whole areas of obscurity in the life history, the clinical picture and the transference situation.

THE ORDERLY SEQUENCE OF MATERIAL

One explanation or description of the way in which the gaining of insight furthers the progress toward recovery is that the realm and freedom of the ego are extended when insight pushes back the barrier of repression and enlarges the area of self-knowledge. This can be shown schematically in our model by a vertical line anterior to the bulk of the childhood zone. As the process develops, this repression barrier (RB) will be repeatedly approached and increasingly penetrated for the recovery of forgotten material. In effect, the line is moved progressively further and further "back"—*i.e.*, to the left.

Along with this progressive regression in the recall of the forgotten and repressed, the correlation process continues, so that the patient is, so to speak, at one moment recalling something from the past, the next moment reporting an attitude toward the doctor and, the next moment, a fantasy (or dream) which identifies the similarity of all three areas.

It is my belief, on the basis of experience, that there is a general *order* in the apparently unstructured presentation of analytic material from these several areas. *In the beginning* of an analysis the patient will often describe some of his contemporary unhappiness and perhaps give a certain anamnestic résumé proceeding from the reality situation back to his childhood. "This happened to me today," he will continue, "just as it did so often when I was a child, for example when . . . etc." This is what I designate as a *clockwise* direction of the order of presenting material; it is typical of good psychiatric histories and of psychotherapy, but not of good psychoanalysis except in the very early stages.

In a "properly going" analysis, on the other hand, the patient will usually describe, for example, an aspect of the *reality* situation which he finds to be unpleasant, and from this go to certain aspects of the *analytic* situation which he may find either pleasant or unpleasant, but probably pleasant in contrast to the unpleasantness of the reality situation. Under the aegis of this pleasant aspect of the analytic situation his mind reverts to childhood, and he recalls something from that area—neither the earliest thing nor the most recent thing but something related. From this area he soon turns again to the present, to something in the contemporary reality situation, and a cycle will have been completed. (Formula: Reality→Analysis→Childhood→Reality→etc.)

Example: "My wife *never* has dinner ready when I get home from work. She always keeps me waiting. Of course, you do too sometimes. But that isn't so serious; I don't wait long. I don't know why I made that little jab at you. I used to tease my mother that way sometimes, ungrateful little cuss that I was. I would accuse her of things she *was* innocent of. My mother would go to great lengths to see that I got enough to eat. I remember the lunches she made for me when I came home from school. My wife wouldn't even—and yet I don't reproach her much. Maybe I'm afraid to. Yes, I think I'm afraid to criticize her. I seem to have more courage about criticizing you than I do my wife; I almost hunt things to find fault with you about."

Any analyst will recognize other things here than the point I wish it to illustrate, which is that the patient successively goes from the contemporary situation to the analytic situation, thence to related aspects of the childhood situation, thence to the reality situation and on around the circle in the same *counterclockwise* direction (as in Figure 15). This is typical, proper, and correct in analysis. We have support for this proposition from Freud's general advice that analysis should proceed from the so-called surface to the so-called depth.[54, 58]

But if successive material tends to move from the depths directly to the present moment, *i.e.,* in what on our diagram is a clockwise direction, something is wrong. Thus any analyst would recognize that a patient who talked in the following way was in some kind of serious resistance difficulty:

"You keep me waiting here. I wonder why that is. Don't you want to see me? My wife keeps me waiting, too, always does. I say nothing—afraid to I guess. My mother never kept me waiting; she'd have lunch ready for me when I got home from school—never any waiting, like here. Why *do* you keep me waiting?"

In this example, the flow of the material is in the wrong direction (Analytic→Reality→Childhood→Analytic). It should roll forward with time along the lines actually experienced and not along trackless, traceless orbits extending from childhood to the analytic situation.

Another common manifestation of resistance is reflected in the tendency for the flow of material to get "stuck" or "hung up," as it were—the "broken record" type of resistance, we call it. A patient will become preoccupied with childhood material, for example, and mull it over and over without insight or progress. The resistance in this case usually has to do with facing something in the contemporary reality situation, and this can be pointed out to the patient and the process moved forward a step. But a patient may also become preoccupied with the reality situation—"reality resistance," as it is sometimes called. In such a case the resistance is usually against recognition of something in the analytic situation, and the patient has to be moved on, so to speak, in that direction. Instead of "How does that operate in your contemporary life?" the analyst would now say, "Is that perhaps reflected in your relationship to your analyst?" But the patient may also become stalled at the point of preoccupation with his *analyst,* and an erotization of the analytic situation. Correction consists, then, in pushing the patient into the past as it were, directing his attention to the fact that "This which you feel toward me is a reflection of something that was once attached to some other person, long ago. But whom?" or "Can you recall ever having felt just this way before?" *

Another way in which the flow of material gets hung up is not on one-point stickiness or resistance or perverseness but on an obsessional seesawing back and forth between any two points. Some patients will incessantly jump from a reality problem to the analytic situation, back to the reality situation, back to the analytic situation, and so forth; never a word is heard about the infantile period. Other patients will speak exhaustively regarding the infantile period and

---

* I believe it was Ferenczi who once said that if the patient talks about the present, he should be directed to the past, and if he talks about the past, he should be directed to the present. This schema is actually only an amplification of the principle implied in this comment of Ferenczi's.

from that to the analytic situation, for a while perhaps making numerous correlations, but never once (or at least not consistently) bringing in the factor of contemporary reality. Such a patient will speak at length about his resentment of a baby brother born two years later than himself and compare this with a new patient the analyst has just taken or with changes in his institute status, without mentioning his own children, perhaps even the recent birth to his wife of a new daughter. In this kind of resistance the young analyst is sometimes at a loss as to where the turning back occurs. If he follows this diagram he need not be (allowing, of course, for certain exceptions for which no rule can be devised).

To take a final look at our schematic diagram, one can say that the cyclic process of comparison, correlation, recollection, correction, etc., seems to move bodily as well as intrinsically. The depth of recall increases, the repression barrier recedes, the analytic situation begins to vanish by absorption into the reality situation, and the patient's progress approaches the ideal goal. Perhaps the Socratic ideal of knowledge, the knowing of things about oneself and one's world correctly, of seeing them objectively, past and present, might be designated the goal of the treatment. But this is only true if with such knowledge goes the appropriate emotional reaction and the sense of freedom for the investment of the creative and constructive powers derived from the life instinct.

In concluding this chapter on the intervention function of the analyst, I am well aware of how sketchy, one-sided, and incomplete it is. But it does contain devices and formulations which I and others have found useful. They have enabled me to convey to aspiring analytic candidates a belief that there is an orderliness even in the disorganized unconscious material with which he is to deal, and a certain orderliness, too, in our methods of dealing with it. This helps him to gain confidence in what he is doing as a therapist. Later he can fit into the scheme the many other views and facts and theories with which his reading and experience will supply him, or he can drop it from his memory. Glover, in his well-known questionnaire survey, discovered a wide variation in the use of "interpretation," its form, timing, quantity, depth, order, and content by practicing analysts. We probably all do it somewhat differently. But we all believe also that there are certain underlying principles which we try to follow, and it is important for the candidate to get a definite idea as to what these are. I have offered him a framework on which to hang them.

VII

THE TERMINATION
OF THE CONTRACT

The Separation of
the Two Parties

WE HAVE DESCRIBED PYSCHOANALYTIC TREATMENT AS A CONTRACTUAL arrangement in the name of treatment in the course of which one party is assisted by another to effect a personality reorganization. His "ego" undergoes a functional splitting or division of duties such that one part of it (*i.e.,* of "them," the ego functions) observes another part progressively abandon all façades of being healthy, mature, realistic, and sensible. This observed part (or set of functions) of the ego may be considered as already to some degree immature, inhibited, unrealistic, and inefficacious in its functioning—hence the patient's need for treatment. But now, in the course of the treatment, this part changes, with many fluctuations, further and further in a retrograde direction, most notably and conspicuously during the daily fifty-minute treatment periods, often taking *some* of the healthy ego functions with it!

During the rest of the day the regression is kept in abeyance or under cover through dominance of the *healthy* ego functions. And at all times this regression, of whatever degree, remains under the scrutiny of the intact portion of the ego, a scrutiny which is supported and assisted by the psychoanalyst.

Along with the scrutiny we may assume that there goes the soft, weak voice of intelligent self-counsel. Though long ignored and resisted, it is *persistent*. Ultimately it is listened to and heeded.

It is a curious thing that the familiar question, "How long does treatment by psychoanalysis last?" which is heard so often inside and outside of analysis, is, at the beginning of analysis, a practical question which is apt to be given a theoretical answer whereas toward the end of analysis it becomes a theoretical question to which a practical answer is usually made. It seems incredible that after fifty years of psychoanalysis there should be such a vast difference of opinion as to what even the average length of analysis is, *or should be!* The three months of analysis advocated by Otto Rank proved to be a farce for some and a tragedy for others. On the other hand, we all know patients who have been in analysis for ten years or more, which seems similarly tragic or farcical. And, of course, these differences reflect differences in the goal of treatment (or mistakes in the assessment of analyzability). In the early days psychoanalysis was very much under the influence of the point of view according to which a disappearance of symptoms indicates a recession of the illness. But today we no longer regard this as an adequate criterion. The patient who has fully recovered from an illness with the aid of psychoanalysis will not have become his old self again; rather he has become (we trust) an enlarged, an improved, indeed a *new* self. But it is hard to say in advance how long this will take.

THE TURNING POINT

In our description of the regression (the "transference neurosis") I discussed the general shape of the curve described by this changing level. When does the descent cease and the ascent or progression back toward "normal" begin? One may pore through the hundreds of articles on technique and on the psychoanalytic process and find few forthright discussions of this question.[24] In the long ago days of our discipline, there used to be a cardinal principle that once the painful, traumatic events of childhood were fully recalled, extracted like splinters from a child's finger, the chronically festering wounds healed up and the patient recovered promptly, to live happily ever afterwards, we hoped.

But as we became more sophisticated—or at least more comprehensive—in our notions of etiology, we spoke less and less in these surgical terms of extracting or evacuating or recovering all painful memories. But we did not put anything in the place of that simple model. One reads very little regarding the process of recovery, of re-regression or progression or reconstitution or reconstruction. We are not even sure what best to call it. Ekstein [25] and Reider [131] inquire into precisely how it is that the observing part of the ego, the healthy part, the stable part, as we assume, becomes enlarged and strengthened by accretions from the formerly affected part. As this occurs, increasingly, the emergency makeshifts can be abandoned.

Every clinician is familiar with the symptomatic evidences of these shifts in the balance—the little day-to-day victories that mean so much to the discouraged, wistful patient. The soft but persistent voice of the intellect, plus the increasingly clearer vision of the practical benefits of better reality adaptation, the fear of pain renewed, the pull of opportunities unrealized, the fruits of better techniques of winning love—all these plus the steadily cumulative burden of the cost of treatment in time, effort, and money combine to turn the direction of the curve from downward to upward, from regression to progression. This is not to exclude the increasingly perceived effect of the example of the psychoanalyst himself—his poise, his patience, his fairness, his consistency, his rationality, his kindliness, in short—his *real* love for the patient.

One can speculate in various ways how to describe this turning point. The change in direction from regression to progression seems to take place through a change in conviction or belief on the part of the patient. He has presumably gotten as far from reality as possible and doesn't like what he finds. We can't quite say that he isn't satisfied; it might be more accurate to say that he is satisfied that he cannot be satisfied by going further in that direction. He comes to see without equivocation that above everything else in life he wants to love and be loved, and realizes that he can give love and can get love and also that he can hate effectively when necessary. He has seen that in many respects he had never grown up, but maintained child-ish attitudes and longings, reaching back into his earliest infancy, which interfered with his present-day life.

Suppose we go back to the very beginning of our theoretical propositions and recollect what it was the patient came for. He came to be relieved of certain distress or certain disability; these were his symptoms. He came, as we diagrammed it, with the proposition, "I want the analyst to *cure* me."

The analyst promised to assist him in getting relief from some of his distress and to set up a treatment program. Then, in the course of this treatment, wherein he was to lose these symptoms, the patient began to discover that his symptoms had a purpose, that he was not so anxious to lose them but that he was, on the other hand, anxious to get something else and impelled moreover to use some very astonish-ing techniques to do so. He wanted to be loved, and to be able to love, but there were unconscious obstacles to both.

The regression induced by the treatment exposed these facts and brought about changes in his goals. At the peak of the regression, at its greatest depth one might say, the patient was aware that he was both blissfully gratified and chronically unsatisfied, and that in cer-tain respects he would always be unsatisfied as compared to his memories and his fantasies. But he also came to realize that his present dissatisfactions need not be as great as his poor techniques had brought about. He progressively approached a point where he could say, in no spirit of sulking or sour grapes:

"I have gained much from this experience; I am still gaining from it, but the law of diminishing returns is operative and the ques-tion is now whether what I have yet to gain will outweigh the prac-tical inconvenience and expense of my continuing to come for my daily sessions. Contrary to what I felt so intensely some time ago, I can say now that I do not seek anything from the analyst. I have his friendship, I have his example, I have his point of view toward illness. That which I *thought* I wanted from him was in part a childish fantasy which I renounced. In the sense of wanting to love and be loved, I realize I can obtain these satisfactions in more likely places and with more appropriate techniques than I have ever used, or than I used during the experience with my analyst. By not giving me what I thought I wanted from him, the analyst gave me what I most needed; namely, a better self-understanding, a better capacity for discrimination, greater tolerance for unavoidable dissatisfaction, a clearer view of my needs. In a symbolic sense, the analyst has given me himself, and I felt free to take his gift. I do not need his help any more. I have gotten what I paid for; I can do for myself. I can assume a mature role in preference to one of expectant pleading; I can substitute hoping for despairing, enjoying for expecting, giving for taking. I can endure foregoing what must be foregone and accept and enjoy without guilt such pleasures as are accessible to me."

Every analyst is happy when a "terminating" patient is able to say something like this and mean it. Many are able to say it, some *do* say it. But they also recognize that there is no such thing as a perfect analysis, a perfect analyst, or a perfect analysand, except in theory, and would be the first to agree with Glover's designation of the myth of the completely analyzed person.

And so, as Marion Milner [111] dryly remarks, "Although there is perhaps no such thing as a completed analysis, patients do sooner or later stop coming to analysis." The daily sessions with the analyst cease by mutual agreement. This is variously referred to as "finishing the analysis," "discontinuing the analysis," "terminating the analysis," "interrupting the analysis," "getting through with the analysis," and so forth. The controlled contractual relationship terminates *insofar as this involves the successive daily session.* The process of self-analysis continues automatically, we think, with increasing freeing and expanding of ego functions, for many months—and even years—following the contractual dissolution. It is understood that the analyst will stand by for a period of time, in case the decision regarding a proper date of interruption of the contract has been faulty, and lend assistance if trouble develops. And even this dependence will usually have been analyzed away.

Now, in all the discussions of termination in the literature (which are actually not very numerous) there is scarcely any mention of the simple question of *why* an analysis must end. Indeed, Ferenczi [34] played with the idea that perhaps it need not end but could perhaps (ideally) go on indefinitely. But does this not imply that the analysis as such is more important than the result? Does it imply that discovering more and more about oneself is increasingly profitable? Is the law of diminishing returns inapplicable to this process?

Both the analyst and analysand are sometimes tempted to evade the question of termination. I shall not stress here the countertransference of the analyst or the unanalyzed reluctance of the patient to leave, but merely point to the general factor of inertia. Some patients have nothing so interesting to do as to continue their self-study, and some analysts seem to think they cannot do better than to permit this! They may both be right.

Ferenczi answered his own question by saying that in most analyses an end point is reached which is perfectly evident to both the analyst and the analysand, that the analysis wears itself out, as it were, and is thus over and done.[36] But this is an intuitive rather than a theoretical criterion.

Balint [3] formulated the theoretical question involved here thus:

> Is health a natural state of equilibrium? Do processes exist in the mind which—if unhampered and undisturbed—would lead the development toward that equilibrium? Or is health the result of a lucky chance, a rare or even an improbable event, the reason being that its conditions are so stringent and so numerous that the chances are very heavily weighted against it? . . . Roughly there are two camps [in the ranks of analysts]. . . . (1) [There are] those who think that mature genitality [he means mental health] is not simply a chance sum-total of a motley mixture of component sexual instincts but a function *per se* [and] that health is a natural equilibrium; [for these] the termination of a psycho-analytic cure is a natural process. (2) The other camp [holds that] health, the termination of an analysis and mature genitality are similarly the result of the interplay of so many forces, tendencies and influences that one is not justified in assuming governing natural processes.

I understand Balint to be attempting here to restate the problem represented by Hippocrates' concept of a *vis medicatrix naturae*. Do the forces of nature tend to make the patient well when the something adventitious which instituted the "disease" is removed? Experience would say sometimes yes, sometimes no; some wounds heal and some gape too large. Freud discovered, and all analysts must constantly remember, that in the case of mental illness the wound is partly self-inflicted and self-maintained; that which is adventitious is largely self-created.

My own point of view in this problem of recovery will be dealt with more extensively elsewhere. It is my belief that one cannot usefully distinguish the process of "recovery" from that of "disease"; these are two aspects of the same thing. I would answer Balint's first question with a "yes," but I would remind my readers that there are those who dispute this, on good grounds.

Of course, certain broad generalities of theory about the spontaneous dissolution of the transference, the reversal of the regression, the increased objectivity of the patient, and so forth have long been current. Perhaps, such descriptions of changes in the patient are the best we can do at present. It is an inescapable fact that if certain pressures are relieved, symptoms sometimes disappear and the sense of "recovery," of increased well-being and relative "independence" force practical considerations to the fore. "The well man hath no need of a physician"—*i.e.*, no need of continuing treatment.*

Estimates of healthiness cannot, however, be based solely upon the patient's subjective appraisal. These are important, but so are the opinions of society and of the physician! In a two-party contract, such as psychoanalytic treatment is, the therapist has access to his own observations and to the patient's judgment regarding the degree of "recovery" but much less access to the opinions of friends, relatives, children, or to the judgment of a more objective or differently-equipped colleague. Insofar as he knows them, the analyst cannot ignore the known discrepancies in these various judgments. If neither

---

* One practical aspect regarding termination, rarely mentioned, relates to the calendar and the vacation custom. Could the statistics be gathered accurately regarding the dates of termination of analyses over the United States, there would be a startling preponderance of patients getting well enough to terminate their analyses at the beginning of summer when so many analysts take their vacation. Most analysts are very conscientious about not interrupting their work any more than necessary, or interrupting it prematurely because of their personal convenience, but vacations are a problem. Patients sometimes say ironically that they ought really to avoid having their illnesses in the summertime!

the patient nor the analyst is satisfied, the contract has obviously not reached a proper termination or interruption point. Nevertheless, for practical reasons—the illness of the analyst, serious financial problems for the patient, illness in the patient's family necessitating a geographic move, and so on—it may become necessary to terminate it. In such cases there is no precise rule of conduct; most analysts would try to leave the opportunity open for the patient to return to him as soon as possible or to assist the patient in finding another analyst as soon as that would be possible.

Sometimes the analyst is satisfied that the analysis has gone as far as it profitably can, but the patient is *not* satisfied. This doesn't happen very often, and it usually means that the analyst has come to the conclusion that one of these interminable or irresolvable problems exists which cannot ever be fully analyzed. Freud discusses them at length in his profound although somewhat pessimistic final paper, "Analysis, Terminable and Interminable." [43]

More frequent is the situation in which the patient is satisfied with the results of the analysis and wishes to discontinue it, but the analyst is not so satisfied that he has reached his potentialities. The analyst attempts to point to the progress remaining to be made, problems not yet solved, attitudes and techniques that could be improved upon; but these the patient refutes or minimizes. This is easily recognized as resistance, but it is not always easily resolved, even with that recognition. An actual physical flight from analysis is more apt to occur during the early months than during the latter months, but every one of us has seen some of the latter,* to our dismay and, if the truth be told, to our considerable anger and sorrow. It would be an interesting psychoanalytic research to follow up a number of these abruptly departing patients, who leave "against medical advice," and see whether in the long run their judgment was perhaps actually better than that of the analyst or, to put it another way, whether the best thing for them to have done in the circumstances was to have evaded the discovery of that final knowledge about themselves which they perhaps could not have borne.

---

* The expression "flight into health" is ascribed by Balint to Freud, but Eduardo Weiss credits it to Tausk. For the references to these sources, and the discussion of the topic, see George F. Train.[155]

Ideally, of course, the situation is one in which the analyst is satisfied with the results of the many months of work together, the patient is satisfied, and reports from friends and associates are favorable. The analyst believes that the patient has achieved his goal —*the goal* of aiming confidently and competently now, for a "better" goal—and the patient feels that he can go on learning by himself. In a moment we shall speak of some of the criteria for such a conviction. But this is a good place to speak again of the fact that both the patient and his analyst undoubtedly have blind spots in this regard, and their best efforts to be objective about the matter are sometimes defeated thereby. It is obviously impossible for them to ask the social environment at large what opinion it may have, but sometimes there are representative figures whom it is not impossible to consult. However, this is a delicate matter. The patient cannot very well go around asking people if he seems to be doing better, and, on the other hand, the analyst cannot very well do it either. To some extent he need not ask; people will inform him of it, often without saying a word about it! Sometimes there is no solution for this, and I have seen instances in which the pride of the analyst or his countertransference and his pressure of work combined with the unconsciously motivated efforts of the patient to embarrass his analyst. At the Menninger Clinic we strongly incline to psychological retesting, an adjuvant which the intelligent patient rarely resists. But, of course, the decision whether or not to terminate the treatment does not rest upon the test results, since they provide (at best) only some of the information needed.

CRITERIA FOR DETERMINING THE APPROPRIATE POINT OF DISCONTINUANCE

We have implied that both the analyst and the analysand do have certain criteria upon which they base their conclusions that maximum therapeutic benefit has been probably obtained and that termination of the contract may be effected. What are these criteria?

Many authors have written on this subject (although it is an interesting commentary that nearly every author who does so begins by saying that very little has ever been written on it). A whole issue of the *International Journal of Psychoanalysis* was given over to the topic a few years ago (1950). Some writers feel confident that it can all be reduced to a few simple points; I mention this to indicate my disagreement.*

Most analysts today rely upon a rather wide variety of criteria for assistance in forming a conclusion which is, at best, approximate, uncertain, and perhaps always partly opportunistic. Everyone agrees that the purpose of the analysis is to enable the individual to deal "better" (*i.e.,* more maturely) with his internal and external problems. Does he demonstrate that he is consistently competent to do this unassisted and unwatched, as it were? One hopes for a subsidence of symptoms or for a better tolerance of them without their becoming his preoccupation or his considerable handicap.

In addition to the disappearance or mitigation or tolerance of the symptoms, what other indication have we that the disintegrative trends have been arrested and self-destructive techniques and purposes replaced with constructive ones? What is the evidence for a better personality integration?

One swallow does not make a summer. The clinical improvement of psychoanalytic patients represented by the successive abandonment of the phases of regression is like birds returning in the spring—first, the one swallow; then a few bluebirds, perhaps; then a flock of warblers. The patient begins to "feel" better. He has more ups than downs, although there are still lags and snags, digressions and delays. But he moves toward new ways, new vistas, new goals. There is a progressive shift from infantile passivity to adult activity, from the assumption that love is something taken to the realization that love is also something given, from the passive expectation of being loved "for one's own sake" to the active satisfaction in giving love without the expectation of a *quid pro quo* in return.

---

* For example, Melanie Klein thinks it is sufficient that "the patient's relations to the external world be sufficiently strengthened to enable him to deal satisfactorily with the situation of mourning arising at this point." But what is "satisfactorily"? Wilhelm Reich thought that the achievement of strong orgastic potency was the essential criterion. The disappearance of the infantile amnesias was considered the index by many of us in the earlier days, although just how we could tell that something negative—*i.e.,* amnesia—is absent poses a problem!

I wish to emphasize that even through what the analysand feels as unending renunciation—to a degree that makes him sometimes cry out that analysis takes away some of his dearest treasures—he senses the indication for and the beginning feeling of obligation and responsibility and a capacity for restitution. One must pay the piper. The long indulgence in infantile fantasies and infantile modes of behavior entail their guilt feelings, some of them appropriate. However much fun the growing child may have in his playroom, he must ultimately pick up his toys. The environment has indeed been injured. It has been smeared, depreciated, hurt, and sometimes destroyed. There is restitution to be made and there is now an increasing capacity for this through the release of creative ambitions and creative activities. The butterfly must emerge from the crawling, devouring, or sleeping stages of larva and pupa.

In a general way, we can say that better relationships with himself, better relationships with others, and better utilizations of work, play, and other sublimations indicate such a satisfactory adjustment.

Let us discuss these somewhat more specifically.

RELATIONS WITH SELF

"Better relations with one's self" *means,* in our theoretical model, that the ego-split is mended, the observing part and the mobile part being once more "united" and harmonious. Nacht describes it as being at peace with oneself.[114] The trend toward depersonalization will have been reduced to a minimum. In a practical sense, it refers to the self-estimate which the patient consciously develops and which he manifests in his relations to others.

With respect to the ego-ideal, one ordinarily sees an elevation of goals as gauged by our cultural standards. On the other hand, in many patients the level of aspiration has been entirely out of balance with attainable goals, and in such individuals the apparent goals and ideals will have been lowered but the likelihood of achievement increased. This does not imply any reduction or change in the value system, of which more will be said later.

The fate of the superego in the analyzed patient has been much discussed in the literature. For a long time it was held that after having been projected upon the analyst, it was gradually but completely eliminated and its function replaced by conscious judgment and perhaps a strengthening of the (conscious) ego-ideal. It was more or less assumed that the superego was "destroyed" and disappeared with the separation from the analyst.

It is pretty well agreed now that this was oversimplified and extreme. Indeed, some patients seem to demonstrate an increased strength of the superego after analysis. It is really naïve to think that value judgments and attitudes can be left to "pure" reason. Many of them have to be made and will continue to be made unconsciously, at the behest of the superego, which should be considered a useful device, causing trouble only when it is ill-formed and ill-functioning (like the gall-bladder.) Typical of the majority of our patients, perhaps, are cases in which the superego has acted with capriciousness or cruelty or gross corruptibility, or all three. Certainly these attitudes and expectations of the superego make for illness, and hence to the extent that the superego is represented by such functioning we would consider a criterion of the successful effects of the analysis that the old superego would have disappeared. The practical effect of this is a *sense of greater freedom, a capacity for more joy in life, a cessation of various compulsive activities* and a *diminution of the tendency to depression.*

RELATIONS WITH OTHERS

It is in the relationships of the patient to other people that we usually see the most conspicuous changes. Quantitatively one expects a widened range or a deepened intensity, or both. Here again, however, one must allow for those patients whose relations to others was (formerly) *impaired* by their diversity and range. Hence we can only speak in a general way of an improvement in the affective satisfactions derived from these relationships through a correction of too little or too great diversity or restriction.

Qualitatively, of course, we expect to see mature, so-called "genital" patterns of sexuality replace the various immature and overly self-centered modes which characterize "illness." One criterion of the achievement of such maturity and the diminution of ambivalence is the improved relationship with the offspring and with those who in a sense represent foster offspring. Maturity has no need to find satisfactions for childish wishes. The "analyzed person" either comes to realize that they can be gratified without such exertions as he had previously made or that they do not need to be gratified or that he has no further feeling of need for such gratification or that there is no prospect of gratifying them and hence they must be renounced without regrets. Having worked this through, the analyzed person is no longer in competition with his own children and with all those who represent his own children. Instead of competing with them, he can now take over his actual role of parent and give to them what they need (which is not necessarily what *he needed,* although this is often an influencing factor). This is reflected in a greater pleasure in being with the children, better judgment in making decisions in regard to them, greater patience with them, increased interest in what they are interested in, and so on. And, by extension, this is reflected in a greater interest on his part in all those peoples of the earth who are weaker or needier than he. One may say that *Agape* has increased at the expense of *Eros* (although it should be noted that Freud sometimes used the latter in the meaning of the former). At any rate, the outside world will very properly continue to judge the efficacy of psychoanalytic treatment in considerable measure by its indirect effect, that is to say, the way in which the former patient deals with those about him. If his analysis was successful, *their* lives, too, will be improved.

The relationships with the actual parents, if they are living, usually show much improvement, simply because the unconscious elements of hostility attached to events of days long gone by have been exposed and decimated. Many patients find that the parent whom they had preferred less now becomes the more interesting. Either parent may have possessed so many unlovable and inacceptable traits in actuality that the patient's continued tolerance of them could be described as more neurotic than realistic. In such instances the ability to sever intimate relations with the parent and deal with him at a distance and more objectively is a great improvement.

The relations with the spouse are considered by many analysts to be the most definitely indicative criterion, representing as they do the expression of the patient's formalized heterosexual adjustment. However, paradoxically enough, the sexual aspects of marriage will, in many instances, have a diminished rather than an increased importance. (Naturally, this is not true of those cases in which there was marked sexual inhibition.) Phallic stage propensities yield to genital stage characteristics. Sexuality in the narrow sense becomes less important because sexuality in the wider sense becomes more important. Sexual relations are usually more satisfactory, more nearly mature in type, freer from anxiety, and freer from overestimation or underestimation. It is misleading, indeed, to follow the thesis of Reich in regard to sexual potency, making the completeness of the orgasm the most important criterion of a completed analysis and hence, by inference, of mental health. Neither psychoanalytic treatment nor life itself can be adequately envisaged in the concept of a frantic search for a better orgasm (a point of view unfortunately not limited to Reich and Kinsey).

In the case of unmarried patients, one expects to see improvement in the love object choices in the direction of those most likely to fulfill the total needs of companionship, mutual love, parenthood, and so forth. Usually this tends toward a marriage situation.

The attitude of both the married and the unmarried toward the principal love object will have changed in the well-analyzed individual from one dominated by possessiveness, opportunism, parasitism, dependency, and the like, to one dominated by the appropriate masculine or feminine attitude. The male patient will have tended to become more masculine in his attitudes, and the female patient more feminine. On the other hand, however, neither will be unaware of or apologetic for those elements conventionally more characteristic of the opposite sex which have come to be an unchangeable part of his own personality. He will strive, rather, to adjust them to the reciprocal characteristics of the partner.

Both male and female members of the partnership will have established toward each other an attitude in which the welfare of the other is the source of the greatest pleasure. To put it another way, the love object will have become an end, and not a means to an end. The husband will cease to use the wife as permissive mother or nurse or masturbational assistant; the wife will cease to use the husband as a slave or monster or penis.

RELATIONS TO THINGS AND IDEAS

The relationships of an individual to the material things of the world constitute the essence of his sublimations of destructive energies unexpendable toward human beings (and animals). As a practical matter, sublimation takes the form of work, play, and thinking. In a general way, it is a criterion of success in analytic treatment that these aspects of life have improved and taken on more importance for the individual. By an improved work pattern, I mean an improved interest in work, a greater satisfaction in work for its own sake rather than as a means to an end, a greater skill, a greater efficiency. And with respect to play, improvement would mean a greater interest if play has been an inhibited modality and a lesser interest if play had occupied too much of the patient's life. In either case he should expect a greater satisfaction from the play and a minimum of guilt feelings connected with it. He should expect a higher degree of sportsmanship and a greater degree of social participation. Important, too, is the achievement of a proper balancing between work interests and play interests. Some people tend to work too much and play too little, some play too much and work too little, and some cannot do either. A trend in the direction of doing both and doing them in a proportion that is both satisfying and effective is usually a dependable criterion of improved integration. The result of this, of course, is an increased productivity and an increased creativity, an increased satisfaction to the individual and to others.

In the light of my concept of sublimation,[105, 107, 75] the improvements just described mean that the ego finds it increasingly possible to effect a neutralization of quantities of aggressive energy with a constructive infusion of "life instinct," that is to say, creativity. In the place of brooding hate, self reproach, or flagellation, or the thinly disguised destruction of the peace or joy or property of fellow beings, the better integrated individual can now expend these energies in their useful disguises as competitive play and constructive work. We are so familiar with the phenomenon of improvement as represented by "getting a job" or "learning to play" or "playing for the first time in my life" that we might forget how logically indicative this is of the sort of change which is predicted by our theory.

Toward possessions and power one sees a change in attitude exactly opposite from that occurring with respect to persons. Whereas the healthiest and most mature object relation with a *human being* is one in which the other person is an end and not a means to an end, toward *things* it is ideal that they be regarded as a means to an end rather than an end. If money or a car or a house or a business or a position of power becomes a love object, adored for its own sake, it represents a substitute for a human love object and to that extent detracts from interpersonal relationships.* For this reason one might say that the result of an analysis is in the direction of making one feel less possessive of one's possessions and to make better use of them.

Similarly, there would be a disappearance or diminution of feelings of covetousness and of power-seeking, not because these are "cardinal sins," but because they indicate an unrealistic attitude and a lack of capacity for satisfaction with those devices for sublimations

---

* Art objects, nature and its phenomena, and the expression of beauty generally constitute an exception to this rule concerning which I am at a loss to supply an explanatory abstraction. A rose, a painting, an essay or poem are indeed adorable for their own sake like love objects and I doubt if they can be equated with, or derived from, human love objects. In this respect I may be somewhat heretical, since the standard teaching relates the rose to the breast, the sculpture to the penis, and so forth, but the sublimation becomes so complete or so isolated that for practical purposes such things fall into a different category. These issues touch upon the complex and often confused theory of narcissism, a topic systematically discussed by my colleague, Dr. H. G. van der Waals.[156, 157] Involved are such considerations as whether these phenomena of love for people and objects and ideas can be conceptualized as quantitative variations in narcissistic libido or whether issues of qualitative difference must be introduced.

and love which one already possesses or which one can, in the course of ordinary enterprise and adventure, obtain for oneself.

OTHER CRITERIA

There are still certain miscellaneous criteria for the termination of an analysis. There is, for example, that well-known criterion of an increased tolerance for personal discomfort.* This discomfort may be physical; it is more often psychological. The latter can either be in the form of that curious uneasiness which we call anxiety or that equally curious discomfort which we call guilt feelings. It is important for young analysts, particularly, to avoid the error made by so many laymen to the effect that psychoanalysis "removes" anxiety and guilt. Psychoanalysis, let us hope, diminishes the anxiety aroused by unresolved unconscious conflicts, but it can never remove anxiety derived from exigencies and pressures yet to develop. Psychoanalysis can indeed alleviate certain guilt feelings which are attached to the idea of an aggression which the individual never committed; it cannot remove guilt feelings properly attached to the aggressions which a person does commit or has committed. Many of the unconscious guilt feelings which people experience are attached to the wrong thing, and one of our objectives might be said to be to get people's guilt feelings attached to the "right" things.

Hence, instead of being free from guilt feelings and anxiety feelings, the psychoanalyzed person may have even more of both than the unanalyzed person, but he will know where they came from and what to do about them instead of developing symptoms. He will know whether or not restitution can be made; whether or not penance is in order; whether or not easement can be found. And if they are not to be had, then he must have the courage to bear them cheerfully.

---

* Surely in the minds of all psychoanalysts there will never be a more magnificent example of this aspect of healthy mindedness than that of Sigmund Freud, who through nearly two decades of constant suffering rarely indulged himself with even so much as a tablet of aspirin. This is to say nothing of the fear, the grief and the sorrow incident to his exile, the loss of his friends and many of his possessions. (See Ernest Jones.[81])

It may perhaps seem to him by now that psychoanalysis is a prodigious hoax. He did not lose his homely looks; he did not get a larger penis; he (she) was not given a baby by the analyst; he was not absolved of his guilt feelings for having mistreated his brother. He was merely shown that he would not be punished for crying; that there are other places to go for help for certain things; that he cannot have the moon but that he can have certain other satisfactions which he had considered equally impossible. In this sense psychoanalysis works to achieve a better discrimination in regard to what is good and what is evil, what is worth having or doing and what is not. In this respect, psychoanalysis must be considered a kind of higher education, the aim of which, according to Arthur Morgan,[113] is "to free us from whatever is trivial, chance, accidental, provincial and misleading in our earlier conditioning, and to replace it with what is true, significant, universal and in accord with the inherent nature of things." Thus freed, we can substitute constructive action—or restraint—for wistful fantasy, awkward aggressiveness or paralyzing indecision.

THE RELATIONSHIP WITH THE PSYCHOANALYST

Finally, criteria for the termination of analysis are discoverable in the transference situation. We have already discussed the changes in the individual and the changes in regard to his relationships with the outside world. His relationship to the analyst has been a special, peculiar, precious thing. In it he has relived all kinds of previous relationships. He has reacted to the analyst as if he were his mother, his father, his brother, his teacher, his sister, his wife. Gradually these illusions have tended to fade in intensity. The analyst becomes more and more just the analyst, "that doctor who has patiently listened to me." The patient begins to be a little bit more considerate of the analyst as a person for his (*i.e.,* the analyst's) own sake. This objectivity toward the analyst increases and the magic omnipotence of the great man begins to diminish. In fantasy this is sometimes conceived of as his death; in a more constructive formulation it represents replacement by a friend, a friend with his own infirmities, his own interests, his own problems, but with a record of consistent and faithful efforts to be helpful. In this way the termination of an analysis often carries with it the thought expressed by Tennyson: "I hope to see my Pilot face to face, when I have crossed the bar."

From another standpoint the termination is less a period of mourning than a period of rejoicing. "The King is dead. Long live the King!" The patient feels, as Balint has put it, that he is going through a kind of rebirth to a period of new life. He has arrived at the end of a dark tunnel, and he sees light again after a long journey. He is almost afraid to feel grateful, lest it be construed as an evasion of gratification, as it well may be. But not entirely, for he has gotten more than he bargained for, more than he paid for, and he will pass its benefits on to someone else.

"It is a deeply moving experience. The general atmosphere is of taking leave forever of something very dear, very precious—with all the corresponding grief and mourning . . . mitigated by the feeling of security, originating from the newly-won possibilities for real happiness. Usually the patient leaves after the last session happy but with tears in his eyes and—I think I may admit—the analyst is apt to be in a very similar mood." [8]

METHODS OF TERMINATION

It remains to say a few words about the *methods* of terminating the analysis, once it has been decided upon. Freud proposed that in those cases where, either because the patient becomes so attached to the analysis, so persistent in his erotization of the process, that he does not want to give it up or where the analysand keeps turning up more and more material which seems to go on forever and ever, the analyst may decide to announce that the analysis will stop on such and such a date. Whether successful or not, this is final and there is nothing more to do about it once one has done it that way.

What I do is usually something like this: When I feel that the point of maximum benefit is approaching, based on criteria discussed, I begin to look for expressions of a similar opinion from the patient. If I get them, I incline to concur with him. Perhaps I answer with a, "Why not, indeed?" Or I may comment to the effect that I see no objection to the possibility of his finishing. I let the inference be that it is not indicative of resistance for him to begin to think (talk) about an ending of the treatment. Sometimes this is a matter of rumination for weeks or even months. If no "protest symptoms" appear, we gradually begin to speak in more definite terms as to just when it might be, and I observe his reactions to this. If he suggests that it might as well be tomorrow, I remark that usually there is some advantage in a little longer time than that to analyze some reactions to the prospect. If he asks me outright how soon I think he could finish, I am apt to ask him how soon *he* thinks, and if he suggests a month or two months, I indicate my concurrence with that as a possibility.

I am always careful to say, "Yes, I think you could finish by then," in order to make it clear to him that this is what I think he *could* do; what he is *going to do* I can't predict. Sometimes I am very explicit in these latter words. "From what I see of you now it looks to me as if you had the capacity for working out the few remaining difficulties by about such a date and from then on could handle your affairs alone." All I can say is how it looks to me. I do not actually know; therefore I say "I think." Furthermore, his unconscious may decide that the analysis is too good a thing to be given up or that it has more material that should come out. In that case, he can't—or doesn't want to—finish by such and such a date, but I don't know that he can't finish.

I think the main thing is for the analyst just to remember that he doesn't know everything and that the patient's unconscious pressures are, in the last analysis, going to settle things. If the analyst, for reasons of opportunism or mistaken judgment or necessity, ends the analysis too abruptly, he will hear about it.

The patient's repressive processes sometimes hold out buried material as long as possible, hoping that the analysis will overlook its existence, so to speak, and that he (the patient) can endure the repression. On the other hand, this may lead to continued high tension in the ego. Some patients, once the date of termination is more or less tentatively agreed on mutually, will suddenly become very much "sicker." Many symptoms will recur, as if the unconscious were protesting vigorously the arbitrary decision of the ego. Usually what is necessary is merely the postponement of the date another thirty or sixty days to get things straightened out. In some cases, a few symptoms which have recurred may remain, only to completely disappear after the patient has gone away.*

Now, a final word on the countertransference problem. One must bear in mind, as I have tried to throughout this book, that there are two parties concerned in the psychoanalytic treatment contract, and that both have an unconscious as well as a conscious. I have already hinted above that the termination may be more difficult for the analyst than for the patient. I recall one of my teachers apologizing for his weariness and disinterest in a control session I was having with him by saying that he happened at that moment to have several patients who were just terminating their analyses and that this was always a very trying experience. As a young analyst who was wistfully hoping at that time for the ultimate termination of his own analysis, to say nothing of the successful completion of *one* patient's analysis *someday*, I felt this to be a most strange remark. It was difficult to conceive of so happy and fortuitous an event as a "trying" experience for the analyst.

Nevertheless all experienced analysts know how difficult the terminal period is. It is difficult because it is fraught with various uncertainties. Has the point of maximum treatment benefit been reached? Has the law of diminishing returns begun to operate? Am I influenced in my inclination to terminate this patient's analysis by certain personal advantages—a new patient clamoring for my time, an impending vacation date, some slightly negative feelings toward this patient, some over-optimistic estimates of my success with him? Is the patient concealing behind the façade of improvement certain sinister seeds of psychic infection? Is the patient merely testing my perspicacity or is he perhaps flattering my vanity? Am I leaning over backward in my conservatism or perhaps even inflicting some mild punishment on this patient by delaying his separation from me? Do I really want to separate from this fine fellow now and see him no more? Am I perhaps favoring a perseverative continuance and an

---

* My colleague, Dr. Ishak Ramzy, comments: "After all, in the 'realistic' profession of being a psychoanalyst one should not expect the satisfaction of having done a 'perfect' job. Moreover if we have liberated the demons of hate, why should we expect them to bid us goodbye without a few wallops?"

unconscious erotization of the process in him for certain gratifications which these afford me?

These are but a few of the questions that a conscientious analyst asks himself at such times. At no other period in the analysis are the countertransference phenomena so disturbing and so potentially dangerous. And it is a paradoxical truth—or at least I think it is a truth—that the less disturbing these thoughts are, the more dangerous the countertransference may be.

An experienced colleague, Annie Reich, has well said:

Sometimes analysts have a tendency to terminate analyses too early. Apart from expediency motives, there is frequently a narcissistic need to achieve results quickly which cannot tolerate the slow pace of analytic work. There are others who have a need to end relationships with patients soon before a danger situation in regard to their own badly controlled homosexual urges can arise; others, on the other hand, cannot give up a patient and enjoy the dependency situation. These counter-transference difficulties, of course, should be eliminated in the analyst's own analysis. But the situation of ending an analysis is seldom one that comes to the attention of the training analyst, as we do not usually see our students that long. Of course, the underlying difficulty should show up in some other fashion.[128]

It is incredible—or it would be were it not for our knowledge of repression—to what degree the most highly proficient and competent analysts will fall into this countertransference trap, defending with the most transparent rationalizations their subsequent pursuit of or proprietary attitude toward their former patients. Some years ago, at the request of the president of the American Psychoanalytic Association, I conducted a series of seminars at our Annual Meetings made up entirely of training analysts. Many valuable considerations were developed, but the signal contribution and conclusion of *all the discussions* might be framed thus: Unrecognized countertransference of an essentially destructive type, even though "positive" in form, is the ever-present threat to successful analysis, particularly the training analysis, and the only dependable remedy is the one recommended by Freud: repeated sessions of post-graduate analysis of the analyst. So far this recommendation has not been as widely and regularly followed as one would wish.

THE UNSUCCESSFUL CASE

Finally, we must not fail to mention the termination of the unsuccessful case. It is a time-honored custom or, let us say, tendency for doctors to take credit when the patient recovers and give the patients (or the intractable disease) the blame when recovery does not ensue. And sometimes it really is the patient's "fault," his rigidity, his fluidity, or his unconquerable fear.

We often start in so bravely with patients whose chief revelation to us in the deep penetration of their "illness" is the poverty of their egos, the frozen impenetrability of their character structure. I often recall the case mentioned in Chapter V—for whom I had such high hopes—who "couldn't bear to look at it." Some of the cases which initially look the most promising disappoint us sadly. On the other hand, among the three cases I count the most successful in my own experience, one was an ignorant (but not unintelligent) colleen, one was a chronic invalid, a spinster who is now a happy grandmother, one was a psychiatrist who had been rejected as unanalyzable by one of our greatest teachers. I shall not register here my failures and my disappointments.

Annie Reich has commented:

> Frequently we do not fail completely, but we can bring about partial mitigation of symptoms and strengthening of the ego. But the time comes when we have to face the fact that it does not make sense to go on. In these cases, it is my impression that a thorough working through of the reaction to the termination of the analysis as described above is not indicated. It is wisest, in these situations, to wait for a period when the ending of analysis seems to be least painful; when, for instance, suffering has subsided, when certain narcissistic gratifications are available. One could say with justification that this way of ending analysis is not really a psychoanalytic but a psychotherapeutic one. It may be so indeed, but it seems to be the most painless procedure.[128]

Freud [43] devoted his last great contribution to an examination of this problem in his paper, "Analysis, Terminable and Interminable." Rereading this paper at least annually should be almost a religious duty of the practicing psychoanalyst in order to foster the humility appropriate to his task.

THE SEPARATION

And so, at last, the stipulations of the psychoanalytic contract are fulfilled. The parties of the first and second part prepare to separate. The party of the second part has the satisfaction of having helped a fellow creature who was in distress. He has learned something—(as one does from *every* case). He is better prepared for his next "contract," his next opportunity to be helpful and to do the work he knows best how to do. He may even have discovered something of value for other colleagues to know—some little or big contribution to science and to the world. How amazed Freud's patient Dora would have been to learn that she had been an agent for the relief of millions of people and for the revolution of psychology and psychiatry.*

Besides all this, the party of the second part has been paid in money by the party of the first part, who, we hope, will feel that he has indeed gotten his money's worth. But it may not be so easy for him to say *wherein* his gain has been. He is poorer and, we hope, wiser. But by the end of his analysis, he had learned that most of the things he hoped for he failed to get. Most of his expectations were never realized. Instead he only learned that one shouldn't expect to get certain things and then cry one's eyes out in disappointment or scratch out other people's eyes in rage. So, as we suggested some pages earlier, the party of the first part will feel defrauded, "let down easy" but very expensively. And some who cannot complete their analyses feel exactly this way.

But the completed analytic experience does *not* leave one in that frame of mind. For, although it is true that his expectations were not met, his gains were *beyond* his expectations! He had learned to live, to love and to live, to love and to be loved and therein to live. This was his great gain.

Learning this simple thing, and recognizing it to be a universal principle, of which his own personal experience is but an example, represents a beginning constructive identification of himself with the universe, with reality, with other people. No one ever gets as much love as he wants, no one gives as much love as he might. Choices can be made but choice involves the assumption of responsibility and the

* For some of the subtle gains and satisfactions of the analyst, see Szasz.[150]

necessity for renunciation. But life is for living and this attitude he has gained the courage to accept.

> "I asked for all things, that I might enjoy life;
> I was given life, that I might enjoy all things. . . ." *

There is thus an implicit philosophy and ethic in the psychoanalytic experience, deny it who may. It is implicit that love is the greatest thing in the world. It is implicit that true love suffereth long and is kind, envieth not, is not puffed up, seeketh not its own (but the welfare of others), and rejoiceth not in iniquity but in the truth.

Thus the intangible gains of psychoanalytic treatment extend out into the universe. They are immeasurable. But the tangible values of the treatment contract have been balanced, usually to the satisfaction and betterment of both parties. Self-improvement will continue, autonomously, but the treatment, as such, is ended. The parties part company. The contract has been fulfilled.

* From "Prayer of an Unknown Confederate Soldier," clipped from a newspaper by Dr. John E. Large.[89-A]

BIBLIOGRAPHY

1. Alexander, Franz, and Others: *Psychoanalytic Therapy*. New York, Ronald, 1946.
2. Anonymous: Zur Vorgeschichte der analytischen Technik. *Internat. Ztschr. f. Psychoanal.*, 6:79-81, 1921. (Included in the *Collected Papers* of Sigmund Freud; see bibliography entry number 51.)
3. Balint, Michael: On the Termination of Analysis. *Internat. J. Psycho-Anal.*, 31:196–199, 1950.
4. ————: *Primary Love and Psychoanalytic Techniques*. New York, Liveright, 1953.
5. Balint, Alice and Michael: On the Transference and Countertransference. *Internat. J. Psycho-Anal.*, 20:223–230, 1939.
6. Barker, Roger, Dembo, Tamara, and Lewin, Kurt: *Studies in Topological and Vector Psychology, II.* (Frustration and Regression, an Experiment with Young Children.) Iowa City, Iowa, University of Iowa, 1941.
7. Bellak, Leopold and Smith, M. Brewster: An Experimental Exploration of the Psychoanalytic Process. *Psychoanalyt. Quart.*, 25:385–414, 1956.
8. Benedek, Therese: Dynamics of the Countertransference. *Bull. Menninger Clin.*, 17:201–208, 1953.
9. Beres, David: Communication in Psychoanalysis and in the Creative Process: A Parallel. *J. Am. Psychoanalyt. A.*, 5:408–423, 1957.
10. Berg, Charles: *Deep Analysis*. New York, Norton, 1947.
11. Berman, Leo: Countertransferences and Attitudes of the Analyst in the Therapeutic Process. *Psychiatry*, 12:159–166, 1949.
12. Bexton, W. H., Heron, W. and Scott, T. H.: Effects of Decreased Variation in the Sensory Environment. *Canad. J. Psychol.*, 8:70–76, 1954.
13. Bibring, Edward: Psychoanalysis and the Dynamic Psychotherapies. *J. Am. Psychoanalyt. A.*, 2:745–770, 1954.

14. Bjerre, Poul: *The History and Practice of Psychoanalysis.* Boston, Badger, 1920, pp. 18–19.

15. Braatöy, Trygve: *Fundamentals of Psychoanalytic Technique.* New York, Wiley, 1954.

16. Cassirer, Ernst: *Language and Myth.* New York, Harper, 1946.

17. Deutsch, Felix: *Applied Psychoanalysis.* New York, Grune & Stratton, 1949.

18. Devereux, George: Some Criteria for the Timing of Confrontations and Interpretations. *Internat. J. Psycho-Anal.,* 32:19–24, 1951.

19. Dimascio, Alberto, Boyd, Richard W., and Greenblatt, Milton: Physiological Correlates of Tension and Antagonism during Psychotherapy. *Psychosom. Med.,* 19:99–104, 1957.

20. Durrell, Lawrence: Studies in Genius: VI. Groddeck. *Horizon,* 17: 384–403, 1948.

21. Edwards, Ward: The Theory of Decision Making. *Psychol. Bull.,* 51:380–417, July 1954.

22. Eissler, K. R.: The Effect of the Structure of the Ego on Psychoanalytic Technique. *J. Am. Psychoanalyt. A.,* 1:104–143, 1953.

23. Ekstein, Rudolf: Psychoanalytic Technique. In *Progress in Clinical Psychology,* Daniel Brower and Lawrence Abt, eds. New York, Grune & Stratton, 1956, Vol. 2, pp. 79–97.

24. ———: Psychoanalytic Theory and Technique. In *Progress in Clinical Psychology,* Daniel Brower and Lawrence Abt, eds. New York, Grune & Stratton, 1952, Vol. 1, pp. 249–267.

25. ———: The Space Child's Time Machine: On "Reconstruction" in the Psychotherapeutic Treatment of a Schizophrenoid Child. *Am. J. Orthopsychiat.,* 24:492–506, 1954.

26. ———: Thoughts Concerning the Nature of the Interpretive Process. To be published.

27. Ellenberger, Henri: A Clinical Introduction to Phenomenology and Existential Analysis. In *Existence: A New Dimension in Psychiatry and Psychology,* Rollo May, Ernest Angel, and Henri F. Ellenberger, eds. New York, Basic Books, 1958.

28. Erikson, Erik H.: The Dream Specimen of Psychoanalysis. *J. Am. Psychoanalyt. A.,* 2:5–56, 1954.

29. Fenichel, Otto (1935): Concerning the Theory of Psychoanalytic Technique. In *Collected Papers of Otto Fenichel,* First Series. New York, Norton, 1953–54, pp. 332–348.

30. ———: Neurotic Acting Out. *Psychoanalyt. Rev.,* 32:197–206, 1945.

31. ———: *Principles of Intensive Psychotherapy.* Chicago, University of Chicago, 1950.

32. ———: *Problems of Psychoanalytic Technique.* New York, Psychoanalytic Quarterly, 1941.

33. Ferenczi, Sandor (1928): The Elasticity of Psychoanalytic Technique. In *Final Contributions to Psychoanalysis*. New York, Basic Books, 1955, pp. 87–101.

34. ———: *Further Contributions to the Theory and Technique of Psychoanalysis*. London, Hogarth, 1926.

35. ——— (1909): Introjection and Transference. In *Sex and Psychoanalysis*. Boston, Badger, 1916.

36. ———: The Problem of the Termination of the Analysis. In *Final Contributions to the Problems and Methods of Psychoanalysis*. New York, Basic Books, 1955, pp. 77–86.

37. Fingert, Hyman H.: Comments on the Psychoanalytic Significance of the Fee. *Bull. Menninger Clin.*, 16:98–104, 1952.

38. Fisher, Charles: Studies on the Nature of Suggestions, Part I. *J. Am. Psychoanalyt. A.*, 1:222–254, 1953.

39. Fliess, Robert: The Metapsychology of the Analyst. *Psychoanalyt. Quart.*, 11:211–227, 1942.

40. Forsyth, David: *The Technique of Psychoanalysis*. London, Paul, Trench, Trubner, 1922.

40-A. French, Thomas M.: *The Integration of Behavior*. Vol. 1 (1952), Vol. 2 (1954). Chicago, Ill., University of Chicago.

41. Freud, Anna: *The Ego and the Mechanisms of Defense*. London, Hogarth, 1937, p. 18.

42. ———: *Psychoanalytic Treatment of Children*. London, Imago Publishing Company, 1946; 2nd Ed., 1947; 3rd Ed., 1951.

43. Freud, Sigmund (1937): Analysis Terminable and Interminable. In *Collected Papers*. London, Hogarth, 1950, Vol. 5, pp. 316–357.

44. ——— (1920): Beyond the Pleasure Principle. In *Standard Edition of the Complete Psychological Works of Sigmund Freud*. London, Hogarth, 1955, Vol. 18, pp. 3–64.

45. ——— (1904): Die Freudsche Psychoanalytische Methode. In *Die Psychischen Zwangerscheinungen,* by Leopold Loewenfeld. Wiesbaden, Bergmann, 1904. Also in *Collected Papers*. 1924, Vol. 1, pp. 264–271.

46. ——— (1912): The Dynamics of Transference. In *Collected Papers*. 1924, Vol. 2, pp. 312–322.

47. ——— (1905): Fragment of an Analysis of a Case of Hysteria. In *Standard Edition*. 1953, Vol. 7, pp. 7–122.

48. ——— (1913): Further Recommendations in the Technique of Psychoanalysis. In *Collected Papers*. 1924, Vol. 2, pp. 342–365.

49. ——— (1910): The Future Prospects of Psychoanalytic Therapy. In *Collected Papers*. 1924, Vol. 2, pp. 285–296.

50. ——— (1926): *Inhibitions, Symptoms, and Anxiety*. London, Hogarth, 1936.

51. Freud, Sigmund (1920): A Note on the Prehistory of the Technique of Analysis. In *Collected Papers*. 1950, Vol. 5, pp. 101–104.

52. —— (1915): Observations on Transference Love. In *Collected Papers*. 1924, Vol. 2, pp. 377–391.

53. —— (1910): Observations on "Wild" Psychoanalysis. In *Collected Papers*. 1924, Vol. 2, pp. 297–304.

54. —— (1913): On Beginning the Treatment. The Question of the First Communication. The Dynamics of the Cure. In *Collected Papers*. 1924, Vol. 2, pp. 343–365.

55. —— (1904): On Psychotherapy. In *Collected Papers*. 1924, Vol. 1, pp. 249–263.

56. —— (1922): Psychoanalysis. In *Collected Papers*. 1950, Vol. 5, pp. 107–130.

57. —— (1914): Recollection, Repetition and Working Through. In *Collected Papers*. 1924, Vol. 2, pp. 366–376.

58. —— (1912): Recommendations for Physicians on the Psychoanalytic Method of Treatment. In *Collected Papers*. 1924, Vol. 2, p. 329.

59. —— (1895 with Josef Breuer): *Studies on Hysteria*. New York, Basic Books, 1957.

60. —— (1919): Turnings in the Ways of Psychoanalytic Therapy. In *Collected Papers*. 1924, Vol. 2, pp. 394–402.

61. Fromm-Reichmann, Frieda: Notes on the Development of Treatment of Schizophrenics by Psychoanalytic Psychotherapy. *Psychiatry*, 11:263–273, 1948.

62. ——: Personal and Professional Requirements of a Psychotherapist. *Psychiatry*, 12:361–378, 1949.

63. ——: *Principles of Intensive Psychotherapy*. Chicago, University of Chicago, 1950; London, Allen and Unwin, 1953, p. 67.

64. GAP Symposium No. 3: *Factors Used to Increase the Susceptibility of Individuals to Forceful Indoctrination: Observation and Experiments*. New York, Group for the Advancement of Psychiatry, 1956.

65. Gill, Merton M.: Psychoanalysis and Exploratory Psychotherapy. *J. Am. Psychoanalyt. A.*, 2:771–797, 1954.

66. ——: Spontaneous Regression on the Induction of Hypnosis. *Bull. Menninger Clin.*, 12:41–48, 1948.

67. Gitelson, Maxwell: The Emotional Position of the Analyst in the Psychoanalytic Situation. *Internat. J. Psycho-Anal.*, 33:1–10, 1952.

68. Glover, Edward: *Psychoanalysis*. 2nd Ed. London, Staples, 1949, p. 309.

69. ——: Therapeutic Results of Psychoanalysis. *Internat. J. Psycho-Anal.*, 18:125–132, 1937.

70. ——: *The Technique of Psychoanalysis*. London, Bailliere, Tindall & Cox, 1928; 2nd Ed. New York, International Universities, 1955.

71. Greenacre, Phyllis: General Problems of Acting Out. *Psychoanalyt. Quart.*, 19:455–467, 1950.
72. ———: The Predisposition to Anxiety, Part II. *Psychoanalyt. Quart.*, 10:610–638, 1941.
73. ———: The Role of Transference. *J. Am. Psychoanalyt. A.*, 2:671–684, 1954.
74. Haak, Nils: Comments on the Analytical Situation. *Internat. J. Psycho-Anal.*, 38:183–195, 1957.
75. Hartmann, Heinz: Notes on the Theory of Sublimation. In *Psychoanalytic Study of the Child.* New York, International Universities, 1955, Vol. 10, pp. 9–29.
76. ———: Technical Implications of Ego Psychology. *Psychoanalyt. Quart.*, 20:31–43, 1951.
77. Hawthorne, Nathaniel: *The Scarlet Letter.* New York, Pocket Books, 1948, p. 127.
78. Hebb, D. O.: The Mammal and His Environment. *Am. J. Psychiat.*, 111:826–831, 1955.
79. Heiman, Paula: On Countertransference. *Internat. J. Psycho-Anal.*, 31:81–84, 1950.
80. Jelliffe, S. E.: *The Technique of Psychoanalysis.* 2nd Ed. New York, Nervous & Mental Disease Pub. Co., 1920.
8ₐ. Jones, Ernest: *The Life and Work of Sigmund Freud,* Vol. III. New York, Basic Books, 1957.
82. ———: *Treatment of the Neuroses.* New York, Wood, 1920.
83. Kaiser, Helmuth: Probleme der Technik. *Internat. Ztschr. f. Psychoanal.*, 20:490–522, 1934.
84. Kant, Immanuel: Von der Macht des Gemüths, durch den blossen Vorsatz seiner krankhaften Gefühle Meister zu sein. *J. d. practischen Arzneykunde u. Wundarzneykunst,* 5:701–751, 1798.
85. Kielholz, Arthur: Vom Kairos. *Schweiz. med. Wschr.*, 86:982–984, 1956.
86. Korzybski, Alfred: *Science and Sanity.* Lakeville, Conn., International non-Aristotelian Library, 1948.
87. Kris, Ernst: On Preconscious Mental Processes. *Psychoanalyt. Quart.*, 19:540–560, 1950.
88. Kubie, L. S.: *Practical Aspects of Psychoanalysis.* New York, Norton, 1936. Second edition was published under the title *Practical and Theoretical Aspects of Psychoanalysis.* New York, International Universities, 1950.
89. Lagache, Daniel: Some Aspects of Transference. *Internat. J. Psycho-Anal.*, 34:1–10, 1953.
89-A. Large, John Ellis: *Think on These Things.* New York, Harper, 1954.

90. Leibniz, G. W. (1704): *Nouveaux essais sur l'entendement humain.* First published in 1765.

91. Lewin, Bertram D.: Dream Psychology and the Analytic Situation. *Psychoanalyt. Quart.*, 24:169–199, 1955.

92. ———: Sleep, Narcissistic Neurosis, and the Analytic Situation. *Psychoanalyt. Quart.*, 23:487–510, 1954.

93. Lifton, Robert J.: "Thought Reform" of Western Civilians in Chinese Communist Prisons. *Psychiatry,* 19:173–195, 1956.

94. Lilly, John C.: Mental Effects of Reduction of Ordinary Levels of Physical Stimuli on Intact, Healthy Persons. *Psychiat. Res. Rep.* 1956, No. 5, 1–9.

95. Little, Margaret: Countertransference and the Patient's Response to It. *Internat. J. Psycho-Anal.,* 32:32–40, 1951.

96. Loewenstein, Rudolph M.: The Problem of Interpretation. *Psychoanalyt. Quart.,* 20:1–14, 1951.

97. ———: Some Remarks on Defences, Autonomous Ego and Psychoanalytic Technique. *Internat. J. Psycho-Anal.,* 35:188–193, 1954.

98. ———: Some Remarks on the Role of Speech in Psychoanalytic Technique. *Internat. J. Psycho-Anal.,* 37:460–468, 1956.

99. Lorand, Sandor: *Technique of Psychoanalytic Therapy.* New York, International Universities, 1946.

100. Macalpine, Ida: The Development of the Transference. *Psychoanalyt. Quart.,* 19:501–539, 1950.

101. ——— and Hunter, Richard A.: *Schizophrenia 1677.* London, Dawson, 1956.

102. McGinley, Phyllis: *Love Letters.* New York, Viking, 1954.

103. Menninger, Karl and Mayman, Martin: Episodic Dyscontrol. *Bull. Menninger Clin.,* 20:153–165, 1956.

104. Menninger, Karl: Impotence and Frigidity from the Standpoint of Psychoanalysis. *J. Urol.,* 34:166–183, 1935.

105. ———: *Love Against Hate.* New York, Harcourt, 1942.

106. ———: Psychological Factors Associated with the Common Cold. *Psychoanalyt. Rev.,* 21:201–207, 1934.

107. ———: Regulatory Devices of the Ego Under Major Stress. *Internat. J. Psycho-Anal.,* 35:412–430, 1954.

108. ———: Somatic Correlations with the Unconscious Repudiation of Femininity in Women. *J. Nerv. & Ment. Dis.,* 89:514–527, 1939. Also in *Bull. Menninger Clin.,* 3:106–121, 1939.

109. ———: Some Observations on the Psychological Factors in Urination and Genitourinary Afflictions. *Psychoanalyt. Rev.,* 28:117–129, 1941.

110. Menninger, William C.: Characterologic and Symptomatic Expressions Related to the Anal Phase of Psychosexual Development. *Psychoanalyt. Quart.,* 12:161–193, 1943.

111. Milner, Marion: A Note on the Ending of Analysis. *Internat. J. Psycho-Anal.,* 31:191–193, 1950.

112. Moloney, James C.: Psychic Self-Abandon and Extortion of Confessions. *Internat. J. Psycho-Anal.,* 36:53–60, 1955.

113. Morgan, Arthur E.: Learning to Learn. Quoted in *Manas,* 11:2, Jan. 22, 1958.

114. Nacht, S.: Introduction au colloque sur les critères de la fin du traitement psychanalytique (Introduction to the Colloquium about the Criteria of the Termination of Psychoanalytic Technique). *Rev. Fr. de Psychanal.,* 18:328–336, 1954.

115. Nunberg, Hermann: *Practice and Theory of Psychoanalysis.* New York, Nervous & Mental Disease Pub. Co., 1948.

116. ——— (1932): *Principles of Psychoanalysis. Their Application to the Neuroses.* New York, International Universities, 1955.

117. ———: Transference and Reality. *Internat. J. Psycho-Anal.,* 32:1–9, 1951.

118. Oberndorf, Clarence P.: *A History of Psychoanalysis in America.* New York, Grune & Stratton, 1953, pp. 15–16.

119. Olinick, Stanley L.: Some Considerations of the Use of Questioning as a Psychoanalytic Technique. *J. Am. Psychoanalyt. A.,* 2:57–66, 1954.

120. Payne, Sylvia: Notes on Developments in the Theory and Practice of Psychoanalytic Technique. *Internat. J. Psycho-Anal.,* 27:12–19, 1946.

121. Plotinus: *The Enneads,* A. Kirchoff, ed. Leipzig, 1856.

122. Racker, Heinrich: The Meanings and Uses of Countertransference. *Psychoanalyt. Quart.,* 26:303–357, 1957.

123. Rado, Sandor: The Economic Principle in Psychoanalytic Technique. *Internat. J. Psycho-Anal.,* 6:35–44, 1925.

124. ———: Recent Advances of Psychoanalytic Therapy. *A. Res. Nerv. & Ment. Dis., Proc.* (1951), 31:42–58, 1953.

125. Rapaport, David. *Organization and Pathology of Thought.* New York, Columbia University, 1951, pp. 689–730.

126. ———: The Theory of Ego Autonomy. *Bull. Menninger Clin.,* 22: 13–35, 1958.

127. Reich, Annie: On Countertransference. *Internat. J. Psycho-Anal.,* 32:25–31, 1951.

128. ———: On the Termination of Analysis. *Internat. J. Psycho-Anal.,* 31:179–183, 1950.

129. Reich, Wilhelm: *Character Analysis.* New York, Orgone Institute, 1933; 2nd Ed., 1945; 3rd Ed., 1949.

130. Reid, John R., and Finesinger, Jacob E.: The Role of Insight in Psychotherapy. *Am. J. Psychiat.,* 108:726–734, 1952.

131. Reider, Norman: Reconstruction and Screen Function. *J. Am. Psychoanalyt. A.,* 1:389–405, 1953.

132. Reik, Theodor: *Listening with the Third Ear.* New York, Farrar, Straus, 1948.

133. ————: *Surprise and the Psychoanalyst.* London, Paul, Trench, Trubner, 1936.

134. Richfield, Jerome: An Analysis of the Concept of Insight. *Psychoanalyt. Quart.,* 23:390–408, 1954.

135. ————: The Role of Philosophy in Theoretical Psychiatry. *Bull. Menninger Clin.,* 17:49–56, 1953.

135-A. Robbins, Lewis L.: A Contribution to the Psychological Understanding of the Character of Don Juan. *Bull. Menninger Clin.* 20:166–180, 1956.

136. Roethlisberger, F. J., and Dickson, W. J.: *Management and the Worker.* Cambridge, Harvard University, 1939.

137. Rogers, Benjamin (tr.): *Fifteen Greek Plays.* New York, New York University Press, 1953, pp. 554, 564, 572–575.

138. Rogers, Carl R.: *Client-Centered Therapy.* Boston, Houghton-Mifflin, 1951.

139. Ruesch, Jurgen: *Disturbed Communication.* New York, Norton, 1957.

140. Sapir, Edward: *Language: An Introduction to the Study of Speech.* New York, Harcourt, 1921.

141. Schein, E. H.: The Chinese Indoctrination Program for Prisoners of War. *Psychiatry,* 19:149–172, 1956.

142. Sechehaye, Marguerite A.: *Symbolic Realization.* New York, International Universities, 1951.

143. Sharpe, Ella: *Collected Papers on Psychoanalysis.* London, Hogarth, 1950.

144. Silverberg, William V.: The Concept of Transference. *Psychoanalyt. Quart.,* 17:303–321, 1948.

145. Solomon, Philip, Leiderman, Herbert, Mendelson, Jack and Wexler, Donald: Sensory Deprivation. *Am. J. Psychiat.,* 114:357–363, Oct. 1957.

146. Spitz, René A.: Countertransference: Comments on Its Varying Role in the Analytic Situation. *J. Am. Psychoanalyt. A.,* 4:256–265, 1956.

147. Sterba, Richard: Character and Resistance. *Psychoanalyt. Quart.,* 20:72–76, 1951.

148. Sullivan, Harry Stack: *Conceptions in Modern Psychiatry.* Washington, William Alanson White Fdn., 1946. Reprinted from *Psychiatry,* 3:1–117, 1940.

149. ————: The Theory of Anxiety and the Nature of Psychotherapy. *Psychiatry,* 12:3–12, 1949.

150. Szasz, Thomas S.: On the Experiences of the Analyst in the Psychoanalytic Situation: A Contribution to the Theory of Psychoanalytic Treatment. *J. Am. Psychoanalyt. A.*, 4:197–223, 1956.

151. Tartakoff, Helen H.: Recent Books on Psychoanalytic Technique. *J. Am. Psychoanalyt. A.*, 4:318–343, 1956.

152. Tillich, Paul: *Kairos.* Darmstadt, Reichl., 1926.

153. Tolstoy, Leo: *War and Peace.* New York, Modern Library, 1931.

154. Tower, Lucia E.: Countertransference. *J. Am. Psychoanalyt. A.*, 4:224–255, 1956.

155. Train, George F.: Flight into Health. *Am. J. Psychotherapy*, 7:463–486, 1953.

156. van der Waals, H. G.: "Narcistische" Problematiek van het Narcisme. *Psychiatrische en Neurolische Blaben,* No. 5/6. 1940.

157. ———: Le Narcissisme. *Rev. Fr. de Psychoanal.*, 13:501–526, 1949.

158. Waelder, Robert: The Function and the Pitfalls of Psychoanalytic Societies. *Bull. Philadelphia A. Psychoanal.*, 5:1–8, 1955.

159. ———: Introduction to the Discussion [of] Problems of Transference. *Internat. J. Psycho-Anal.*, 37:367–368, 1956.

160. Winnicott, D. W.: Hate in Countertransference. *Internat. J. Psycho-Anal.*, 30:69–74, 1949.

161. ———: Metapsychological and Clinical Aspects of Regression Within the Psychoanalytic Set-up. *Internat. J. Psycho-Anal.*, 36:16–26, 1955.

162. Zilboorg, Gregory: *Sigmund Freud.* New York, Scribner's, 1951.

163. ———: Some Sidelights on Free Associations. *Internat. J. Psycho-Anal.*, 33:489–496, 1952.

INDEX

72 73   12 11 10 9 8

hARPER ✷ τORChBOOKS

American Studies: General

HENRY ADAMS Degradation of the Democratic Dogma. ‡ *Introduction by Charles Hirschfeld.* TB/1450

LOUIS D. BRANDEIS: Other People's Money, *and How the Bankers Use It. Ed. with Intro, by Richard M. Abrams* TB/3081

HENRY STEELE COMMAGER, Ed.: The Struggle for Racial Equality TB/1300

CARL N. DEGLER: Out of Our Past: *The Forces that Shaped Modern America* CN/2

CARL N. DEGLER, Ed.: Pivotal Interpretations of American History
Vol. I TB/1240; Vol. II TB/1241

A. S. EISENSTADT, Ed.: The Craft of American History: *Selected Essays*
Vol. I TB/1255; Vol. II TB/1256

LAWRENCE H. FUCHS, Ed.: American Ethnic Politics TB/1368

MARCUS LEE HANSEN: The Atlantic Migration: 1607-1860. *Edited by Arthur M. Schlesinger. Introduction by Oscar Handlin* TB/1052

MARCUS LEE HANSEN: The Immigrant in American History. *Edited with a Foreword by Arthur M. Schlesinger* TB/1120

ROBERT L. HEILBRONER: The Limits of American Capitalism TB/1305

JOHN HIGHAM, Ed.: The Reconstruction of American History TB/1068

ROBERT H. JACKSON: The Supreme Court in the American System of Government TB/1106

JOHN F. KENNEDY: A Nation of Immigrants. *Illus. Revised and Enlarged. Introduction by Robert F. Kennedy* TB/1118

LEONARD W. LEVY, Ed.: American Constitutional Law: *Historical Essays* TB/1285

LEONARD W. LEVY, Ed.: Judicial Review and the Supreme Court TB/1296

LEONARD W. LEVY: The Law of the Commonwealth and Chief Justice Shaw: *The Evolution of American Law, 1830-1860* TB/1309

GORDON K. LEWIS: Puerto Rico: *Freedom and Power in the Caribbean. Abridged edition* TB/1371

HENRY F. MAY: Protestant Churches and Industrial America TB/1334

RICHARD B. MORRIS: Fair Trial: *Fourteen Who Stood Accused, from Anne Hutchinson to Alger Hiss* TB/1335

GUNNAR MYRDAL: An American Dilemma: *The Negro Problem and Modern Democracy. Introduction by the Author.*
Vol. I TB/1443; Vol. II TB/1444

GILBERT OSOFSKY, Ed.: The Burden of Race: *A Documentary History of Negro-White Relations in America* TB/1405

CONYERS READ, Ed.: The Constitution Reconsidered. *Revised Edition. Preface by Richard B. Morris* TB/1384

ARNOLD ROSE: The Negro in America: *The Condensed Version of Gunnar Myrdal's* An American Dilemma. *Second Edition* TB/3048

JOHN E. SMITH: Themes in American Philosophy: *Purpose, Experience and Community* TB/1466

WILLIAM R. TAYLOR: Cavalier and Yankee: *The Old South and American National Character* TB/1474

American Studies: Colonial

BERNARD BAILYN: The New England Merchants in the Seventeenth Century TB/1149

ROBERT E. BROWN: Middle-Class Democracy and Revolution in Massachusetts, 1691-1780. *New Introduction by Author* TB/1413

JOSEPH CHARLES: The Origins of the American Party System TB/1049

HENRY STEELE COMMAGER & ELMO GIORDANETTI, Eds.: Was America a Mistake? *An Eighteenth Century Controversy* TB/1329

WESLEY FRANK CRAVEN: The Colonies in Transition: 1660-1712† TB/3084

CHARLES GIBSON: Spain in America † TB/3077

CHARLES GIBSON, Ed.: The Spanish Tradition in America + HR/1351

LAWRENCE HENRY GIPSON: The Coming of the Revolution: 1763-1775. † *Illus.* TB/3007

JACK P. GREENE, Ed.: Great Britain and the American Colonies: 1606-1763. + *Introduction by the Author* HR/1477

AUBREY C. LAND, Ed.: Bases of the Plantation Society + HR/1429

JOHN LANKFORD, Ed.: Captain John Smith's America: *Selections from his Writings* ‡ TB/3078

LEONARD W. LEVY: Freedom of Speech and Press in Early American History: *Legacy of Suppression* TB/1109

---

† The New American Nation Series, edited by Henry Steele Commager and Richard B. Morris.
‡ American Perspectives series, edited by Bernard Wishy and William E. Leuchtenburg.
a History of Europe series, edited by J. H. Plumb.
§ The Library of Religion and Culture, edited by Benjamin Nelson.
‖ Researches in the Social, Cultural, and Behavioral Sciences, edited by Benjamin Nelson.
Σ Harper Modern Science Series, edited by James A. Newman.
° Not for sale in Canada.
+ Documentary History of the United States series, edited by Richard B. Morris.
# Documentary History of Western Civilization series, edited by Eugene C. Black and Leonard W. Levy.
Λ The Economic History of the United States series, edited by Henry David et al.
¶ European Perspectives series, edited by Eugene C. Black.
** Contemporary Essays series, edited by Leonard W. Levy.
* The Stratum Series, edited by John Hale.

PERRY MILLER: Errand Into the Wilderness
TB/1139
PERRY MILLER & T. H. JOHNSON, Eds.: The Puritans: *A Sourcebook of Their Writings*
Vol. I TB/1093; Vol. II TB/1094
EDMUND S. MORGAN: The Puritan Family: *Religion and Domestic Relations in Seventeenth Century New England* TB/1227
RICHARD B. MORRIS: Government and Labor in Early America TB/1244
WALLACE NOTESTEIN: The English People on the Eve of Colonization: 1603-1630. † *Illus.*
TB/3006
FRANCIS PARKMAN: The Seven Years War: *A Narrative Taken from Montcalm and Wolfe, The Conspiracy of Pontiac, and* A Half-Century of Conflict. *Edited by John H. McCallum* TB/3083
LOUIS B. WRIGHT: The Cultural Life of the American Colonies: 1607-1763. † *Illus.*
TB/3005
YVES F. ZOLTVANY, Ed.: The French Tradition in America + HR/1425

American Studies: The Revolution to 1860

JOHN R. ALDEN: The American Revolution: 1775-1783. † *Illus.* TB/3011
MAX BELOFF, Ed.: The Debate on the American Revolution, 1761-1783: *A Sourcebook*
TB/1225
RAY A. BILLINGTON: The Far Western Frontier: 1830-1860. † *Illus.* TB/3012
STUART BRUCHEY: The Roots of American Economic Growth, 1607-1861: *An Essay in Social Causation. New Introduction by the Author.*
TB/1350
WHITNEY R. CROSS: The Burned-Over District: *The Social and Intellectual History of Enthusiastic Religion in Western New York, 1800-1850* TB/1242
NOBLE E. CUNNINGHAM, JR., Ed.: The Early Republic, 1789-1828 + HR/1394
GEORGE DANGERFIELD: The Awakening of American Nationalism, 1815-1828. † *Illus.*
TB/3061
CLEMENT EATON: The Freedom-of-Thought Struggle in the Old South. *Revised and Enlarged. Illus.* TB/1150
CLEMENT EATON: The Growth of Southern Civilization, 1790-1860. † *Illus.* TB/3040
ROBERT H. FERRELL, Ed.: Foundations of American Diplomacy, 1775-1872 + HR/1393
LOUIS FILLER: The Crusade against Slavery: 1830-1860. † *Illus.* TB/3029
DAVID H. FISCHER: The Revolution of American Conservatism: *The Federalist Party in the Era of Jeffersonian Democracy* TB/1449
WILLIAM W. FREEHLING, Ed.: The Nullification Era: *A Documentary Record* ‡ TB/3079
WILLIM W. FREEHLING: Prelude to Civil War: *The Nullification Controversy in South Carolina, 1816-1836* TB/1359
PAUL W. GATES: The Farmer's Age: *Agriculture, 1815-1860* △ TB/1398
FELIX GILBERT: The Beginnings of American Foreign Policy: *To the Farewell Address*
TB/1200
ALEXANDER HAMILTON: The Reports of Alexander Hamilton. ‡ *Edited by Jacob E. Cooke*
TB/3060
THOMAS JEFFERSON: Notes on the State of Virginia. ‡ *Edited by Thomas P. Abernethy*
TB/3052
FORREST MCDONALD, Ed.: Confederation and Constitution, 1781-1789 + HR/1396

BERNARD MAYO: Myths and Men: *Patrick Henry, George Washington, Thomas Jefferson*
TB/1108
JOHN C. MILLER: Alexander Hamilton and the Growth of the New Nation TB/3057
JOHN C. MILLER: The Federalist Era: 1789-1801. † *Illus.* TB/3027
RICHARD B. MORRIS, Ed.: Alexander Hamilton and the Founding of the Nation. *New Introduction by the Editor* TB/1448
RICHARD B. MORRIS: The American Revolution Reconsidered TB/1363
CURTIS P. NETTELS: The Emergence of a National Economy, 1775-1815 △ TB/1438
DOUGLASS C. NORTH & ROBERT PAUL THOMAS, Eds.: *The Growth of the American Economy to 1860* + HR/1352
R. B. NYE: The Cultural Life of the New Nation: 1776-1830. † *Illus.* TB/3026
GILBERT OSOFSKY, Ed.: Puttin' On Ole Massa: *The Slave Narratives of Henry Bibb, William Wells Brown, and Solomon Northup* ‡
TB/1432
JAMES PARTON: The Presidency of Andrew Jackson. *From Volume III of the* Life of Andrew Jackson. *Ed. with Intro. by Robert V. Remini* TB/3080
FRANCIS S. PHILBRICK: The Rise of the West, 1754-1830. † *Illus.* TB/3067
MARSHALL SMELSER: The Democratic Republic, 1801-1815 † TB/1406
TIMOTHY L. SMITH: Revivalism and Social Reform: *American Protestantism on the Eve of the Civil War* TB/1229
JACK M. SOSIN, Ed.: The Opening of the West + HR/1424
GEORGE ROGERS TAYLOR: The Transportation Revolution, 1815-1860 △ TB/1347
A. F. TYLER: Freedom's Ferment: *Phases of American Social History from the Revolution to the Outbreak of the Civil War. Illus.*
TB/1074
GLYNDON G. VAN DEUSEN: The Jacksonian Era: 1828-1848. † *Illus.* TB/3028
LOUIS B. WRIGHT: Culture on the Moving Frontier TB/1053

American Studies: The Civil War to 1900

W. R. BROCK: An American Crisis: *Congress and Reconstruction, 1865-67* ° TB/1283
T. C. COCHRAN & WILLIAM MILLER: The Age of Enterprise: *A Social History of Industrial America* TB/1054
W. A. DUNNING: Reconstruction, Political and Economic: 1865-1877 TB/1073
HAROLD U. FAULKNER: Politics, Reform and Expansion: 1890-1900. † *Illus.* TB/3020
GEORGE M. FREDRICKSON: The Inner Civil War: *Northern Intellectuals and the Crisis of the Union* TB/1358
JOHN A. GARRATY: The New Commonwealth, 1877-1890 † TB/1410
JOHN A. GARRATY, Ed.: The Transformation of American Society, 1870-1890 + HR/1395
WILLIAM R. HUTCHISON, Ed.: American Protestant Thought: *The Liberal Era* ‡ TB/1385
HELEN HUNT JACKSON: A Century of Dishonor: *The Early Crusade for Indian Reform.* † *Edited by Andrew F. Rolle* TB/3063
ALBERT D. KIRWAN: Revolt of the Rednecks: *Mississippi Politics, 1876-1925* TB/1199
WILLIAM G. MCLOUGHLIN, Ed.: The American Evangelicals, 1800-1900: An Anthology ‡
TB/1382
ARTHUR MANN: Yankee Reforms in the Urban Age: *Social Reform in Boston, 1800-1900*
TB/1247

ARNOLD M. PAUL: Conservative Crisis and the Rule of Law: *Attitudes of Bar and Bench, 1887-1895*. New Introduction by Author
TB/1415

JAMES S. PIKE: The Prostrate State: *South Carolina under Negro Government.* ‡ *Intro. by Robert F. Durden*
TB/3085

WHITELAW REID: After the War: *A Tour of the Southern States, 1865-1866.* ‡ *Edited by C. Vann Woodward*
TB/3066

FRED A. SHANNON: The Farmer's Last Frontier: *....Agriculture, 1860-1897*
TB/1348

VERNON LANE WHARTON: The Negro in Mississippi, 1865-1890
TB/1178

American Studies: The Twentieth Century

RICHARD M. ABRAMS, Ed.: The Issues of the Populist and Progressive Eras, 1892-1912 +
HR/1428

RAY STANNARD BAKER: Following the Color Line: *American Negro Citizenship in Progressive Era.* ‡ *Edited by Dewey W. Grantham, Jr. Illus.*
TB/3053

RANDOLPH S. BOURNE: War and the Intellectuals: *Collected Essays, 1915-1919.* ‡ *Edited by Carl Resek*
TB/3043

A. RUSSELL BUCHANAN: The United States and World War II. † *Illus.*
Vol. I TB/3044; Vol. II TB/3045

THOMAS C. COCHRAN: The American Business System: *A Historical Perspective, 1900-1955*
TB/1080

FOSTER RHEA DULLES: America's Rise to World Power: 1898-1954. † *Illus.*
TB/3021

JEAN-BAPTISTE DUROSELLE: From Wilson to Roosevelt: *Foreign Policy of the United States, 1913-1945. Trans. by Nancy Lyman Roelker*
TB/1370

HAROLD U. FAULKNER: The Decline of Laissez Faire, 1897-1917
TB/1397

JOHN D. HICKS: Republican Ascendancy: 1921-1933. † *Illus.*
TB/3041

ROBERT HUNTER: Poverty: *Social Conscience in the Progressive Era.* ‡ *Edited by Peter d'A. Jones*
TB/3065

WILLIAM E. LEUCHTENBURG: Franklin D. Roosevelt and the New Deal: 1932-1940. † *Illus.*
TB/3025

WILLIAM E. LEUCHTENBURG, Ed.: The New Deal: *A Documentary History* +
HR/1354

ARTHUR S. LINK: Woodrow Wilson and the Progressive Era: 1910-1917. † *Illus.*
TB/3023

BROADUS MITCHELL: Depression Decade: *From New Era through New Deal, 1929-1941* Λ
TB/1439

GEORGE E. MOWRY: The Era of Theodore Roosevelt and the Birth of Modern America: 1900-1912. † *Illus.*
TB/3022

WILLIAM PRESTON, JR.: Aliens and Dissenters: *Federal Suppression of Radicals, 1903-1933*
TB/1287

WALTER RAUSCHENBUSCH: Christianity and the Social Crisis. ‡ *Edited by Robert D. Cross*
TB/3059

GEORGE SOULE: Prosperity Decade: *From War to Depression, 1917-1929* Λ
TB/1349

GEORGE B. TINDALL, Ed.: A Populist Reader: *Selections from the Works of American Populist Leaders*
TB/3069

TWELVE SOUTHERNERS: I'll Take My Stand: *The South and the Agrarian Tradition. Intro. by Louis D. Rubin, Jr.; Biographical Essays by Virginia Rock*
TB/1072

Art, Art History, Aesthetics

CREIGHTON GILBERT, Ed.: Renaissance Art **
Illus.
TB/1465

EMILE MALE: The Gothic Image: *Religious Art in France of the Thirteenth Century.* § *190 illus.*
TB/344

MILLARD MEISS: Painting in Florence and Siena After the Black Death: *The Arts, Religion and Society in the Mid-Fourteenth Century. 169 illus.*
TB/1148

ERWIN PANOFSKY: Renaissance and Renascences in Western Art. *Illus.*
TB/1447

ERWIN PANOFSKY: Studies in Iconology: *Humanistic Themes in the Art of the Renaissance. 180 illus.*
TB/1077

JEAN SEZNEC: The Survival of the Pagan Gods: *The Mythological Tradition and Its Place in Renaissance Humanism and Art. 108 illus.*
TB/2004

OTTO VON SIMSON: The Gothic Cathedral: *Origins of Gothic Architecture and the Medieval Concept of Order. 58 illus.*
TB/2018

HEINRICH ZIMMER: Myths and Symbols in Indian Art and Civilization. *70 illus.*
TB/2005

Asian Studies

WOLFGANG FRANKE: China and the West: *The Cultural Encounter, 13th to 20th Centuries. Trans. by R. A. Wilson*
TB/1326

L. CARRINGTON GOODRICH: A Short History of the Chinese People. *Illus.*
TB/3015

DAN N. JACOBS, Ed.: The New Communist Manifesto and Related Documents. *3rd revised edn.*
TB/1078

DAN N. JACOBS & HANS H. BAERWALD, Eds.: Chinese Communism: *Selected Documents*
TB/3031

BENJAMIN I. SCHWARTZ: Chinese Communism and the Rise of Mao
TB/1308

BENJAMIN I. SCHWARTZ: In Search of Wealth and Power: *Yen Fu and the West*
TB/1422

Economics & Economic History

C. E. BLACK: The Dynamics of Modernization: *A Study in Comparative History*
TB/1321

STUART BRUCHEY: The Roots of American Economic Growth, 1607-1861: *An Essay in Social Causation. New Introduction by the Author.*
TB/1350

GILBERT BURCK & EDITORS OF *Fortune:* The Computer Age: *And its Potential for Management*
TB/1179

JOHN ELLIOTT CAIRNES: The Slave Power. ‡ *Edited with Introduction by Harold D. Woodman*
TB/1433

SHEPARD B. CLOUGH, THOMAS MOODIE & CAROL MOODIE, Eds.: Economic History of Europe: *Twentieth Century* #
HR/1388

THOMAS C. COCHRAN: The American Business System: *A Historical Perspective, 1900-1955*
TB/1180

ROBERT A. DAHL & CHARLES E. LINDBLOM: Politics, Economics, and Welfare: *Planning and Politico-Economic Systems Resolved into Basic Social Processes*
TB/3037

PETER F. DRUCKER: The New Society: *The Anatomy of Industrial Order*
TB/1082

HAROLD U. FAULKNER: The Decline of Laissez Faire, 1897-1917 Λ
TB/1397

PAUL W. GATES: The Farmer's Age: *Agriculture, 1815-1860* Λ
TB/1398

WILLIAM GREENLEAF, Ed.: American Economic Development Since 1860 +
HR/1353

J. L. & BARBARA HAMMOND: The Rise of Modern Industry. || *Introduction by R. M. Hartwell*
TB/1417

3

ROBERT L. HEILBRONER: The Future as History: *The Historic Currents of Our Time and the Direction in Which They Are Taking America* TB/1386

ROBERT L. HEILBRONER: The Great Ascent: *The Struggle for Economic Development in Our Time* TB/3030

FRANK H. KNIGHT: The Economic Organization TB/1214

DAVID S. LANDES: Bankers and Pashas: *International Finance and Economic Imperialism in Egypt. New Preface by the Author* TB/1412

ROBERT LATOUCHE: The Birth of Western Economy: *Economic Aspects of the Dark Ages* TB/1290

ABBA P. LERNER: Everbody's Business: *A Reexamination of Current Assumptions in Economics and Public Policy* TB/3051

W. ARTHUR LEWIS: Economic Survey, 1919-1939 TB/1446

W. ARTHUR LEWIS: The Principles of Economic Planning. *New Introduction by the Author*° TB/1436

ROBERT GREEN MC CLOSKEY: American Conservatism in the Age of Enterprise TB/1137

PAUL MANTOUX: The Industrial Revolution in the Eighteenth Century: *An Outline of the Beginnings of the Modern Factory System in England*° TB/1079

WILLIAM MILLER, Ed.: Men in Business: *Essays on the Historical Role of the Entrepreneur* TB/1081

GUNNAR MYRDAL: An International Economy. *New Introduction by the Author* TB/1445

HERBERT A. SIMON: The Shape of Automation: *For Men and Management* TB/1245

PERRIN STRYER: The Character of the Executive: *Eleven Studies in Managerial Qualities* TB/1041

RICHARD S. WECKSTEIN, Ed.: Expansion of World Trade and the Growth of National Economies ** TB/1373

Education

JACQUES BARZUN: The House of Intellect TB/1051

RICHARD M. JONES, Ed.: Contemporary Educational Psychology: *Selected Readings* ** TB/1292

CLARK KERR: The Uses of the University TB/1264

Historiography and History of Ideas

HERSCHEL BAKER: The Image of Man: *A Study of the Idea of Human Dignity in Classical Antiquity, the Middle Ages, and the Renaissance* TB/1047

J. BRONOWSKI & BRUCE MAZLISH: The Western Intellectual Tradition: *From Leonardo to Hegel* TB/3001

EDMUND BURKE: On Revolution. Ed. by Robert A. Smith TB/1401

WILHELM DILTHEY: Pattern and Meaning in History: *Thoughts on History and Society.*° *Edited with an Intro. by H. P. Rickman* TB/1075

ALEXANDER GRAY: The Socialist Tradition: *Moses to Lenin* ° TB/1375

J. H. HEXTER: More's Utopia: *The Biography of an Idea. Epilogue by the Author* TB/1195

H. STUART HUGHES: History as Art and as Science: *Twin Vistas on the Past* TB/1207

ARTHUR O. LOVEJOY: The Great Chain of Being: *A Study of the History of an Idea* TB/1009

JOSE ORTEGA Y GASSET: The Modern Theme. *Introduction by Jose Ferrater Mora* TB/1038

RICHARD H. POPKIN: The History of Scepticism from Erasmus to Descartes. *Revised Edition* TB/1391

G. J. RENIER: History: *Its Purpose and Method* TB/1209

MASSIMO SALVADORI, Ed.: Modern Socialism # HR/1374

GEORG SIMMEL et al.: Essays on Sociology, Philosophy and Aesthetics. *Edited by Kurt H. Wolff* TB/1234

BRUNO SNELL: The Discovery of the Mind: *The Greek Origins of European Thought* TB/1018

W. WARREN WAGER, ed.: European Intellectual History Since Darwin and Marx TB/1297

W. H. WALSH: Philosophy of History: In Introduction TB/1020

History: General

HANS KOHN: The Age of Nationalism: *The First Era of Global History* TB/1380

BERNARD LEWIS: The Arabs in History TB/1029

BERNARD LEWIS: The Middle East and the West ° TB/1274

History: Ancient

A. ANDREWS: The Greek Tyrants TB/1103

ERNST LUDWIG EHRLICH: A Concise History of Israel: *From the Earliest Times to the Destruction of the Temple in A.D. 70* ° TB/128

ADOLF ERMAN, Ed.: The Ancient Egyptians: *A Sourcebook of their Writings. New Introduction by William Kelly Simpson* TB/1233

THEODOR H. GASTER: Thespis: *Ritual Myth and Drama in the Ancient Near East* TB/1281

MICHAEL GRANT: Ancient History ° TB/1190

A. H. M. JONES, Ed.: A History of Rome through the Fifgth Century # *Vol. I: The Republic* HR/1364

Vol. II The Empire: HR/1460

SAMUEL NOAH KRAMER: Sumerian Mythology TB/1055

NAPHTALI LEWIS & MEYER REINHOLD, Eds.: Roman Civilization *Vol. I: The Republic* TB/1231

Vol. II: The Empire TB/1232

History: Medieval

MARSHALL W. BALDWIN, Ed.: Christianity Through the 13th Century # HR/1468

MARC BLOCH: Land and Work in Medieval Europe. *Translated by J. E. Anderson* TB/1452

HELEN CAM: England Before Elizabeth TB/1026

NORMAN COHN: The Pursuit of the Millennium: *Revolutionary Messianism in Medieval and Reformation Europe* TB/1037

G. G. COULTON: Medieval Village, Manor, and Monastery HR/1022

HEINRICH FICHTENAU: The Carolingian Empire: *The Age of Charlemagne. Translated with an Introduction by Peter Munz* TB/1142

GALBERT OF BRUGES: The Murder of Charles the Good: *A Contemporary Record of Revolutionary Change in 12th Century Flanders. Translated with an Introduction by James Bruce Ross* TB/1311

F. L. GANSHOF: Feudalism TB/1058

F. L. GANSHOF: The Middle Ages: *A History of International Relations. Translated by Rémy Hall* TB/1411

W. O. HASSALL, Ed.: Medieval England: *As Viewed by Contemporaries* TB/1205

DENYS HAY: The Medieval Centuries ° TB/1192

DAVID HERLIHY, Ed.: Medieval Culture and Socitey # HR/1340

4

J. M. HUSSEY: The Byzantine World TB/1057
ROBERT LATOUCHE: The Birth of Western Economy: *Economic Aspects of the Dark Ages* ° TB/1290
HENRY CHARLES LEA: The Inquisition of the Middle Ages. || *Introduction by Walter Ullmann* TB/1456
FERDINAND LOT: The End of the Ancient World and the Beginnings of the Middle Ages. *Introduction by Glanville Downey* TB/1044
H. R. LOYN: The Norman Conquest TB/1457
ACHILLE LUCHAIRE: Social France at the time of Philip Augustus. *Intro. by John W. Baldwin* TB/1314
GUIBERT DE NOGENT: Self and Society in Medieval France: *The Memoirs of Guibert de Nogent.* || Edited by John F. Benton TB/1471
MARSILIUS OF PADUA: The Defender of Peace. *The Defensor Pacis. Translated with an Introduction by Alan Gewirth* TB/1310
CHARLES PETET-DUTAILLIS: The Feudal Monarchy in France and England: *From the Tenth to the Thirteenth Century* ° TB/1165
STEVEN RUNCIMAN: A History of the Crusades Vol. I: *The First Crusade and the Foundation of the Kingdom of Jerusalem. Illus.* TB/1143
Vol. II: *The Kingdom of Jerusalem and the Frankish East 1100-1187. Illus.* TB/1243
Vol. III: *The Kingdom of Acre and the Later Crusades. Illus.* TB/1298
J. M. WALLACE-HADRILL: The Barbarian West: *The Early Middle Ages, A.D. 400-1000* TB/1061

History: Renaissance & Reformation

JACOB BURCKHARDT: The Civilization of the Renaissance in Italy. *Introduction by Benjamin Nelson and Charles Trinkaus. Illus.* Vol. I TB/40; Vol. II TB/41
JOHN CALVIN & JACOPO SADOLETO: A Reformation Debate. *Edited by John C. Olin* TB/1239
FEDERICO CHABOD: Machiavelli and the Renaissance TB/1193
THOMAS CROMWELL: Thomas Cromwell on Church and Commonwealth,: *Selected Letters 1523-1540.* ¶ *Ed. with an Intro. by Arthur J. Slavin* TB/1462
⟩R. TREVOR DAVIES: The Golden Century of Spain, 1501-1621 ° TB/1194
J. H. ELLIOTT: Europe Divided, 1559-1598 *a* ° TB/1414
G. R. ELTON: Reformation Europe, 1517-1559 ° *a* TB/1270
DESIDERIUS ERASMUS: Christian Humanism and the Reformation: *Selected Writings. Edited and Translated by John C. Olin* TB/1166
DESIDERIUS ERASMUS: Erasmus and His Age: *Selected Letters. Edited with an Introduction by Hans J. Hillerbrand. Translated by Marcus A. Haworth* TB/1461
WALLACE K. FERGUSON et al.: Facets of the Renaissance TB/1098
WALLACE K. FERGUSON et al.: The Renaissance: *Six Essays. Illus.* TB/1084
FRANCESCO GUICCIARDINI: History of Florence. *Translated with an Introduction and Notes by Mario Domandi* TB/1470
WERNER L. GUNDERSHEIMER, Ed.: French Humanism, 1470-1600. * *Illus.* TB/1473
MARIE BOAS HALL, Ed.: Nature and Nature's Laws: *Documents of the Scientific Revolution* # HR/1420
HANS J. HILLERBRAND, Ed., The Protestant Reformation # HR/1342
JOHAN HUIZINGA: Erasmus and the Age of Reformation. *Illus.* TB/19

JOEL HURSTFIELD: The Elizabethan Nation TB/1312
JOEL HURSTFIELD, Ed.: The Reformation Crisis TB/1267
PAUL OSKAR KRISTELLER: Renaissance Thought: *The Classic, Scholastic, and Humanist Strains* TB/1048
PAUL OSKAR KRISTELLER: Renaissance Thought II: *Papers on Humanism and the Arts* TB/1163
PAUL O. KRISTELLER & PHILIP P. WIENER, Eds.: Renaissance Essays TB/1392
DAVID LITTLE: Religion, Order and Law: *A Study in Pre-Revolutionary England.* § *Preface by R. Bellah* TB/1418
NICCOLO MACHIAVELLI: History of Florence and of the Affairs of Italy: *From the Earliest Times to the Death of Lorenzo the Magnificent. Introduction by Felix Gilbert* TB/1027
ALFRED VON MARTIN: Sociology of the Renaissance. ° *Introduction by W. K. Ferguson* TB/1099
GARRETT MATTINGLY et al.: Renaissance Profiles. *Edited by J. H. Plumb* TB/1162
J. E. NEALE: The Age of Catherine de Medici ° TB/1085
J. H. PARRY: The Establishment of the European Hegemony: 1415-1715: *Trade and Exploration in the Age of the Renaissance* TB/1045
J. H. PARRY, Ed.: The European Reconnaissance: *Selected Documents* # HR/1345
BUONACCORSO PITTI & GREGORIO DATI: Two Memoirs of Renaissance Florence: *The Diaries of Buonaccorso Pitti and Gregorio Dati. Edited with Intro. by Gene Brucker. Trans. by Julia Martines* TB/1333
J. H. PLUMB: The Italian Renaissance: *A Concise Survey of Its History and Culture* TB/1161
A. F. POLLARD: Henry VIII. *Introduction by A. G. Dickens.* ° TB/1249
RICHARD H. POPKIN: The History of Scepticism from Erasmus to Descartes TB/139
PAOLO ROSSI: Philosophy, Technology, and the Arts, in the Early Modern Era 1400-1700. || *Edited by Benjamin Nelson. Translated by Salvator Attanasio* TB/1458
FERDINAND SCHEVILL: The Medici. *Illus.* TB/1010
FERDINAND SCHEVILL: Medieval and Renaissance Florence. *Illus.* Vol. I: *Medieval Florence* TB/1090
Vol. II: *The Coming of Humanism and the Age of the Medici* TB/1091
R. H. TAWNEY: The Agrarian Problem in the Sixteenth Century. *Intro. by Lawrence Stone* TB/1315
H. R. TREVOR-ROPER: The European Witch-craze of the Sixteenth and Seventeenth Centuries and Other Essays ° TB/1416
VESPASIANO: Rennaissance Princes, Popes, and XVth Century: *The Vespasiano Memoirs. Introduction by Myron P. Gilmore. Illus.* TB/1111

History: Modern European

RENE ALBRECHT-CARRIE, Ed.: The Concert of Europe # HR/1341
MAX BELOFF: The Age of Absolutism, 1660-1815 TB/1062
OTTO VON BISMARCK: Reflections and Reminiscences. *Ed. with Intro. by Theodore S. Hamerow* ¶ TB/1357
EUGENE C. BLACK, Ed.: British Politics in the Nineteenth Century # HR/1427

EUGENE C. BLACK, Ed.: European Political History, 1815-1870: *Aspects of Liberalism* ¶ TB/1331

ASA BRIGGS: The Making of Modern England, 1783-1867: *The Age of Improvement* ° TB/1203

D. W. BROGAN: The Development of Modern France ° Vol. I: *From the Fall of the Empire to the Dreyfus Affair* TB/1184
Vol. II: *The Shadow of War, World War I, Between the Two Wars* TB/1185

ALAN BULLOCK: Hitler, A Study in Tyranny. ° *Revised Edition. Illus.* TB/1123

EDMUND BURKE: On Revolution. *Ed. by Robert A. Smith* TB/1401

E. R. CARR: International Relations Between the Two World Wars. 1919-1939 ° TB/1279

E. H. CARR: The Twenty Years' Crisis, 1919-1939: *An Introduction to the Study of International Relations* ° TB/1122

GORDON A. CRAIG: From Bismarck to Adenauer: *Aspects of German Statecraft. Revised Edition* TB/1171

LESTER G. CROCKER, Ed.: The Age of Enlightenment # HR/1423

DENIS DIDEROT: The Encyclopedia: *Selections. Edited and Translated with Introduction by Stephen Gendzier* TB/1299

JACQUES DROZ: Europe between Revolutions, 1815-1848. ° *a Trans. by Robert Baldick* TB/1346

JOHANN GOTTLIEB FICHTE: Addresses to the German Nation. *Ed. with Intro. by George A. Kelly* ¶ TB/1366

FRANKLIN L. FORD: Robe and Sword: *The Re-Louis XIV* TB/1217

ROBERT & ELBORG FORSTER, Eds.: European Society in the Eighteenth Century # HR/1404

C. C. GILLISPIE: Genesis and Geology: *The Decades before Darwin* § TB/51

ALBERT GOODWIN, Ed.: The European Nobility in the Enghteenth Century TB/1313

ALBERT GOODWIN: The French Revolution TB/1064

ALBERT GUERARD: France in the Classical Age: *The Life and Death of an Ideal* TB/1183

JOHN B. HALSTED, Ed.: Romanticism # HR/1387

J. H. HEXTER: Reappraisals in History: *New Views on History and Society in Early Modern Europe* ° TB/1100

STANLEY HOFFMANN et al.: In Search of France: *The Economy, Society and Political System In the Twentieth Century* TB/1219

H. STUART HUGHES: The Obstructed Path: *French Social Thought in the Years of Desperation* TB/1451

JOHAN HUIZINGA: Dutch Civilisation in the 17th Century and Other Essays TB/1453

LIONAL KOCHAN: The Struggle for Germany: *1914-45* TB/1304

HANS KOHN: The Mind of Germany: *The Education of a Nation* TB/1204

HANS KOHN, Ed.: The Mind of Modern Russia: *Historical and Political Thought of Russia's Great Age* TB/1065

WALTER LAQUEUR & GEORGE L. MOSSE, Eds.: Education and Social Structure in the 20th Century. ° *Volume 6 of the Journal of Contemporary History* TB/1339

WALTER LAQUEUR & GEORGE L. MOSSE, Ed.: International Fascism, 1920-1945. ° *Volume 1 of the* Journal of Contemporary History TB/1276

WALTER LAQUEUR & GEORGE L. MOSSE, Eds.: Literature and Politics in the 20th Century. ° *Volume 5 of the* Journal of Contemporary History. TB/1328

WALTER LAQUEUR & GEORGE L. MOSSE, Eds.: The New History: *Trends in Historical Research and Writing Since World War II.* ° *Volume 4 of the* Journal of Contemporary History TB/1327

WALTER LAQUEUR & GEORGE L. MOSSE, Eds.: 1914: *The Coming of the First World War.* ° *Volume3 of the* Journal of Contemporary History TB/1306

C. A. MACARTNEY, Ed.: The Habsburg and Hohenzollern Dynasties in the Seventeenth and Eighteenth Centuries # HR/1400

JOHN MCMANNERS: European History, 1789-1914: *Men, Machines and Freedom* TB/1419

PAUL MANTOUX: The Industrial Revolution in the Eighteenth Century: *An Outline of the Beginnings of the Modern Factory System in England* TB/1079

FRANK E. MANUEL: The Prophets of Paris: *Turgot, Condorcet, Saint-Simon, Fourier, and Comte* TB/1218

KINGSLEY MARTIN: French Liberal Thought in the Eighteenth Century: *A Study of Political Ideas from Bayle to Condorcet* TB/1114

NAPOLEON III: Napoleonic Ideas: *Des Idées Napoléoniennes, par le Prince Napoléon-Louis Bonaparte. Ed. by Brison D. Gooch* ¶ TB/1336

FRANZ NEUMANN: Behemoth: *The Structure and Practice of National Socialism, 1933-1944* TB/1289

DAVID OGG: Europe of the Ancien Régime, 1715-1783 ° *a* TB/1271

GEORGE RUDE: Revolutionary Europe, 1783-1815 ° *a* TB/1272

MASSIMO SALVADORI, Ed.: Modern Socialism # TB/1374

HUGH SETON-WATSON: Eastern Europe Between the Wars, 1918-1941 TB/1330

DENIS MACK SMITH, Ed.: The Making of Italy, 1796-1870 # HR/1356

ALBERT SOREL: Europe Under the Old Regime. *Translated by Francis H. Herrick* TB/1121

ROLAND N. STROMBERG, Ed.: Realism, Naturalism, and Symbolism: *Modes of Thought and Expression in Europe, 1848-1914* # HR/1355

A. J. P. TAYLOR: From Napoleon to Lenin: *Historical Essays* ° TB/1268

A. J. P. TAYLOR: The Habsburg Monarchy, 1809-1918: *A History of the Austrian Empire and Austria-Hungary* ° TB/1187

J. M. THOMPSON: European History, 1494-1789 TB/1431

DAVID THOMSON, Ed.: France: Empire and Republic, 1850-1940 # HR/1387

ALEXIS DE TOCQUEVILLE & GUSTAVE DE BEAUMONT: Tocqueville and Beaumont on Social Reform. *Ed. and trans. with Intro. by Seymour Drescher* TB/1343

G. M. TREVELYAN: British History in the Nineteenth Century and After: 1792-1919 ° TB/1251

H. R. TREVOR-ROPER: Historical Essays ° TB/1269

W. WARREN WAGAR, Ed.: Science, Faith, and MAN: *European Thought Since 1914* # HR/1362

MACK WALKER, Ed.: Metternich's Europe, 1813-1848 # HR/1361

ELIZABETH WISKEMANN: Europe of the Dictators, 1919-1945 ° *a* TB/1273

JOHN B. WOLF: France: 1814-1919: *The Rise of a Liberal-Democratic Society* TB/3019

Literature & Literary Criticism

JACQUES BARZUN: The House of Intellect TB/1051

W. J. BATE: From Classic to Romantic: *Premises of Taste in Eighteenth Century England* TB/1036

VAN WYCK BROOKS: Van Wyck Brooks: The Early Years: *A Selection from his Works, 1908-1921* Ed. with Intro. by Claire Sprague TB/3082

ERNST R. CURTIUS: European Literature and the Latin Middle Ages. *Trans. by Willard Trask* TB/2015

RICHMOND LATTIMORE, Translator: The Odyssey of Homer TB/1389

JOHN STUART MILL: On Bentham and Coleridge. *Introduction by F. R. Leavis* TB/1070

SAMUEL PEPYS: The Diary of Samuel Pepys. ° *Edited by O. F. Morshead. 60 illus. by Ernest Shepard* TB/1007

ROBERT PREYER, Ed.: Victorian Literature ** TB/1302

ALBION W. TOURGEE: A Fool's Errand: *A Novel of the South during Reconstruction. Intro. by George Fredrickson* TB/3074

BASIL WILEY: Nineteenth Century Studies: *Coleridge to Matthew Arnold* ° TB/1261

RAYMOND WILLIAMS: Culture and Society, 1780-1950 ° TB/1252

Philosophy

HENRI BERGSON: Time and Free Will: *An Essay on the Immediate Data of Consciousness* ° TB/1021

LUDWIG BINSWANGER: Being-in-the-World: *Selected Papers. Trans. with Intro. by Jacob Needleman* TB/1365

H. J. BLACKHAM: Six Existentialist Thinkers: *Kierkegaard, Nietzsche, Jaspers, Marcel, Heidegger, Sartre* ° TB/1002

J. M. BOCHENSKI: The Methods of Contemporary Thought. *Trans. by Peter Caws* TB/1377

CRANE BRINTON: Nietzsche. *Preface, Bibliography, and Epilogue by the Author* TB/1197

ERNST CASSIRER: Rousseau, Kant and Goethe. *Intro. by Peter Gay* TB/1092

FREDERICK COPLESTON, S. J.: Medieval Philosophy TB/376

F. M. CORNFORD: From Religion to Philosophy: *A Study in the Origins of Western Speculation* § TB/20

WILFRID DESAN: The Tragic Finale: *An Essay on the Philosophy of Jean-Paul Sartre* TB/1030

MARVIN FARBER: The Aims of Phenomenology: *The Motives, Methods, and Impact of Husserl's Thought* TB/1291

MARVIN FARBER: Basic Issues of Philosophy: *Experience, Reality, and Human Values* TB/1344

MARVIN FARBER: Phenomenology and Existence: *Towards a Philosophy within Nature* TB/1295

PAUL FRIEDLANDER: Plato: *An Introduction* TB/2017

MICHAEL GELVEN: A Commentary on Heidegger's "Being and Time" TB/1464

J. GLENN GRAY: Hegel and Greek Thought TB/1409

W. K. C. GUTHRIE: The Greek Philosophers: *From Thales to Aristotle* ° TB/1008

G. W. F. HEGEL: On Art, Religion Philosophy: *Introductory Lectures to the Realm of Absolute Spirit.* || *Edited with an Introduction by J. Glenn Gray* TB/1463

G. W. F. HEGEL: Phenomenology of Mind. ° || *Introduction by George Lichtheim* TB/1303

MARTIN HEIDEGGER: Discourse on Thinking. *Translated with a Preface by John M. Anderson and E. Hans Freund. Introduction by John M. Anderson* TB/1459

F. H. HEINEMANN: Existentialism and the Modern Predicament TB/28

WERNER HEISENBERG: Physics and Philosophy: *The Revolution in Modern Science. Intro. by F. S. C. Northrop* TB/549

EDMUND HUSSERL: Phenomenology and the Crisis of Philosophy. § *Translated with an Introduction by Quentin Lauer* TB/1170

IMMANUEL KANT: Groundwork of the Metaphysic of Morals. *Translated and Analyzed by H. J. Paton* TB/1159

IMMANUEL KANT: Lectures on Ethics. § *Introduction by Lewis White Beck* TB/105

WALTER KAUFMANN, Ed.: Religion From Tolstoy to Camus: *Basic Writings on Religious Truth and Morals* TB/123

QUENTIN LAUER: Phenomenology: *Its Genesis and Prospect. Preface by Aron Gurwitsch* TB/1169

MAURICE MANDELBAUM: The Problem of Historical Knowledge: *An Answer to Relativism* TB/1338

GEORGE A. MORGAN: What Nietzsche Means TB/1198

H. J. PATON: The Categorical Imperative: *A Study in Kant's Moral Philosophy* TB/1325

MICHAEL POLANYI: Personal Knowledge: *Towards a Post-Critical Philosophy* TB/1158

KARL R. POPPER: Conjectures and Refutations: *The Growth of Scientific Knowledge* TB/1376

WILLARD VAN ORMAN QUINE: Elementary Logic *Revised Edition* TB/577

WILLARD VAN ORMAN QUINE: From a Logical Point of View: *Logico-Philosophical Essays* TB/566

JOHN E. SMITH: Themes in American Philosophy: *Purpose, Experience and Community* TB/1466

MORTON WHITE: Foundations of Historical Knowledge TB/1440

WILHELM WINDELBAND: A History of Philosophy *Vol. I: Greek, Roman, Medieval* TB/38 *Vol. II: Renaissance, Enlightenment, Modern* TB/39

LUDWIG WITTGENSTEIN: The Blue and Brown Books ° TB/1211

LUDWIG WITTGENSTEIN: Notebooks, 1914-1916 TB/1441

Political Science & Government

C. E. BLACK: The Dynamics of Modernization: *A Study in Comparative History* TB/1321

KENNETH E. BOULDING: Conflict and Defense: *A General Theory of Action* TB/3024

DENIS W. BROGAN: Politics in America. *New Introduction by the Author* TB/1469

CRANE BRINTON: English Political Thought in the Nineteenth Century TB/1071

ROBERT CONQUEST: Power and Policy in the USSR: *The Study of Soviet Dynastics* ° TB/1307

ROBERT A. DAHL & CHARLES E. LINDBLOM: Politics, Economics, and Welfare: *Planning and Politico-Economic Systems Resolved into Basic Social Processes* TB/1277

HANS KOHN: Political Ideologies of the 20th Century TB/1277

ROY C. MACRIDIS, Ed.: Political Parties: *Contemporary Trends and Ideas* ** TB/1322

ROBERT GREEN MC CLOSKEY: American Conservatism in the Age of Enterprise, 1865-1910 TB/1137

MARSILIUS OF PADUA: The Defender of Peace. *The Defensor Pacis. Translated with an Introduction by Alan Gewirth* TB/1310

KINGSLEY MARTIN: French Liberal Thought in the Eighteenth Century: *A Study of Political Ideas from Bayle to Condorcet* TB/1114

BARRINGTON MOORE, JR.: Political Power and Social Theory: *Seven Studies* || TB/1221

BARRINGTON MOORE, JR.: Soviet Politics—The Dilemma of Power: *The Role of Ideas in Social Change* || TB/1222

BARRINGTON MOORE, JR.: Terror and Progress—USSR: *Some Sources of Change and Stability*

JOHN B. MORRALL: Political Thought in Medieval Times TB/1076

KARL R. POPPER: The Open Society and Its Enemies *Vol. I: The Spell of Plato* TB/1101 *Vol. II: The High Tide of Prophecy: Hegel, Marx, and the Aftermath* TB/1102

CONYERS READ, Ed.: The Constitution Reconsidered. *Revised Edition, Preface by Richard B. Morris* TB/1384

JOHN P. ROCHE, Ed.: Origins of American Political Thought: *Selected Readings* TB/1301

JOHN P. ROCHE, Ed.: American Political Thought: *From Jefferson to Progressivism* TB/1332

HENRI DE SAINT-SIMON: Social Organization, The Science of Man, and Other Writings. || *Edited and Translated with an Introduction by Felix Markham* TB/1152

CHARLES SCHOTTLAND, Ed.: The Welfare State ** TB/1323

JOSEPH A. SCHUMPETER: Capitalism, Socialism and Democracy TB/3008

PETER WOLL, Ed.: Public Administration and Policy: *Selected Essays* TB/1284

Psychology

ALFRED ADLER: The Individual Psychology of Alfred Adler: *A Systematic Presentation in Selections from His Writings. Edited by Heinz L. & Rowena R. Ansbacher* TB/1154

ALFRED ADLER: Problems of Neurosis: *A Book of Case Histories. Introduction by Heinz L. Ansbacher* TB/1145

LUDWIG BINSWANGER: Being-in-the-World: *Selected Papers.* || *Trans. with Intro. by Jacob Needleman* TB/1365

ARTHUR BURTON & ROBERT E. HARRIS: Clinical Studies of Personality Vol. I TB/3075 Vol. II TB/3076

HADLEY CANTRIL: The Invasion from Mars: *A Study in the Psychology of Panic* || TB/1282

MIRCEA ELIADE: Cosmos and History: *The Myth of the Eternal Return* § TB/2050

MIRCEA ELIADE: Myth and Reality TB/1369

MIRCEA ELIADE: Myths, Dreams and Mysteries: *The Encounter Between Contemporary Faiths and Archaic Realities* § TB/1320

MIRCEA ELIADE: Rites and Symbols of Initiation: *The Mysteries of Birth and Rebirth* § TB/1236

HERBERT FINGARETTE: The Self in Transformation: *Psychoanalysis, Philosophy and the Life of the Spirit* || TB/1177

SIGMUND FREUD: On Creativity and the Unconscious: *Papers on the Psychology of Art, Literature, Love, Religion.* § *Intro. by Benjamin Nelson* TB/45

J. GLENN GRAY: The Warriors: *Reflections on Men in Battle. Introduction by Hannah Arendt* TB/1294

WILLIAM JAMES: Psychology: *The Briefer Course. Edited with an Intro. by Gordon Allport* TB/1034

C. G. JUNG: Psychological Reflections. *Ed. by J. Jacobi* TB/2001

KARL MENNINGER, M.D.: Theory of Psychoanalytic Technique TB/1144

JOHN H. SCHAAR: Escape from Authority: *The Perspectives of Erich Fromm* TB/1155

MUZAFER SHERIF: The Psychology of Social Norms. *Introduction by Gardner Murphy* TB/3072

HELLMUT WILHELM: Change: *Eight Lectures on the I Ching* TB/2019

Religion: Ancient and Classical, Biblical and Judaic Traditions

W. F. ALBRIGHT: The Biblical Period from Abraham to Ezra TB/102

SALO W. BARON: Modern Nationalism and Religion TB/818

C. K. BARRETT, Ed.: The New Testament Background: *Selected Documents* TB/86

MARTIN BUBER: Eclipse of God: *Studies in the Relation Between Religion and Philosophy* TB/12

MARTIN BUBER: Hasidism and Modern Man. *Edited and Translated by Maurice Friedman* TB/839

MARTIN BUBER: The Knowledge of Man. *Edited with an Introduction by Maurice Friedman. Translated by Maurice Friedman and Ronald Gregor Smith* TB/135

MARTIN BUBER: Moses. *The Revelation and the Covenant* TB/837

MARTIN BUBER: The Origin and Meaning of Hasidism. *Edited and Translated by Maurice Friedman* TB/835

MARTIN BUBER: The Prophetic Faith TB/73

MARTIN BUBER: Two Types of Faith: *Interpenetration of Judaism and Christianity* ° TB/75

MALCOLM L. DIAMOND: Martin Buber: *Jewish Existentialist* TB/840

M. S. ENSLIN: Christian Beginnings TB/5

M. S. ENSLIN: The Literature of the Christian Movement TB/6

ERNST LUDWIG EHRLICH: A Concise History of Israel: *From the Earliest Times to the Destruction of the Temple in A.D. 70* ° TB/128

HENRI FRANKFORT: Ancient Egyptian Religion: *An Interpretation* TB/77

MAURICE S. FRIEDMAN: Martin Buber: *The Life of Dialogue* TB/64

ABRAHAM HESCHEL: The Earth Is the Lord's & The Sabbath. *Two Essays* TB/828

ABRAHAM HESCHEL: God in Search of Man: *A Philosophy of Judaism* TB/807

ABRAHAM HESCHEL: Man Is not Alone: *A Philosophy of Religion* TB/838

ABRAHAM HESCHEL: The Prophets: *An Introduction* TB/1421

T. J. MEEK: Hebrew Origins TB/69

JAMES MUILENBURG: The Way of Israel: *Biblical Faith and Ethics* TB/133

H. J. ROSE: Religion in Greece and Rome TB/55

H. H. ROWLEY: The Growth of the Old Testament TB/107

D. WINTON THOMAS, Ed.: Documents from Old Testament Times TB/85

Religion: General Christianity

ROLAND H. BAINTON: Christendom: *A Short History of Christianity and Its Impact on Western Civilization. Illus.* Vol. I TB/131; Vol. II TB/132

JOHN T. MCNEILL: Modern Christian Movements. *Revised Edition* TB/1402

ERNST TROELTSCH: The Social Teaching of the Christian Churches. *Intro. by H. Richard Niebuhr* Vol. TB/71; Vol. II TB/72

Religion: Early Christianity Through Reformation

ANSELM OF CANTERBURY: Truth, Freedom, and Evil: *Three Philosophical Dialogues. Edited and Translated by Jasper Hopkins and Herbert Richardson* TB/317
MARSHALL W. BALDWIN, Ed.: Christianity through the 13th Century # HR/1468
W. D. DAVIES: Paul and Rabbinic Judaism: *Some Rabbinic Elements in Pauline Theology. Revised Edition* ° TB/146
ADOLF DEISSMAN: Paul: *A Study in Social and Religious History* TB/15
JOHANNES ECKHART: Meister Eckhart: *A Modern Translation by R. Blakney* TB/8
EDGAR J. GOODSPEED: A Life of Jesus TB/1
ROBERT M. GRANT: Gnosticism and Early Christianity TB/136
WILLIAM HALLER: The Rise of Puritanism TB/22
GERHART B. LADNER: The Idea of Reform: *Its Impact on the Christian Thought and Action in the Age of the Fathers* TB/149
ARTHUR DARBY NOCK: Early Gentile Christianity and Its Hellenistic Background TB/111
ARTHUR DARBY NOCK: St. Paul ° TB/104
ORIGEN: On First Principles. *Edited by G. W. Butterworth. Introduction by Henri de Lubac* TB/311
GORDON RUPP: Luther's Progress to the Diet of Worms ° TB/120

Religion: The Protestant Tradition

KARL BARTH: Church Dogmatics: *A Selection. Intro. by H. Gollwitzer. Ed. by G. W. Bromiley* TB/95
KARL BARTH: Dogmatics in Outline TB/56
KARL BARTH: The Word of God and the Word of Man TB/13
HERBERT BRAUN, et al.: God and Christ: *Existence and Province. Volume 5 of Journal for Theology and the Church, edited by Robert W. Funk and Gerhard Ebeling* TB/255
WHITNEY R. CROSS: The Burned-Over District: *The Social and Intellectual History of Enthusiastic Religion in Western New York, 1800-1850* TB/1242
NELS F. S. FERRE: Swedish Contributions to Modern Theology. *New Chapter by William A. Johnson* TB/147
WILLIAM R. HUTCHISON, Ed.: American Protestant Thought: *The Liberal Era* ‡ TB/1385
ERNST KASEMANN, et al.: Distinctive Protestant and Catholic Themes Reconsidered. *Volume 3 of Journal for Theology and the Church, edited by Robert W. Funk and Gerhard Ebeling* TB/253
SOREN KIERKEGAARD: On Authority and Revelation: *The Book on Adler, or a Cycle of Ethico-Religious Essays. Introduction by F. Sontag* TB/139
SOREN KIERKEGAARD: Crisis in the Life of an Actress, *and Other Essays on Drama. Translated with an Introduction by Stephen Crites* TB/145
SOREN KIERKEGAARD: Edifying Discourses. *Edited with an Intro. by Paul Holmer* TB/32
SOREN KIERKEGAARD: The Journals of Kierkegaard. ° *Edited with an Intro. by Alexander Dru* TB/52
SOREN KIERKEGAARD: The Point of View for My Work as an Author: *A Report to History.* § *Preface by Benjamin Nelson* TB/88

SOREN KIERKEGAARD: The Present Age. § *Translated and edited by Alexander Dru. Introduction by Walter Kaufmann* TB/94
SOREN KIERKEGAARD: Purity of Heart. *Trans. by Douglas Steere* TB/4
SOREN KIERKEGAARD: Repetition: *An Essay in Experimental Psychology* § TB/117
SOREN KIERKEGAARD: Works of Love: *Some Christian Reflections in the Form of Discourses* TB/122
WILLIAM G. MCLOUGHLIN, Ed.: The American Evangelicals: 1800-1900: *An Anthology* TB/1382
WOLFHART PANNENBERG, et al.: History and Hermeneutic. *Volume 4 of Journal for Theology and the Church, edited by Robert W. Funk and Gerhard Ebeling* TB/254
JAMES M. ROBINSON, et al.: The Bultmann School of Biblical Interpretation: New Directions? *Volume 1 of Journal for Theology and the Church, edited by Robert W. Funk and Gerhard Ebeling* TB/251
F. SCHLEIERMACHER: The Christian Faith. *Introduction by Richard R. Niebuhr.*
Vol. I TB/108; Vol. II TB/109
F. SCHLEIERMACHER: On Religion: Speeches to *Its Cultured Despisers. Intro. by Rudolf Otto* TB/36
TIMOTHY L. SMITH: Revivalism and Social Reform: *American Protestantism on the Eve of the Civil War* TB/1229
PAUL TILLICH: Dynamics of Faith TB/42
PAUL TILLICH: Morality and Beyond TB/142
EVELYN UNDERHILL: Worship TB/10

Religion: The Roman & Eastern Christian Traditions

A. ROBERT CAPONIGRI, Ed.: Modern Catholic Thinkers II: *The Church and the Political Order* TB/307
G. P. FEDOTOV: The Russian Religious Mind: *Kievan Christianity, the tenth to the thirteenth Centuries* TB/370
GABRIEL MARCEL: Being and Having: *An Existential Diary. Introduction by James Collins* TB/310
GABRIEL MARCEL: Homo Viator: *Introduction to a Metaphysic of Hope* TB/397

Religion: Oriental Religions

TOR ANDRAE: Mohammed: *The Man and His Faith* § TB/62
EDWARD CONZE: Buddhism: *Its Essence and Development.* ° *Foreword by Arthur Waley* TB/58
EDWARD CONZE: Buddhist Meditation TB/1442
EDWARD CONZE et al, Editors: Buddhist Texts through the Ages TB/113
ANANDA COOMARASWAMY: Buddha and the Gospel of Buddhism TB/119
H. G. CREEL: Confucius and the Chinese Way TB/63
FRANKLIN EDGERTON, Trans. & Ed.: The Bhagavad Gita TB/115
SWAMI NIKHILANANDA, Trans. & Ed.: The Upanishads TB/114
D. T. SUZUKI: On Indian Mahayana Buddhism. ° *Ed. with Intro. by Edward Conze.* TB/1403

Religion: Philosophy, Culture, and Society

NICOLAS BERDYAEV: The Destiny of Man TB/61
RUDOLF BULTMANN: History and Eschatology: *The Presence of Eternity* ° TB/91
RUDOLF BULTMANN AND FIVE CRITICS: Kerygma and Myth: *A Theological Debate* TB/80

RUDOLF BULTMANN and KARL KUNDSIN: Form Criticism: *Two Essays on New Testament Research. Trans. by F. C. Grant* TB/96

WILLIAM A. CLEBSCH & CHARLES R. JAEKLE: Pastoral Care in Historical Perspective: *An Essay with Exhibits* TB/148

FREDERICK FERRE: Language, Logic and God. *New Preface by the Author* TB/1407

LUDWIG FEUERBACH: The Essence of Christianity. § *Introduction by Karl Barth. Foreword by H. Richard Niebuhr* TB/11

C. C. GILLISPIE: Genesis and Geology: *The Decades before Darwin* § TB/51

ADOLF HARNACK: What Is Christianity? § *Introduction by Rudolf Bultmann* TB/17

KYLE HASELDEN: The Racial Problem in Christian Perspective TB/116

MARTIN HEIDEGGER: Discourse on Thinking. *Translated with a Preface by John M. Anderson and E. Hans Freund. Introduction by John M. Anderson* TB/1459

IMMANUEL KANT: Religion Within the Limits of Reason Alone. § *Introduction by Theodore M. Greene and John Silber* TB/FG

WALTER KAUFMANN, Ed.: Religion from Tolstoy to Camus: *Basic Writings on Religious Truth and Morals. Enlarged Edition* TB/123

JOHN MACQUARRIE: An Existentialist Theology: *A Comparison of Heidegger and Bultmann.* ° *Foreword by Rudolf Bultmann* TB/125

H. RICHARD NIERUHR: Christ and Culture TB/3

H. RICHARD NIEBUHR: The Kingdom of God in America TB/49

ANDERS NYGREN: Agape and Eros. *Translated by Philip S. Watson* ° TB/1430

JOHN H. RANDALL, JR.: The Meaning of Religion for Man. *Revised with New Intro. by the Author* TB/1379

WALTER RAUSCHENBUSCHS Christianity and the Social Crisis. ‡ *Edited by Robert D. Cross* TB/3059

JOACHIM WACH: Understanding and Believing. *Ed. with Intro. by Joseph M. Kitagawa* TB/1399

Science and Mathematics

JOHN TYLER BONNER: The Ideas of Biology. Σ *Illus.* TB/570

W. E. LE GROS CLARK: The Antecedents of Man: *An Introduction to the Evolution of the Primates.* ° *Illus.* TB/559

ROBERT E. COKER: Streams, Lakes, Ponds. *Illus.* TB/586

ROBERT E. COKER: This Great and Wide Sea: *An Introduction to Oceanography and Marine Biology. Illus.* TB/551

W. H. DOWDESWELL: Animal Ecology. *61 illus.* TB/543

C. V. DURELL: Readable Relativity. *Foreword by Freeman J. Dyson* TB/530

GEORGE GAMOW: Biography of Physics. Σ *Illus.* TB/567

F. K. HARE: The Restless Atmosphere TB/560

S. KORNER: The Philosophy of Mathematics: *An Introduction* TB/547

J. R. PIERCE: Symbols, Signals and Noise: *The Nature and Process of Communication* Σ TB/574

WILLARD VAN ORMAN QUINE: Mathematical Logic TB/558

Science: History

MARIE BOAS: The Scientific Renaissance, 1450-1630 ° TB/583

W. DAMPIER, Ed.: Readings in the Literature of Science. *Illus.* TB/512

STEPHEN TOULMIN & JUNE GOODFIELD: The Architecture of Matter: *The Physics, Chemistry and Physiology of Matter, Both Animate and Inanimate, as it has Evolved since the Beginnings of Science* TB/584

STEPHEN TOULMIN & JUNE GOODFIELD: The Discovery of Time TB/585

STEPHEN TOULMIN & JUNE GOODFIELD: The Fabric of the Heavens: *The Development of Astronomy and Dynamics* TB/579

Science: Philosophy

J. M. BOCHENSKI: The Methods of Contemporary Thought. *Tr. by Peter Caws* TB/1377

J. BRONOWSKI: Science and Human Values. *Revised and Enlarged. Illus.* TB/505

WERNER HEISENBERG: Physics and Philosophy: *The Revolution in Modern Science. Introduction by F. S. C. Northrop* TB/549

KARL R. POPPER: Conjectures and Refutations: *The Growth of Scientific Knowledge* TB/1376

KARL R. POPPER: The Logic of Scientific Discovery TB/576

STEPHEN TOULMIN: Foresight and Understanding: *An Enquiry into the Aims of Science. Foreword by Jacques Barzun* TB/564

STEPHEN TOULMIN: The Philosophy of Science: *An Introduction* TB/513

Sociology and Anthropology

REINHARD BENDIX: Work and Authority in Industry: *Ideologies of Management in the Course of Industrialization* TB/3035

BERNARD BERELSON, Ed., The Behavioral Sciences Today TB/1127

JOSEPH B. CASAGRANDE, Ed.: In the Company of Man: *Twenty Portraits of Anthropological Informants. Illus.* TB/3047

KENNETH B. CLARK: Dark Ghetto: *Dilemmas of Social Power. Foreword by Gunnar Myrdal* TB/1317

KENNETH CLARK & JEANNETTE HOPKINS: A Relevant War Against Poverty: *A Study of Community Action Programs and Observable Social Change* TB/1480

W. E. LE GROS CLARK: The Antecedents of Man: *An Introduction to the Evolution of the Primates.* ° *Illus.* TB/559

LEWIS COSER, Ed.: Political Sociology TB/1293

ROSE L. COSER, Ed.: Life Cycle and Achievement in America ** TB/1434

ALLISON DAVIS & JOHN DOLLARD: Children of Bondage: *The Personality Development of Negro Youth in the Urban South* ‖ TB/3049

ST. CLAIR DRAKE & HORACE R. CAYTON: Black Metropolis: *A Study of Negro Life in a Northern City. Introduction by Everett C. Hughes. Tables, maps, charts, and graphs* Vol. I TB/1086; Vol. II TB/1087

PETER E. DRUCKER: The New Society: *The Anatomy of Industrial Order* TB/1082

CORA DU BOIS: The People of Alor. *With a Preface by the Author* Vol. I *Illus.* TB/1042; Vol. II TB/1043

EMILE DURKHEIM et al.: Essays on Sociology and Philosophy: *with Appraisals of Durkheim's Life and Thought.* ‖ *Edited by Kurt H. Wolff* TB/1151

LEON FESTINGER, HENRY W. RIECKEN, STANLEY SCHACHTER: When Prophecy Fails: *A Social and Psychological Study of a Modern Group that Predicted the Destruction of the World* ‖ TB/1132

CHARLES Y. GLOCK & RODNEY STARK: Christian Beliefs and Anti-Semitism. *Introduction by the Authors* TB/1454

ALVIN W. GOULDNER: The Hellenic World TB/1479

ALVIN W. GOULDNER: Wildcat Strike: *A Study in Worker-Management Relationships* || TB/1176

CESAR GRANA: Modernity and Its Discontents: *French Society and the French Man of Letters in the Nineteenth Century* TB/1318

L. S. B. LEAKEY: Adam's Ancestors: *The Evolution of Man and His Culture. Illus.* TB/1019

KURT LEWIN: Field Theory in Social Science: *Selected Theoretical Papers.* || *Edited by Dorwin Cartwright* TB/1135

RITCHIE P. LOWRY: Who's Running This Town? *Community Leadership and Social Change* TB/1383

R. M. MACIVER: Social Causation TB/1153

GARY T. MARX: Protest and Prejudice: *A Study of Belief in the Black Community* TB/1435

ROBERT K. MERTON, LEONARD BROOM, LEONARD S. COTTRELL, JR., Editors: Sociology Today: *Problems and Prospects* ||
Vol. I TB/1173; Vol. II TB/1174

GILBERT OSOFSKY, Ed.: The Burden of Race: A Documentary History of Negro-White Relations in America TB/1405

GILBERT OSOFSKY: Harlem: The Making of a Ghetto: *Negro New York 1890-1930* TB/1381

TALCOTT PARSONS & EDWARD A. SHILS, Editors: Toward a General Theory of Action: *Theoretical Foundations for the Social Sciences* TB/1083

PHILIP RIEFF: The Triumph of the Therapeutic: *Uses of Faith After Freud* TB/1360

JOHN H. ROHRER & MUNRO S. EDMONSON, Eds.: The Eighth Generation Grows Up: *Cultures and Personalities of New Orleans Negroes* || TB/3050

ARNOLD ROSE: The Negro in America: *The Condensed Version of Gunnar Myrdal's* An American Dilemma. *Second Edition* TB/3048

GEORGE ROSEN: Madness in Society: *Chapters in the Historical Sociology of Mental Illness.* || *Preface by Benjamin Nelson* TB/1337

PHILIP SELZNICK: TVA and the Grass Roots: *A Study in the Sociology of Formal Organization* TB/1230

PITIRIM A. SOROKIN: Contemporary Sociological Theories: *Through the First Quarter of the Twentieth Century* TB/3046

MAURICE R. STEIN: The Eclipse of Community: *An Interpretation of American Studies* TB/1128

WILLIAM I. THOMAS: The Unadjusted Girl: *With Cases and Standpoint for Behavior Analysis. Intro. by Michael Parenti* TB/1319

EDWARD A. TIRYAKIAN, Ed.: Sociological Theory, Values and Sociocultural Change: *Essays in Honor of Pitirim A. Sorokin* ° TB/1316

FERDINAND TONNIES: Community and Society: *Gemeinschaft und Gesellschaft. Translated and Edited by Charles P. Loomis* TB/1116

SAMUEL E. WALLACE: Skid Row as a Way of Life TB/1367

W. LLOYD WARNER and Associates: Democracy in Jonesville: *A Study in Quality and Inequality* || TB/1129

W. LLOYD WARNER: Social Class in America: *The Evaluation of Status* TB/1013

FLORIAN ZNANIECKI: The Social Role of the Man of Knowledge. *Introduction by Lewis A. Coser* TB/1372